To: My Friend
Kenny
Dusty Rhodes

Shooter

Shooter
Copyright © 2004
Dusty Rhodes
All rights reserved.

Cover Art
Copyright © 2004 Holly Smith
Bookskins
All rights reserved.

SUNDOWNERS
A division of
Treble Heart Books
1284 Overlook Dr.
Sierra Vista, AZ 85635-5512
http://www.trebleheartbooks.com

The characters and events in this book are fictional, and any resemblance to persons, whether living or dead, is strictly coincidental.

All rights reserved. No part of this book may be reproduced or transmitted in any form by any means, electronic or mechanical, including photocopying, recording, scanning to a computer disk, or by any informational storage and retrieval system, without express permission in writing from the publisher.

ISBN: 1-931742-49-9

Other Books by Dusty Rhodes

Man Hunter
Shiloh
Jedidiah Boone
Death Rides a Pale Horse

Shooter
by
Dusty Rhodes

Sundowners
A
division of
Treble Heart Books

Author's Foreword

Amid birthing pains of a new nation, hardy, and sometimes desperate, men and women struggled and all too often paid the ultimate price to blaze new frontiers. When the Civil War ended in 1865 many bitter and disillusioned survivors returned home to find nothing left. Some of these took to the outlaw trail. Robbers, cutthroats, murderers, rapists, and outlaw gangs ran rampant; crime became an epidemic.

Those seeking to escape the "long arm of the law" found a safe-haven in what was called, the Indian Territory, or by some, the Nations, home of the Five Civilized Tribes. The Choctaw, Cherokee, Chickasaw, Creek, and Seminole tribes, as well as portions of numerous other tribes, had been moved by force-of-arms to this God-forsaken land.

This vast area, which we now know as Oklahoma, encompassed some 74,000 square miles and was a lawless land beyond the reach of conventional justice. Bounded by Arkansas, Kansas, Texas, and New Mexico Territory, the Nations became the base of operations for outlaw gangs that looted and plundered surrounding states.

Under tremendous pressure to curb this lawlessness, President Ulysses S. Grant appointed Judge Isaac C. Parker and gave him unfettered jurisdictional authority over the Federal District Court of Western Arkansas, which included all of the Indian Territory and roughly half of the state of Arkansas.

Judge Parker was given unprecedented authority. For fourteen of the twenty-one years on the bench, his decisions were final and irrevocable. Upon his appointment he became the only jurist in the history of the United States from which there was no appeal. Certainty of arrest and surety of punishment became the rule of his court.

His first act upon arriving at his court in Fort Smith, Arkansas on May 2, 1875 was to order the construction of a gallows; not just any gallows, this one must be capable of hanging as many as 12 condemned at a time. It took only eight days for the press to dub him, "The Hanging Judge," a name which stuck, and which struck fear in the heart of many an outlaw.

On May 10, 1875, just eight days after arriving, eighteen men came before him charged with murder. Eight were convicted and sentenced to die on the brand new gallows. Before the sentence could be carried out, one was shot and killed attempting to escape, a second's sentence was commuted to life in prison because of his age—he was only sixteen.

On September 3, 1875, the remaining six men were hanged.

During his tenure, Judge Parker sentenced one hundred-sixty-eight men and four women to hang. In pronouncing sentence, he always concluded with the statement:

"May God, whose laws you have broken and before whose tribunal you must now appear, have mercy on your soul."

To enforce his orders, he authorized the United States Marshal, James F. Fagan, to hire two hundred U. S. Deputy Marshals. This is the story of one of those men. His name was Johnny Shooter, but he became known to every fugitive simply as, "Shooter"—the most dreaded name in the territory. Among wanted men, he was known as the deadliest of all manhunters. They knew if there was a price on your head, death was chasing you—and his name was *Shooter*. It was said around many outlaw campfires:

"The only thing worse than standing before the "Hanging Judge" is finding out "Shooter" is on your trail."

Chapter I

They called the dungeon-like basement jail "Hell on the Border." It lived up to its name. The nauseating stench of urine, excrement, vomit, and sweat from his eighty-seven fellow prisoners made breathing near impossible. The dankness of a fall night wrapped itself around Johnny Shooter and chilled him to the bone. He drew his long legs up into a tighter fetal position and shivered from the cold of the bare concrete floor.

But maybe the worst thing of all was the noise; the constant uproar of curses, screams, and shouting never stopped. He had resigned himself that his date with the hangman at high noon tomorrow would almost be a relief.

Near a week had passed since his trial, which lasted less than an hour. The only witness to testify on his behalf was his cousin, Sam Thurman, one of Judge Parker's deputy marshals and Johnny's best friend. All Sam could say was that Johnny came from a good family and had never been in serious trouble.

"He never would have shot the Kimes boys if they hadn't murdered his folks in cold blood," Sam told the court. But his testimony fell on deaf ears and hadn't made a whit of difference. It was clear the jury had already made up their minds.

"Guilty," the short, bald headed foreman said after the jury deliberated all of fifteen minutes. A self-satisfying smirk lifted one corner of the little man's cruel mouth and he glanced quickly at Johnny before he said it. They were right, too. He shot Ed and Slim Kimes down like the dogs they were. When the judge asked him if he had anything to say before he pronounced sentence, Johnny said as much.

"They had it coming," he told the court. "That lowdown scum murdered both of my elderly parents. My folks gave them shelter on a cold, rainy night and the Kimes brothers repaid their kindness by slitting their throats and robbing them. Twenty-one lousy dollars. They murdered my ma and pa for twenty-one dollars. What was I supposed to do, just forget it? If I had it to do over I'd do the same thing and so would most of you if you're any kind of man, and that's all I got to say about that."

To say the least, his impassioned lecture to the jury hadn't exactly helped his case.

The words of Judge Isaac C. Parker still rang in his ears; he would never forget them.

"Johnny Shooter, you have been found guilty of the murders of Ed and Slim Kimes. Although I sympathize with your reasons for what you did, under the law I am left with no choice. Therefore, I hereby sentence you to hang by your neck until you are dead. May God, whose laws you have broken and before whose tribunal you must now appear, have mercy on your soul."

Well, I'll hang for what I done, but the Kimes brothers beat me to hell by a whole month.

Johnny's thoughts were interrupted when he heard the heavy steel door at the end of the hallway squeak open on its rusty hinges, and then bang shut. It was a common occurrence and he paid it little mind. Something caused Johnny to swing a look.

James Fagan, the United States Marshal, and Jack Bascom, the jailer, trudged wearily down the narrow passageway and stopped in front of the cramped cell Johnny shared with a dozen other men. The jailer lifted a coal-oil lantern and peered into the cage. The jagged circle of flickering light illuminated the cell and projected eerie shadows against the wall. Men in varied degrees of dress and undress huddled on the cold, filthy concrete floor in their own squalor.

"Shooter," the jailer bellowed out with his bullfrog voice. "Front and center!"

Bascom was a bear of a man that sniffled like he had a head cold all the time. It was likely too, since he spent most of his time in the cold, dungeon-like jail breaking up fights and seeing to the prisoners.

The Marshal stood nearby. He was a tall, sledge-shouldered fellow somewhere on the sundown side of forty. He had a square jaw and a chiseled face. His eyes were colder than an outhouse in dead winter. Even in his declining years, he was an imposing man. He looked like a man that had been up and down a lot of trails and a fellow you'd walk around if you had a lick of sense.

Johnny uncurled stiffly from his spot on the floor and pushed to his knees, then to his bare feet. Stepping carefully over the other prisoners, he approached the cell door.

"Here," the big jailer said, holding a pair of wrist and leg shackles through the bars. "Put these on. The Marshal's taking you for a walk."

"A walk, huh? Business so good you're hanging folks at night now?" Johnny complained sarcastically, puzzled by being taken from his cell this late.

"Shut your trap and get into those bracelets," the jailer growled. "We ain't got all night."

Johnny clamped the shackles in place, and then held them close to the bars so the locks could be snapped on. A short chain held his ankle shackles close together. A second chain connected his wrist bracelets to the ankle shackles so his hands couldn't be raised more than waist-high. Bascom took a big key ring from his belt, inserted a key, and swung the cell door open.

Unable to walk normally with his ankles chained together, Johnny shuffled in baby-steps through the door into the hallway. Scooting his feet along, he followed the marshal as the little procession headed toward the outside door at the end of the long hallway. Bascom followed closely.

The jailer unlocked and swung the heavy outside door open. It was pitch dark. The murky blackness was as thick as week-old coffee. A chilly October breeze slapped Johnny in the face and smelled sweet and fresh and clean. Johnny took a deep inhale. It was the first good breath he had had in a week. Better enjoy it, he thought sadly. Likely I ain't got many more left.

Marshal Fagan took Johnny's arm and led him up the steps from the basement dungeon. They turned left toward a flight of steps leading to the two-story courthouse above the jail.

"Mind telling me where we're headed?" Johnny asked.

"Judge wants to see you."

Shackled like he was, it was a pure-de effort climbing all those steps. When they finally pushed through the front door, they faced yet another flight of stairs leading to the second floor. It took awhile.

They moved slowly down a long, wood-floored hallway and stopped in front of a door with frosted glass in the top half. Johnny read what was painted on the glass in black letters, it said; ISAAC C. PARKER-JUDGE.

Fagan tapped lightly on the door and waited.

Shooter

"Come in," a voice called from inside.

The Judge looked different without the big, black robe Johnny remembered from court. He now wore a black, broadcloth suit and white shirt with a stiff-starched collar cinched tight with a black cravat. He looked more like a preacher than the one known as the "Hanging Judge."

He was an average sized fellow that seemed to be straddling forty. He wore a wide mustache and a small goatee that, like his dark hair, was sprinkled with flecks of gray. His dark, penetrating eyes and no-nonsense, business-like manner told Johnny to keep his mouth shut unless he was asked a question.

The only chair in the office was the red leather high-backed chair where the judge sat. Johnny stood in front of the judge's desk, trussed up like a plucked chicken.

For a long space of time the judge studied the man before him without saying a word. Barefooted, his shirt in tatters, his pants sported more holes than a watering trough on Saturday night and was ragged around the edges. But even in his bare feet, this man stood taller than most men, at least three inches over six feet. He was whipcord lean, yet broad through the shoulders and chest. His work-hardened hands spoke of long hard days on a farm. His skin was weathered tough like good saddle leather and sun browned. A firm jaw sat just below easy, slightly mocking lips with a slight twist in the righthand corner. A shock of hair hung to his shoulders and was sun bleached copper, most likely from too many hours following a team of mules and a breaking plow.

Right now, though, his features were stony. He stared down. His pale-green eyes that never seemed to blink studied the floor. When he lifted a look to meet the judge's stare, his piercing gaze was intense, penetrating as though he looked at nothing and saw everything. His mouth was set in a tight line of resignation. Something about that look sent an icy shiver down the Judge's spine.

Johnny waited uneasily, shifting his weight from one foot to the other nervously, as if wondering what was going through the judge's mind. Had he resigned himself to the inevitable? He looked cold and sleepy and tired clear down to his bones. Maybe that rope will be a blessing for such a man.

The Judge raked Johnny's long frame up and down and up again, finally settling his gaze on the condemned man's face. It was stony-cold, expressionless.

"How old are you, Mr. Shooter?"

"I just turned twenty-one, sir,"

Again the judge stared in silent contemplation for another long minute. Finally he leaned forward, rested his elbows on his desk and steepled his hands in front of him as if in prayer.

"I spent some time with Deputy Thurmon after your trial the other day," Judge Parker said. "He told me some interesting things about you. He said you are a fair minded sort of fellow. He also said you are the best gun hand he'd ever seen and that you had ice water in your veins when it come to using your gun.

"From what I gather, he felt like you could have taken him easily when he came to arrest you. Surely you knew you'd hang if you let him bring you in. If you're as good with a gun as he said, why did you come with him without a fight?"

"He's my cousin. I'd never throw down on my own kin. I also count him my best friend. He's been good to me and my family."

"So you'd hang before you'd do harm to your cousin, is that what you're telling me?"

"Like I said, he's my friend."

"I'm afraid I've got some bad news. Deputy Thurmon was gunned down over near Fort Gibson a few days ago. They shot him ten times. I thought you'd want to know."

Johnny tensed and started.

Sam? Dead? The sudden shock of the news stunned Johnny. Shock quickly gave birth to anger. It started as a balled up knot deep in the pit of his belly and churned its way up through his chest, flushing his neck and face crimson red. His jaw set, his eyes narrowed, muscles worked silently in his cheeks.

"Who done it?" he asked through clenched teeth.

"It was a renegade they call the Choctaw Kid and them that run with him, we ain't sure how many," the marshal said, speaking up for the first time since they walked into the room. "He fancies himself a gun slick. We've been after him for six months. Your cousin was the second Deputy Marshal he's killed."

"Why are you telling me all this? There ain't nothing I can do about it. I've got a date with the hangman tomorrow at noon."

The judge turned to Marshal Fagan.

"Marshal, would you mind waiting outside? I'd like to talk with Mr. Shooter alone for a few minutes."

The marshal laid the key to Johnny's chains on the desk in front of the judge and turned to go. As he did he slanted a look at Johnny, the faintest hint of a smile lifted one corner of his lips. The smile puzzled Johnny. When the door closed, the judge continued.

"Young man, I've been in Fort Smith exactly seven months. With the killing of deputy Thurmon, that makes thirty-one deputies I've lost. I'm tired of burying good men. Marshal Fagan has only two hundred deputies to cover well over 74,000 square miles, an impossible task. What I'm about to say must never be repeated to a living soul. Do you understand?"

Johnny didn't understand, but he nodded his head. *I'm going to hang tomorrow. This very man sentenced me to die. Why is he talking all of a sudden like I ain't?*

"You see," the judge said. "My position as an officer of the court requires that I place certain restraints upon my deputies. I must insist they make every effort possible to capture the fugitives I send them after and bring them back alive to stand trial.

"Nevertheless, I've become convinced that sometimes, when dealing with certain individuals, those restraints may not be justified and I'm losing good men because of those restraints. Let me speak frankly, Mr. Shooter. I need someone, just one man that is not hampered by any such rules. I need a man I can trust, a man that would work directly for me and report only to me. I need a man I can send after the worst of the worst, who will pursue his assignment relentlessly until the fugitive is either dead or brought back to stand trial. In short, I need a man like you.

"I want to make you an offer, Mr. Shooter. I am willing to commute your sentence and parole you to Marshal Fagan for a period of six months. During that time, you would work for me and me alone as a Deputy United States Marshal. No one, I repeat, absolutely no one is to know the details of our arrangement. If you do the job and last out the six months, I'll give you a full pardon.

"Your assignments would come directly from me or from Marshal Fagan. We would communicate with each other only at night. Under no circumstances would you come to my office during the day. To the other two hundred deputies you will just be one of them. Neither the news people nor our other deputies must learn of our arrangement. You will be free to handle your assignment any way you see fit, as long as you get the job done. However, should you fail to complete any of your assignments you will be hunted down and the original sentence will be carried out. Do you understand?"

"Yes sir," Johnny breathed, a flicker of hope blossoming to life in his mind.

"In return, you would be paid regular deputy's wages. My deputies draw no salary but are paid two dollars for each prisoner they deliver to the court here in Fort Smith, plus six cents a mile for transporting prisoners. In addition, unlike our other deputies, you would be entitled to any rewards your assignments might have posted on them."

Opening a desk drawer, the judge withdrew more money than Johnny had ever seen at one time in his whole life. He laid the money in a neat stack on his desk, using a finger to align the edges perfectly. On top of the money he laid a shiny new U. S. Deputy Marshal's badge.

"There's six hundred dollars there," Judge Parker said. "The Kimes brothers had three hundred dollars reward apiece on them, dead or alive. It's yours, providing we have an agreement."

"Sounds like an offer I can't refuse," Johnny said, a wellspring of hope bubbling up inside him. "What have I got to lose? I was gonna hang tomorrow anyway."

"Fine," the judge said, lifting from the chair. "Splendid."

He came quickly around the desk, removed the shackles and let them drop at Johnny's feet, then stuck out his hand. Johnny took it. The bargain was sealed with a firm handshake.

"You'll have to provide yourself with a good horse and properly arm yourself and...some new clothes might be in order too. I can't have my Deputy Marshals going around half-naked. Return here tomorrow night at nine for your first assignment."

"Marshal Fagan," Judge Parker called out. "You can come in now."

Scooping up the money and the badge, Johnny stuffed them in his pants pocket.

"I've decided to commute Mr. Shooter's sentence," the judge told the marshal. "I'm paroling him into your custody. He'll be working as one of your deputy marshals on special assignments. He will work for and report directly to me. If he does the job and lasts out the term of his parole, his record will be completely expunged and he will be given a full pardon. No one outside this room is to know of this arrangement, is that understood?"

"Yes, sir," the marshal replied.

"Marshal, I'd appreciate it if you'd take Mr. Shooter and get him cleaned up and see he has a place to stay. He's to report back here tomorrow night at nine, sufficiently armed and mounted and ready for his first assignment. Is that clear?"

"Yes, sir."

"Then you're both excused."

Turning on bare feet, Johnny padded along behind the marshal as they exited the judge's chambers and made their way down the stairs. The chilly night air danced around them as they pushed through the front doors. Leaving the yellowish patch of light of the courthouse, they were swallowed up by an inky blackness.

"Johnny, I'm shore sorry about your folks and your cousin. Sam Thurmon was a good deputy, one of the best I had. You're a lucky young man," Marshal Fagan commented as they walked side by side across the wide courtyard and headed the few blocks toward downtown Fort Smith. "I don't know all the details of your arrangement with the judge–and I don't want to know–but at least it got you out of your date with the hangman tomorrow."

"That's a fact."

"Johnny, I don't know for shore, but the way I got it figured the judge is gonna give you the worst assignments we got—the ones nobody else wants—the ones that are too dangerous for the other deputies. I've got to be honest with you, son, most likely all you've done tonight is buy yourself a little more time.

"If I'm right, he'll likely send you after the Choctaw Kid and his bunch. They tell me the kid's got a temper that's as quick as his gun and he runs with a bad bunch. Going up against the likes of them is the next thing to suicide. If you're planning on lasting very long you're going to need every edge you can get."

"What do you mean?"

"Well, to be honest with you, I can't rightly say I wouldn't have done the same as you if the Kimes brothers had killed my folks like they did yours. To my way of thinking, they should have given you a medal instead of sentencing you to hang. I kind of get the feeling the judge feels the same way. I think that badge you've got in your pocket is his way of giving you that medal. I figure what he's doing is giving you a badge just to make legal what he's sending you out to do.

"The point is I want to help you all I can, but the other deputies can never be allowed to find out about your arrangement with the judge. If news ever gets out, I'll have to deny I know anything about it."

"So you're saying I can't expect help from the other deputies? That I'm on my own?"

"Not exactly, but that's the long and short of it, son. They'll know you are a United States Deputy Marshal, of course, but they can't know about your arrangement with the judge."

Johnny digested this bit of information and it went down hard. His voice thickened as he spoke, the words coming out sharp and determined.

"Well, I'll tell you one thing, Marshal, I intend to be around to get that pardon the judge promised me."

"I hope so, Johnny. I truly hope so. I like you, boy. Personally, I think you got a raw deal. So I'm gonna give you a piece of advice. I've been doing law work a lot of years. I've worn a badge off and on most of my life. I've been up and down the trail a few times, son. I've put shackles on some real bad hombres and put more'n a few in the ground. I've been almighty lucky, but luck won't keep you alive very long nowadays, especially in this line of work. If you're as good with a gun as Deputy Thurmon said, you might last awhile. But being fast ain't enough. Believe me, son, there's always somebody faster."

"I don't reckon I understand."

"Well, if I was you, kid, I'd work real hard at building me a reputation. Most of those hardcases out there are no different than the rest of us. They ain't anxious to make that one-way trip to Boot Hill. A lawman wears a reputation just like he wears a badge and it will help keep you alive a whole lot longer than that star you got in your pocket. It can give you that edge, that split second that means the difference between living and dying.

"Even the men you'll be going after get nervous when they're facing someone they think might be faster or deadlier than they are, and nervous men make mistakes."

For a long space of time Johnny said nothing. He walked in silent contemplation beside the marshal, his downcast eyes unconsciously counting the cracks in the wooden boardwalk beneath his bare feet. The glare from kerosene lamps in several late-night shops cast checkered patches of yellow light into the darkened and mostly deserted street. The reverberation of a tinny-sounding piano and drunken laughter spilled from some of Fort Smith's thirty saloons and drifted on the night air, reaching his hearing.

"How can I build a reputation like you talked about?" Johnny finally asked, completely bumfuzzled.

"A reputation is built by talk. When it comes to a reputation, what a man is don't matter near as much as what others think he is. If I was you, I'd start with my clothes. Somebody said, 'clothes make the man.' Obviously that ain't altogether true, but they can shore help create an impression. Sometimes just looking like a gun hand is enough to keep you out of a whole bunch of gunfights."

As they walked, the marshal received three or four howdies as they made their way down the street, which he returned with a nod of his head. He pulled the makings from a shirt pocket. He creased a rolling paper and sprinkled tobacco into the fold. With expert adeptness he rolled the cigarette and sealed it with the tip of his tongue. Popping the top of a match with a thumbnail, he cupped it in a hand, put fire to the twirly, then drew a deep inhale. Then tilting his head back, he released the blue smoke into the air in a long, thin slide before continuing.

"When you're out there in the field, Johnny, you're the law. Aps-as-not you're the only law most of them will ever even hear about, let alone see. That star on your chest and the gun in your hand is the only law west of the Arkansas River. Right now they got no respect for law.

"We've lost thirty-one good deputies in the last eight months. The men you'll be going after ain't afraid of killing a United States Deputy Marshal. That's got to change. I figure the only way we can change it is to put the fear of God in 'em. They've got to know if they kill one of us, they're gonna die for it, one way or the other.

"Never give the men you'll be going after an even chance. If he'll let you take him alive, fine. If not, kill him before he kills you. Don't ever give a man the edge on you. There's only the winners and the losers, there ain't no in between. Have you got any place in mind to stay?"

"No, sir, I've never been to Fort Smith. The hotel, I reckon."

"Since my wife died about a year ago, I've been living over on Third Street at Miss Lila's boarding house. She charges less than a hotel and puts out better grub than any café in town. I think you'd like it there."

"Sounds good to me."

"Good, then we'll walk over together and get you squared away," Marshal Fagan said. "If you want me to, tomorrow morning I'll help you find yourself a horse, some clothes, and some new weapons. If you're gonna last anytime in this new job of yours, you're going to need something better than that old Navy .36 caliber Colt pistol and plow horse you had when you were arrested."

It was only about eight blocks to the boarding house. The marshal and Johnny talked every step of the way. Johnny discovered he liked the old marshal.

Miss Lila's boarding house was a large, two-story structure of white clapboard that sat on the corner of the street. A single covered street lantern cast a jagged circle of light and lit the area. Green shutters framed the tall windows and the roofline was bordered with design-laden trim. A wide porch with white, high railings skirted three sides. Several rocking chairs and a swing made the porch a homey looking place. A black wrought-iron fence with spearhead posts guarded the yard, which was filled with all sorts of fall flowers and bushes. A gray tendril of smoke wafted lazily from the brick chimney and billowed up to swirl quickly away, sharply bent by a westerly breeze. It was the most inviting looking house Johnny Shooter had ever seen.

"Come on in," the marshal said. "I'll introduce you to Miss Lila and her daughter, Libby. They run the place."

Pushing through the front door, they entered a long, oak hardwood hallway. The floor was polished to a high shine. Johnny was amazed that he could actually see his own reflection when he glanced down. A stairway to the second floor stood against the lefthand wall. A giant grandfather clock stood against the white wall and filled the quietness with its rhythmic ticking.

The place carried a clean smell about it. Johnny drew a deep breath. He liked the place immediately.

Veering to their right, they passed through an open doorway into a large sitting area. It was a cozy room. A heavy, wine-colored rug with blue flowers covered the floor. Two large sofas faced each other in front of a blazing fire in the fireplace. A painting of a beautiful young woman with flaming red hair hung above the mantle. An older and much heavier version of the same woman rose from one of the sofas to greet them.

Johnny judged her to be the better part of fifty years old and her weight to be four times that. Her jowls hung heavy and a second chin folded over the stiff, buttoned collar of a dark blue dress. Obviously she was a victim of her own good cooking. Her reddish, gray-streaked hair formed a bun that clung to the back of her head. There was a friendly look about her, but also something that suggested she could be tough as a she-bear when the occasion called for it.

"You're running late tonight, James," the woman greeted in a husky, boisterous voice.

"Yeah, we had some late business to settle before the hanging tomorrow."

"Who's your friend?" she asked, her hazel eyed gaze flicking to settle on Johnny.

"Miss Lila, this is Johnny Shooter. He wants to talk to you about bed and board."

"Johnny Shooter, huh?" she said. "Unusual name."

He cringed under the weight of her appraising gaze that crawled slowly along his tall frame, pausing at his unshaven face, stringy hair, and ragged clothes. Her nose wrinkled.

"If you don't mind me saying so, Mr. Shooter, you look a sight, and smell even worse. If you weren't with Mr. Fagan, I'd send you on down the street."

"Yes, ma'am. I've...it's been awhile since I was able to clean up."

"Well, no matter. I'll not have you sleep in one of my beds until you bathe. Room and board is two dollars a day, twelve dollars a week, or fifty a month paid in advance. I allow no drinking, fighting or taking the Lord's name in vain in my home. We're church-going folks. Meals are served twice daily, breakfast from five till six, suppers at six sharp. If you ain't at the table, you don't eat, but I'll make an exception just this once.

"I'll have Libby rustle you fellows up something to eat. It'll be on the table after you finish your bath. You'll be in room number four. Top of the stairs, second door on the right. Bathroom's at the end of the hall. How do you want to pay?"

"Reckon I ought to just pay by the day for now," Johnny said, fishing the money from his pocket. "I've got to make a trip. Don't know how long I'll be gone. Do you have a stable for a horse?"

"Out back, but that'll cost you an extra dollar a day for stall and feed."

Johnny counted out the money into the woman's outstretched hand. She folded the bills, stuck them down the front of her bodice, and settled back down on the sofa. Marshal Fagan poured himself a cup of coffee from a shiny pot on the buffet and folded onto the sofa across from Miss Lila.

"I've got an extra pair of pants and a shirt I'll loan you until you can pick up some new clothes tomorrow," the marshal said. "I'll lay them outside the bathroom door. Don't have any boots that would fit you, though. You're welcome to use my razor and shaving mug if you want, it's on the washstand in the bathroom. Come back down when you finish your bath, we'll eat together."

"I'll have Libby bring up some towels," Miss Lila told

him. "There's water in the tub. We keep a fresh bath poured once a day."

"I'm obliged," Johnny said, lifting one of the glass lamps from the buffet and lighting it to take with him.

Turning, he padded from the room and climbed the steep stairs. He found room number four and pushed inside. The light from his coal oil lamp lit the room with a yellowish hue and revealed a bed with a pink and white snowball pattern quilt over it. There was a dresser with mirror and a white water pitcher and washbasin. A straight-backed chair sat near the bed. Pretty lace curtains covered the single window that faced the street. It was the nicest room he had ever seen in all his twenty-one years. He could already tell he was going to like it here.

Punching the bed with a finger, his lip curled in a half-smile. It was one of those featherbeds he had heard about. It was soft. He could hardly wait to sprawl out on it for a good night's rest. It had been way too long.

I'd better hurry, he thought. The marshal's waiting on me. He went to find the bathroom. It was a small room that contained a washstand, mirror, and an oversized washtub. Testing the water, he found it to be less than lukewarm. Quickly shucking his ragged excuse for clothes, he climbed into the clean water. It was absolutely heavenly. Using the big bar of soap and bristle brush he found beside the tub, he set in scrubbing off a week's worth of dirt from the filthy jail floor.

Finally stepping from the tub, he dripped a trail of water on his way to the door. Intent on getting a towel and his borrowed clothes from outside, he pushed the door open and reached out to find the clothes, but no towel.

Sensing a presence, he glanced up, right into the face of an angel.

Light from the lamp she carried bounced off of her flaming red hair that spiraled about her shoulders and seemed to set it ablaze. She wore a white blouse that buttoned all the way up to her creamy white neck. A wine-colored skirt hung to the floor. She had an armload of folded towels and a beautiful face that now blushed crimson to match her hair. She had the biggest, brightest, emerald-green eyes he had ever seen. Right now they were widened in surprised and focused somewhere just shy of his waist. A hand flew to her mouth to stifle a silent, embarrassed gasp and caused her to drop the armload of towels.

"Oh, I'm sorry, ma'am!" Johnny blurted out. Suddenly realizing his nakedness, he quickly ducked back inside the bathroom.

He leaned against the door, closed his eyes and listened to the rapidly retreating footsteps outside in the hallway. He swallowed hard and silently wished he could die. *Well, that sure cooked my goose. Miss Lila will throw me out on my behind. I haven't been here a half-hour and her daughter sees me in my birthday suit. Way to go, Johnny.*

It took a few minutes to recover and get up enough nerve to crack the door open again. He retrieved the towels and clothes from the hall floor where they had been dropped by the daughter's hasty retreat. He shaved quickly, then dried off and shrugged into the tight-fitting borrowed clothes. Reluctantly, he trudged downstairs to face the music.

He found Marshal Fagan, Miss Lila, and a short, bald fellow sipping coffee at a large table in the dining room. They all glanced up from their cups when Johnny padded barefooted into the room.

"Now that's a heap better, son," Miss Lila said, looking him over approvingly. "You clean up right nice. Pour yourself a cup of coffee and have a seat. Libby will have you menfolk some grub in a minute or two. This is Silas Elliott. He's one of our local barbers. He's in room number three, right next door to yours. Looks like you could put his services to good use."

Shooter

Johnny shook the barber's outstretched hand and nodded a *howdy*.

"Sorry the clothes ain't quite big enough," Marshal Fagan said, as Johnny filled a cup from the pot on the table.

"They'll do fine," he replied, scraping out a chair and settling into it. Judging by their reaction, the daughter must not have told them about the incident upstairs, at least not yet.

"Miss Lila, you've got a right nice place. I shore do appreciate getting to stay here."

"Glad to have you, son. Mr. Fagan tells me you're gonna be working with him some."

"Yes, ma'am. Some, I reckon."

"You gonna go to the big hanging tomorrow, Miss Lila?" the marshal quickly asked, anxious to change the subject.

"I should say not. I can't imagine why anybody would want to see such a gruesome thing. I swear to my time, since that Judge Parker came, seems there's a hanging most every week or two."

"Yes, ma'am," the marshal said, "but all those men are cold-blooded murderers and worse."

"I suppose, but that don't change nothing. It still ain't a fit sight for good folks to see."

At that moment the daughter walked into the room. She carried two plates brimming with leftovers from supper. Johnny took one look and his breath caught in his throat. His heart skipped a beat then thundered inside his chest; he felt sure everyone in the room could hear it. It pleasured him to look at her. She was the most beautiful woman he had ever laid eyes on.

The spitting image of the lady in the painting over the fireplace, she was her mother made over. Long, auburn curls cascaded over her shoulders and wreathed a creamy-white, angelic face. Her tall, lithe body was slender but rounded in all the right places. She moved with the grace of a mountain lioness. Budding young breasts strained with innocent allure against the white blouse she wore. Her emerald-green eyes sparkled as they met his for the briefest instant, then darted quickly away under his frankly appraising stare. Johnny had never seen eyes like that. A rose hue flushed her cheeks as she set one of the plates in front of him.

"Libby," her mother said. "This is Johnny Shooter. He's a new boarder. This is my daughter, Libby Russell."

Her glance swung his way. Again her gaze worked their way over him, for the briefest slice of eternity, their gazes touching. She quickly raised a hand to brush away a stray lock of hair from her face. Her blush brightened and the slightest hint of a smile lifted one corner of those beautiful lips.

"It's nice to meet you, Mr. Shooter," she said barely above a whisper.

Her brief gaze tore away as she finished the words. The sweet sound of her voice breached the distance between them and found lodging in his heart. He swallowed a huge lump in his throat.

"It's good to meet you, too," he choked out, somehow knowing that from that moment on his life would never be the same, and that there would never be another woman for Johnny Shooter.

Chapter II

It was a lousy day for a hanging. Bloated dark clouds hung heavy and a cold drizzle driven by a stiff westerly wind kept the expected crowds away. Still, more than a thousand sadistic souls crowded the courtyard in front of the gallows.

Off to the southwest, a low rumbling thunder muffled the jovial voices of the celebratory spectators. A circus atmosphere prevailed, with vendors hawking everything from popcorn and boiled peanuts to replicas of a hangman's noose.

Fathers with small sons astride their shoulders jostled for room so their children could witness the big event.

One observer stood alone some distance away and watched the proceedings from a grassy knoll that rose from the Arkansas River behind him. He leaned against the trunk of a large sycamore tree and pulled the collar of his black duster up against the damp air. A cold wind flogged him and fluttered the tail of the long coat about his legs. Water dripped off a flat-brimmed black Stetson that mostly hid his features. The crown sported a ring of silver conchos. Strapped about his waist were matching bone handled Colt Peacemakers resting in black, notched holsters tied low on either leg—a gunfighter's rig.

In his hand he held the reins of a magnificent black gelding. The liveryman he bought it from said his name was Blackjack. The black saddle on the horse's back was studded with silver Conchos. A Winchester 73 rested in a saddle boot. A pair of sawed-off, double barrel Stevens ten gauge shotguns hung in matching holsters that straddled the horse's neck just in front of the saddle. The gelding pawed the rain-soaked ground impatiently and tossed its big head, but the man paid it little mind. His gaze was focused on the little procession emerging from the jail and making its way slowly toward the gallows.

United States Marshal James Fagan led the way. Behind him, with legs and hands manacled, and escorted by three deputy marshals with Winchesters carried at the ready, shuffled three condemned men.

The gallows toward which they headed was an elevated structure constructed of heavy timber. An overhead beam where the hangman's ropes were suspended traversed the entire length of the structure. A shingled roof assured inclement weather wouldn't prevent or delay the condemned's appointment with death. Four trapdoors, each three feet wide and twenty feet long spanned the length of the platform and provided adequate space for twelve men to be sent into eternity at the same time.

The little procession reached the foot of the steps and started their climb. They ascended the twelve steps slowly. Waiting at the top stood the hangman, a small German named George Maldon. As the condemned reached the platform they were positioned underneath a heavy rope fashioned into a noose. George slipped the ropes over each man's head, positioned behind their left ears, and cinched it tight.

Marshal Fagan stood on the top step and raised his hand

asking for quiet. When the crowd fell silent he read loudly from a paper he held in his hands.

"Abner Manley, you have been tried and convicted of the murder of Ellis McVay. By order of the Federal Court for the Western District of Arkansas, you have been sentenced to hang by the neck until you are dead.

"Amos Manley, you have been tried and convicted of the murder of Ellis McVay. By order of the Federal Court for the Western District of Arkansas, you have been sentenced to hang by the neck until you are dead.

"Te-o-lit-se, you have been tried and convicted of the murder of E. R. Cochran and of robbing him of seven dollars and forty cents. By order of the Federal Court for the Western District of Arkansas, you have been sentenced to hang by the neck until you are dead.

"May God have mercy on your souls."

George Maldon placed black hoods over each man's head, then walked to the end of the long platform and placed a hand on a long trip lever. He paused. His head swiveled to fix a gaze at the man standing just inside a second story window of the courthouse.

An eerie hush fell over the crowd. For a long moment time seemed to stand still.

Every eye was glued on the three men in the black hoods.

Judge Parker stood in front of his office window and stared for a long minute, contemplating what he was about to do. The decision weighed heavily on him. *I never wanted the kind of power that's been placed upon me—the power of life or death.*

Finally, with a long sigh, he gave a slight nod of his head and turned away from the window. The hangman's hand moved.

The lever tripped. The trapdoors collapsed. Three men plunged downward into eternity to face their Maker.

Long after the doctor entered the enclosed room underneath the gallows and examined the deceased, long after the three bodies were hauled away by the undertaker, long after the crowds disbursed, the mysterious spectator in black still stood underneath the sycamore tree. His gaze fixed not on the gallows or the spectacle he just witnessed, but on the fourth noose that hung from the overhead beam—the empty noose—the noose that would have been his.

Johnny Shooter slammed his eyes tightly shut and turned away.

Libby Russell's eyes lifted her heart from the lonely place where it held itself and danced inside her chest. Her heart on her sleeve, she watched from an upstairs window as the new boarder left the house, climbed on that magnificently beautiful black horse, and slowly rode away.

Johnny Shooter, she thought, what an unusual name, what an unusual man. She had never met a man like him. She had known him less than two days, yet in that short time, her whole life seemed changed.

Her face flushed red at the thoughts that raced through her mind: the brief, embarrassing encounter outside the bathroom that first night, the glances they exchanged at the dinner table and again at breakfast. Glances that hinted at unasked questions she dared not utter—fantasies she dared not dream. Or had her eyes played tricks on her heart, and seen something that wasn't there?

Tiny goose bumps prickled her skin as some strange, indefinable emotion she never felt before flushed without warning over her like a flood, frightening her, exciting her, bewildering her, setting her heart racing.

He left the house that first morning barefooted and in ill-fitting clothes borrowed from the Marshal. Yet, even then, there was a rugged handsomeness about him. He was tall, with broad shoulders, muscled arms and clean cut features. But it was those pale green eyes that haunted her and sent a strange excitement washing through her, so wondrous and sweet, so irresistible and strong it stole her breath away.

The man who returned late that same night bore no resemblance to the man who walked away that morning. This man was dressed in black from head to toe, wore twin pistols tied low on his hips, and rode a magnificent black horse. It was a miraculous re-birth, a metamorphosis of both looks and character. The shy young man in the hallway looked nothing like the self-assured man who returned. Yet, the transformation only served to heighten the mystery that surrounded him and swell her interest even more.

Now she stood at the upstairs window and watched him ride away, and for a long time after he disappeared from sight she remained at the window, as if her staring could bring him back.

Who was this tall stranger who came into her life and changed everything? Would she ever see him again?

Absently she brushed a tear from her eyes and turned slowly away.

Chapter III

A blustery wind moaned through the cottonwood trees along the riverbank and lashed Johnny's face with a steady downpour of rain. He tilted his new black Stetson lower and swiped water from his eyes with the back of a gloved hand. Pulling the collar of his long, black rain slicker tighter around his neck, he kicked free of the stirrup, lifted a leg over the back of his prancing mount and slowly lowered himself to the ground.

The Arkansas River was wide and roughly paralleled the boundary separating Arkansas from the Indian Territory. The only means of crossing the broad stream was the ferryboat. It shuttled freight wagons, horses, and passengers on foot from one side of the swift running river to the other. Right now the boat stood empty, rocked gently from the current, and awaited its first crossing of the day.

Several would-be passengers gathered along the wooden dock. They stood huddled together in little clusters, immersed in the heavy fog that hovered over the river.

As he rode up they cast appraising looks in Johnny's

direction, then quickly tore their gaze away as if they were glimpsing the devil himself. It was a mixed lot who—like himself—were all bound for the Indian Territory. Johnny's searching gaze took their measure: a farmer—his worn out shoes and patched bib overalls a sure sign of a life of hardship—stood with his family. Two small children shivered from the cold and clutched at their mother's ragged coat. She looked like a woman old before her time.

A puffy cheeked drummer with his bowler hat and suitcase no doubt filled with samples of his wares shifted nervously and avoided contact with Johnny's gaze.

Three men standing apart from the others earned a prolonged examination from Johnny's searching stare. They were tough looking men, hardcases, men whose faces either already decorated a wanted poster or soon would. Johnny studied their faces for future reference. Even these toughs averted their eyes and avoided eye contact.

Their reaction still surprised him, though he witnessed it often since his appearance transformation the day before. "Clothes make the man," Marshal Fagan said, and now Johnny experienced firsthand the truth of that statement. Tough looking men wearing low-tied guns stepped aside to make room when Johnny walked down the street. Folk's staring eyes followed his progress everywhere, and then whispered hurried questions in nearby ears inquiring as to his identity. Whoever he was, this man in black with the twin, bone-handled Peacemakers commanded respect, if not outright fear. This was something new for Johnny Shooter.

He hunkered inside his slicker and toyed with the reins in his hand, intent on waiting until the others boarded. But the bearded ferry master cast a patronizing look and waved him aboard ahead of the waiting passengers who skulked aside, clearing a path to the loading ramp.

The high-strung black gelding showed no reluctance and climbed the ribbed gangplank without hesitation. Johnny flipped a half-dollar to the operator and led his mount to the far end of the large barge. The remaining passengers came aboard and huddled together at the opposite end, seemingly wanting to locate as far from the pale-eyed man in black as they could get.

That suited Johnny just fine. He turned his back to them and stared into the murky denseness of a fog that hovered above the river. The damp air chilled Johnny to the bone and reminded him of his week in the basement prison.

What lay ahead for him out there? Why had he been spared a quick death at the end of a short hangman's rope? Most likely his end would come in a hail of gunfire or a bullet in the back from a man whose face decorated a wanted poster. The thought made him remember the flier Judge Parker gave him.

Unconsciously, he reached a hand to a pocket inside his slicker and felt the United States Deputy Marshal's badge. He still found it hard to believe it belonged to him. Also in his pocket were two pieces of folded paper. One was an arrest warrant. The other was the poster.

Pulling the second paper from his pocket he stared down at it for a long moment. The boyish face of the Choctaw Kid stared back at him. It was a face most would call handsome with a look of youthful innocence that belied his deadly reputation. He had high cheekbones and a cocky smile. Long, straight hair held in place by a leather headband framed the young face. But it was the boy's eyes, those dark, piercing eyes that betrayed the innocent look and revealed the evil that lurked somewhere behind their fixed stare—the evil of a cold blooded killer.

Johnny Shooter's job was to find the Kid, bring him in if possible, or kill him if he had to. The judge never actually said so, but it made clear which of the two options he preferred.

Six months. How can I hope to last that long, going up against the likes of the Choctaw Kid?

Swift running water tugged at the ferry. Thick ropes strained, creaking as they held the barge from being swept downstream. Somewhere behind them the muffled shrill of a factory whistle pierced the early morning quietness. The ferry moved slowly toward the distant bank, buffeted by the choppy waters.

After long minutes the ferry gave a shudder and came to a sudden stop against the sloped bank. The bowlines were secured and the gangplank lowered. Johnny led his mount ashore. Without so much as a backward glance he toed a stirrup and swung into the saddle.

Gathering the reins, he feathered the big gelding in the flanks and reined him up the unloading ramp and onto Indian Territory, then gave him his head and settled into the gently rocking motion of a five-beat, ground-eating gait. The liveryman said the horse possessed staying power and plenty of speed. He would see.

"You can shore cover the ground can't you, big fellow?"

The sound of his own voice seemed odd to his ears, as if from a stranger, someone Johnny had never met nor cared to know. This new creation he became was as frightful to him as to those he encountered. An uneasy feeling settled somewhere in the pit of his stomach and found a home.

Johnny followed a wagon trail northwest. Flat river bottom land appeared choked with heavy growth of willow, sycamore, and an occasional stand of oak trees. Swampy marshland stretched as far as he could see and slowed his progress.

By noon the rain stopped and the sun poked holes through the low hanging clouds; it was hot on his shoulders. He shrugged out of his rain gear and tied it behind his saddle. A soft westerly breeze felt good against his face. His eyes narrowed against the sun's harsh glare. He rode on toward an uncertain destiny.

Chapter IV

Three riders sat their saddles, peered from a thick stand of scrub oak trees, and waited. Their gazes were fixed on a small log farmhouse in the valley below. A thin tendril of smoke from a supper fire rose from a rock chimney, bent, and scattered by the wind.

The steady ring of a chopping ax drifted across the small valley and reached the onlookers' hearing as a bare chested man cut firewood. The happy laughter of a small boy and a teen-age girl playing hide-and-go-seek painted a peaceful scene.

"What we waiting fer, Kid?" the oldest of the three questioned, clearly irritated at the delay. "We been sittin' here on our backsides watchin' that cabin fer the best part of an hour. We could have had it over and done with by now."

Choctaw Kid eyed a man with massive shoulders and a cannonball head that was mostly hidden by a shock of dirty, shaggy hair and facial hair to match. His buckskins were filthy and ragged. Tobacco stains painted trails through his scraggly beard. Cruel eyes flashed from under bushy eyebrows. An evil grin curled his lips as he toyed with the long Bowie knife in his hand; Zack Thibodeaux dearly loved to cut folks. For him, death was a way of life.

The Choctaw Kid heard the question, but delayed his response. He was in no hurry. Waiting was something he understood all too well. In one way or another he had spent his whole life waiting. As the youngest of ten children he was last in line for just about everything.

He never knew who his pa was. What difference would it make anyway? he figured. Men beat a path to their door, a different one most every night. One of his ma's nightly visitors had been his first kill when he was only twelve years old.

When he finally spoke, the answer cut through the fading twilight like a knife through hot butter. The words were little more than a whisper, yet they were spoken with chilling authority and deadly meaning. A small smile played around the Choctaw Kid's lips as he spoke.

"We'll do it when I say we do it."

"Ain't nobody down there but that feller, his woman, and them two brats. They ain't gonna be no trouble."

This time the Kid didn't bother to reply. He touched heels to his black-and-white pinto and headed slowly down the hillside toward the cabin. His two companions followed.

The third man in the threesome wasn't a man at all, barely in his mid-teens. His dark hair and peach-fuzz whiskers gave him a school-boy appearance. But at fifteen, Joshua Thibodeaux had been eyewitness to murder more times than men twice his age. Most of those times were since he started riding with his uncle Zack and the Choctaw Kid. He sucked in a ragged breath and tried to quell the flood of fear that tore at his guts. He was about to see death again.

The two children spotted the approaching riders first. The boy alerted his pa who leaned his ax against a log, swiped sweat from his face with an arm, and picked up his nearby rifle and levered a shell. He watched suspiciously as they approached.

"Who are you and what you want?" he called out as the three riders drew near.

"Jest lookin' to water our horses, friend," Chocktaw shouted in an overly friendly tone. "We don't mean no harm."

"There's water in the trough and you're welcome to it," the farmer replied, relaxing somewhat and lowering his rifle.

That proved to be the last mistake the man would ever make. With no warning and lightning speed, the Choctaw Kid drew his pistol. His gun belched two orange streaks of flame. A surprised expression overtook the farmer's face. He gazed, unbelieving, and grabbed at the two holes in his chest that spurted bright crimson life from his body. For a long moment he teetered like a tree rocking in the wind before his legs gave way like they had been chopped from beneath him, and he pitched facedown in the dusty yard. The young teenage girl screamed and bolted for the house.

"Get them kids!" Zack ordered his nephew with a shout.

Leaping from his horse, Joshua tore out after the girl. She was fast. She sped on bare feet across the yard. Her long, golden colored hair flew in the breeze as she ran. He barely caught her before she reached the cabin. Then he wished he hadn't.

Chocktaw grinned as she lit into Joshua like a wildcat. Tiny, balled fists pummeled him. Her fingernails scratched at his eyes. Bare feet lashed out. Piercing screams escaped her lips. Her breath came in great gasps between sobs and racked her body.

Joshua finally subdued her by wrapping both arms around her in a bear hug. Apparently exhausted from the struggle and overcome with emotion, he felt her go limp in his grasp. She must have fainted.

Shooter

The farm boy, who looked to be maybe eleven or twelve, rushed to his pa's side screaming his name. Tears streamed down the boy's face and great sobs shook his small body as he held his dying father's head in his lap and kept screaming.

Climbing down from his sway-backed horse, Zack Tribodeaux's face took on a sinister look and a wide grin curled his lips as he strode to the boy. Without so much as a word he grasped a handful of the boy's blond hair and yanked his head back savagely with his left hand. An evil laugh broke from his throat as his right hand swiped the long Bowie across the helpless boy's throat.

A woman's scream pierced the air from the doorway of the cabin. She was trying frantically to lever a shell into the rifle in her hands when the Choctaw Kid reached her. Snatching the weapon from her grasp, he backhanded her across the face, sending her sprawling backwards through the door. He stalked inside after her and slammed the door shut.

Riley Buckner whistled happily as he trudged through the thick woods on his way home. His pa would be proud of him. At fourteen he was already an accomplished hunter. The six squirrels in the tow sack slung over his shoulder proved that once again. They would make a good meal for the Buckner family. A feeling of pride swelled his chest.

His thoughts were scattered by the sound of gunfire coming from the direction of their cabin.

What in blazes is Pa be shooting at? he wondered, hurrying his steps.

A feeling of fear rushed over him like an icy chill. He swung the twelve-gauge shotgun off his shoulder and broke into a run. Their cabin was still a good mile and a half away.

Caution slowed him as he topped a wooded hill overlooking their cabin. Three strange horses stood ground hitched in their yard.

A big, grizzly looking man slouched on the ground with his back against the side of the barn, sipping from a bottle. Cathy, and some boy about Riley's own age, sat leaning against a tree. Something was wrong with Cathy; she never sat that still in her whole life.

Then he saw his pa and Billy. He knew immediately they were dead. His breath caught, and came harsh and quivery. Fear clamped its sharp talons deep in his chest. He tried swallowing down his fear, but it wouldn't go. He stifled a great sob that boiled up from the depths of his soul and threatened to erupt as a scream. Tears blurred his vision. He mopped them away with the back of a hand.

Then anger overtook him, hot anger that burned a path to his face. Killing anger. Anger like he had never known before. With shaky hands he broke open the double-barreled shotgun and fumbled two shells from his pocket. He thumbed them into the openings and slammed the shotgun shut with a flick of his wrist.

His first instinct was to charge down the hillside and kill those who murdered his pa and little brother. Somewhere in his troubled mind reason took control. He would only get himself killed too, and then who would be left to help his ma and sister? What would pa expect him to do?

He was too far away for the shotgun. He knew he had to get closer. Besides, there were three horses, but he only saw two strangers. That means the other one must be inside the house. That thought sent waves of new fear flooding over him. Ma must be inside the house.

Drawing a deep breath, he pushed to his feet. Sweeping a quick gaze at the space between himself and the house told him he would have to circle along the shoulder of the hill in order to use the cover of the trees. There was an open space between the trees and a gully that ran along the valley floor. If he could make it to the gully without being seen, then he could work his way pretty close to the barn, maybe even slip inside through the back door. He had to give it a try.

It was the better part of a half-hour before the Choctaw Kid emerged from the cabin. Joshua sat beside the girl under a big oak tree. He had tied her hands like his uncle told him. She seemed to be awake but sat motionless, her eyes fixed with a glassy stare like she was looking but wasn't seeing anything.

Joshua watched as Zack finally drained the whiskey bottle he was working on while they waited. For the last half hour he had been casting hungry looks at the girl. Joshua didn't want his uncle to hurt her; he liked her. But what could he do to stop him?

"Did you leave anything for me, Kid?" Zack slurred, an evil laugh breaking from his throat. "Or do I get this pretty little girl here?"

"You can have what's left of the woman. Finish her off when you're through, but leave the girl be. We're taking her with us."

"I won't be long," Zack promised, staggering as he pushed to his feet and headed for the cabin. "Don't take me all day to get it done."

"Want me to catch up that horse over yonder in the corral?" Josh asked anxiously. "If the girl's going with us, she'll need a horse to ride."

The Choctaw Kid threw a quick sideways glance at the girl.

"Might as well, I reckon, unless you want her riding double with you. What's wrong with her, she looks kind of funny or something. If she can't cook and stuff, ain't no use taking her."

"Don't know. She's been like that ever since she woke up. She'll be all right. I'll take care of her—I mean if it's okay with you."

"Just keep an eye on her. That uncle of yours would give his eye teeth to get ahold of that little gal."

"Reckon I could have the man's rifle?" Joshua asked. "I could help with the hunting if I had a gun."

"Don't know why not, another gun might come in handy. Time I was your age, I'd already killed a half dozen men."

Joshua tried his best not to look at the murdered man and young boy when he snatched up the rifle and slid it into the saddle boot on his horse. By the time he had a saddle cinched on the only horse in the corral and the girl in the saddle, Zack stumbled from the cabin pulling up his pants and wiping his bloody knife on a britches leg.

"You find any money or anything?" he asked, climbing stiffly on his horse.

"Weren't hardly worth the effort," the Choctaw Kid replied, heeling his pinto forward. "All they had was twelve dollars."

Riley was halfway along the gully when he heard the pounding hooves. He rose to peek over the bank in time to see them riding away. He jerked the shotgun to his shoulder but couldn't fire. Cathy was riding pa's horse and was the last one in line. She was slumped over in the saddle like she was half-asleep. The boy had the horse's reins, leading Cathy's horse behind his own. Riley felt helpless. All he could do was watch them ride away.

Scrambling up the bank, he ran as fast as he could to check on his pa and Billy. As he fell to his knees beside his pa he already knew the answer even before the question formed in his mind—they were both dead.

His pa lay on his back. Two dark holes in his chest still oozed blood. His sightless eyes were wide in a chalky face, blank with horror, open, staring into nothingness. Riley touched his pa's face with a trembling hand. It felt cold and lifeless.

Turning on his knees, Riley looked for the first time at his little brother. His sight blurred with tears. A sharp cry escaped his lips. His breath came in labored gasps. His heartbeat thundered and pounded against the wall of his chest as if it would burst. Billy's throat had been cut from ear to ear. He lay in a pool of blood.

Then Riley remembered his mother. Leaping to his feet, he raced to the open door of the cabin. He didn't go inside. One look and he froze in his tracks, grasping at the door facing to keep from falling.

She lay naked in a puddle of blood. Her throat, too, had been cut.

Riley's stomach emptied its contents. An unbearable pain twisted his guts. Again and again the retching racked his body. Great sobs tore from his throat. Ruthless, clutching fingers crushed his heart. He sank to his knees.

How long he knelt there weeping, he didn't know nor care. What was left to live for now anyway? Everyone he loved had been taken from him.

Cathy! He remembered Cathy. She was still alive. Somehow he had to save her. But how? He was just a boy. I've got to think. What would Pa do? What would he want me to do? Go get help. He would want me to go get help.

Leaping to his feet he raced to the corral. Jake was there. The old plow mule would have to do, all that was left, and it was twelve miles to Fort Gibson. Hurriedly he slipped the extra bridle in place, his fingers fumbling to fasten the neck strap. There was no saddle. Clutching the shotgun in one hand, he grabbed a handful of mane and swung onto the mule's bare back.

Chapter V

The burning sun-ball hung blood-red and slid gently behind the line of rolling, blue hills and was swallowed up by the horizon. Long shadows crept across the land.

Johnny Shooter reined up on the crest of a hill overlooking Fort Gibson and watched the amazing spectacle unfold before his eyes. From early childhood, he always marveled at the beauty of the heavens. As sunset faded to twilight, he shifted his gaze to the ramshackle community below. He endured two days of hard riding since leaving Fort Smith. The day before he camped near the small settlement of Webbers Falls. From there he followed the Arkansas River as it meandered through the heavily wooded countryside.

He knew that Fort Gibson was the oldest Army Fort in the Indian Territory. The army outpost hugged a hillside along the Arkansas River. A settlement had quickly sprung up around the fort.

Johnny had never been there, but heard plenty about it. Its reputation as one of the toughest towns in the Mid-West was known far and wide. Rumors said men were shot in Fort Gibson just for target practice. Johnny hoped to find the Choctaw Kid here, or at least be able to pick up his trail. The Kid was known to be a frequent visitor.

Lengthening shadows were claiming the last hint of day when he reined up in front of the livery. He was bone tired after his two-day ride from Fort Smith. His body felt leaden, wrung dry of strength as he climbed from the saddle. A grizzled old timer, whose face was mostly hidden behind a mask of tangled gray hair, limped out to take his horse.

"Mighty fine lookin' black ye be riding there, young fellow. Ye be new in these parts. I'd remember a gelding like that if'n I'd ever seen it before."

"Just passing through," Johnny said, stomping feeling back into his feet. "Where might a fellow find a bed and grub around here?"

"Ward Hotel right up the street's got rooms that are tolerable, I reckon. Cost ye three dollars. Ye can bunk up in my hayloft for fifty cents, but ye don't look the type. Best place to eat in town is the Chow Hall Café. Course, it's the only place to eat in Fort Gibson. It's right across the street from the hotel. Gonna be staying long?"

"Doubt it. Kinda looking for a man. You might have seen him. Calls himself the Choctaw Kid?"

Johnny watched the old timer's reaction. Those shifty old eyes cut a quick look at Johnny. The hosteler's appraising gaze crawled along Johnny's six foot-three inches, pausing briefly at the pistols tied to his legs.

"Ye the law or a bounty hunter?"

"I'm a fellow looking for the Choctaw Kid," Johnny said, flipping a silver dollar in the old fellow's direction.

The man's gnarled hand shot forward, plucking the coin out of mid-air with surprising deftness. The whiskers parted as a squirt of tobacco juice streamed out, dousing a nearby horsefly with the brown liquid. A wide grin settled across the old man's lips.

"He's in and out. Right now he's out. Rides a black-and-white pinto. Usually rides with a bunch of hardcases. This time he just had a grizzly bear looking fellow and a young kid with him when he pulled out couple of days back. Headed south. That's all I know."

"You've been a help. I'm obliged. Double grain and stall my horse. I'll be leaving before first light."

Johnny slid the Winchester from its saddle boot and slung his saddlebags over one shoulder. The old fellow gathered Blackjack's reins.

"Be smart to keep ye eyes peeled and your gun hand empty while ye in town, young fellow. There's more'n a few hereabouts that might take a notion to see if'n ye's any good with them pistols ye's packin'."

"Thanks old timer, but I ain't looking for trouble," Johnny said, turning to head up the street.

"Man don't have to look for trouble in Fort Gibson. It comes looking for him," the hosteler said, raising his voice as Johnny walked away.

He lifted a hand to acknowledge the old fellow's warning. All he wanted right now was a soft, clean bed and a thick steak. He was so hungry his belt buckle was rubbing his backbone.

As he strode up the boardwalk toward the hotel, his searching gaze took in his surroundings. It wasn't dark yet and already the predictable transition was evident in the streets. The day folks—the businessmen, the shoppers, and the upstanding people of Fort Gibson—had all but disappeared to their respective homes. In their place came the night people: the soldiers, the drinkers, the gamblers, and the troublemakers.

The tinny sound of a piano floated on a soft breeze. Throaty laughter from female voices mixed with slurred curses of soldiers who'd already drank too much filled the creeping darkness. Johnny pushed through the door of the Ward Hotel.

A buxom redhead slouching behind the desk lifted her gaze and pulled herself upright. She pushed a hank of hair from her face and pasted an overly generous smile on heavy-painted lips. Pulling her shoulders back, she unashamedly pushed forward her best assets.

"What might I do for you, handsome?"

"Hoping you got a room with a soft bed and clean sheets."

"Just so happens my best room is still available."

"How much?"

"Three dollars for the room."

Johnny fished three silver dollars from his pocket and signed his name in the book. The red head took a key from a rack and sashayed around the counter. Johnny followed the exaggerated swinging of generous hips up the stairs to room number six. She unlocked the door and stood aside.

"Is there anything else I could do for you, handsome?" she purred, flashing wide, hazel eyes.

Johnny allowed himself a wry grin.

"Not unless you serve supper, too."

The pasted smile on the woman's face disappeared and was abruptly replaced by an ugly scowl. Without so much as a word she spun on her heels and left.

Johnny smothered a chuckle and tossed his saddlebags on the bed. He checked the bed, somewhat surprised to find the sheets clean and fresh. He stood his Winchester against the wall and walked from the room.

The Chow Hall café was mostly empty when Johnny pushed through the door and selected a table near the back wall. He scraped out a straight-backed chair and settled into it as an Indian girl looking to be in her late teens set a coffee cup in front of him and filled it from a blackened pot.

She was a pretty thing. She looked to be Cherokee. Her flawless olive skin and high cheekbones gave her face a look more mature than her apparent years. Shiny black braids hung down her back and reached below her tiny waist. Her lips quivered nervously and a look of fear clouded her dark eyes. Johnny smiled broadly to help allay her fears.

"Do you have a beef steak back there you could cook up for a hungry fellow?"

"Yes, sir," she said softly, seeming to relax a bit.

"Then that's what I'll have."

Without a word she turned away. Johnny blew the steam from his coffee and chanced a sip. Over the lip of his cup, he swept the room with a searching gaze.

Two other tables were occupied. At one table was a drummer. He wore the look as surely as if he had a sign hanging around his neck. The woman sitting with him was clearly a lady of the night. Her face had too much makeup and her dress was too short at both ends.

Three tough looking soldiers slouched at the other table. One wore the stripes of a sergeant. He was a bear of a man. His large head sat on massive shoulders. A barrel chest strained against the blue jacket of his uniform. All three stared hard at Johnny and talked in low tones. They looked like trouble with a capitol T. That was the last thing Johnny needed right now.

He sipped his coffee and tried not to notice the stares. All he wanted was a meal and a good night's sleep. He drained his cup and poured another. By the time he finished it his food came. It was good.

He'd consumed about half of his steak when the soldiers pushed up from their table and headed for the door. Johnny relaxed. He sure wasn't anxious to tangle with that bunch. Their leaving made him the only remaining customer. He took his time enjoying one more cup, left a generous tip, and then headed back to the hotel. He looked forward to sleeping in a real bed.

For a long time he lay there, staring into the darkness of his room. Quietness wrapped itself around him. Even the cornshuck mattress emitted only soft whispers when he moved. His mind drifted. Like a leaf on still water pushed by a gentle breeze, his thoughts flitted here and there.

What a difference a week makes.

Only a week ago he was a condemned man facing a long drop on a short rope. Now, here he was, a Unites States Deputy Marshal on the trail of a killer they called the Choctaw Kid. A man possibly not a great deal unlike himself.

Finally, as sleep tumbled closer, the haunting image of a beautiful lady with auburn hair and emerald eyes, and a little lift at one corner of a smile, sought and found lodging in his mind. She was a pleasing thought.

A loud banging on the door woke Johnny from a sound sleep. He grabbed his pistol even before he opened his eyes, then swung his bare feet to the floor.

"Who is it?"

"It's Lester from the livery." A familiar voice called from outside the door. "I got a boy here what needs to talk to ye."

"Can't it wait till morning?"

"Ye the law ain't ye? Killin' don't wait till mornin'"

Striking a match, Johnny lit a coal oil lamp, jammed the pistol in the waistband of his pants and opened the door.

A young boy looking to be in his early-teens stood beside the grizzled old hosteler. Johnny stood aside to allow them entrance and set the lamp on the bureau.

"What's this about a killing?" Johnny asked.

"The boy come riding in hell-bent-for-leather on a plow mule just now. Mule looks plumb tuckered out. The boy don't look much better. Seems there's been a killin'. Well, I'll let him tell it."

"They killed my ma and pa and little brother," the excited young boy blurted out. "They just killed 'em for no reason! They took my sis with them when they rode off."

"Who's they?" Johnny asked. "Who killed your folks?"

"There was three of 'em. Don't know who they was. They just killed 'em for no reason. They cut my little brother's throat. My ma's too. They didn't have no reason a' tall! Why would they do that mister?"

"Where'd this happen, son? Where do you live?"

"'Bout twelve miles north. You gotta come and help me, mister. They killed my folks and took my sis and I don't know what to do."

Johnny turned to face the hosteler.

"Is that mule of his fit to ride?"

"He's tired and lathered up, but a good mule can outlast any horse on four legs."

"Then saddle my horse. Let me get some clothes on and I'll be along directly. Son, do you feel like riding with me and showing me where you live?"

"Yes, sir."

"Good. You go on with the old timer. I'll be right along. You can tell me all about it while we're riding."

As Lester and the boy left, Johnny stomped his boots on and shrugged into his shirt. He strapped his pistols around his waist, slung his saddlebags over a shoulder and snatched up his Winchester. Looked like it was gonna be a long night.

Chapter VI

Joshua Thibodeaux twisted in his saddle. His dark eyes darted again at the girl on the horse behind him. She still slumped badly, barely managing to stay in the saddle. *I should have tied her on.*

His gaze lingered on her for a long moment. Her long, corn silk hair splashed across slumped shoulders and hung down her back. Even in their fixed stare, her blue eyes sparkled. Flushed cheeks, with tear trails turned silver by the sun, bore witness to the recent traumatic events. The creamy whiteness of her neck, the youthful breasts that pushed against the faded gingham dress—all this Joshua took in with one slow, searching stare.

She was pretty, maybe the prettiest girl he had ever seen. Course that wasn't saying a whole lot, he could probably count on one hand the girls he'd known in his young life. There hadn't been many worth a second glance on the Atchafalaya River in the Louisiana bayou where he grew up.

Then a thought struck terror in Joshua's heart. Without a doubt they will kill her, or worse. He gasped at the thought and felt nauseous in the pit of his stomach. He knew when she was no longer useful to the Kid, he would either kill her himself, or even worse, turn her over to Uncle Zack. Joshua already saw how his Uncle looked at her.

Joshua swung his attention back to the riders in front of him. His Uncle was next in line with the Choctaw Kid leading the way. All day the Kid pushed on northwest at an unrelenting pace. It was obvious he wanted to put some tracks between them and the murdered farm family. Joshua figured they were headed somewhere to meet the rest of the gang.

Joshua wished for the thousandth time he had never gone with his Uncle after his pa died, but what else could he have done? *I ought to have run off into the swamps, nobody could have found me there.* Joshua knew the swamps like he knew the back of his hand. He'd hunted there since he was knee-high to a swamp rabbit.

Joshua threw a quick glance at the sky; it was near sunset. *We should be stopping soon. Shore hope the girl is able to help with the chores around camp. If she don't earn her keep, they won't keep her around long.*

The country they were riding through was mostly hilly and heavily wooded. Small, fresh running streams threaded through thick growth of pine and scrub cedar, and wound their way lazily around rocky outcroppings of moss covered rocks. The waters seemed mysteriously drawn to some unknown rendezvous and seemed in no hurry to get there.

The Choctaw Kid suddenly reined left toward a pocket of large rocks with a stream nearby. Joshua knew this would be their campsite for the night. It was a good one. Cabin-size boulders formed a wall around a grassy opening. The rocks would hide their campfire.

Joshua reined his horse through the opening between two big rocks and sprang quickly to the ground. Two quick strides took him beside the girl's horse. Reaching up, he gently lifted her to the ground. Slipping an arm around her waist, he led her to a large boulder, lowered her to the soft cushion of grass and leaned her back against the rock. He had chores to do.

Hurriedly, he rustled up wood and built a fire. By the time it was going good he had the blackened coffeepot filled with water from the nearby stream and sitting over the flames. Rummaging through the food sack, he withdrew the small hand-size piece of salt pork. Withdrawing his hunting knife from its scabbard on his belt, he sliced the last of the meat into the frying pan.

Glancing up from his chores, he noted with disgust that Uncle Zack was already sprawled against a rock, guzzling golden liquid from a half-empty bottle and eyeing the girl. He would be drunk before supper. The Choctaw Kid wandered off somewhere, as usual. He seldom stayed around camp long, but often returned with something to add to their sparse meals.

Peering once again into the sack, Joshua removed the last two potatoes and wrinkled his nose; one was half-rotten. A quick slice of his blade disposed of the spoiled half. Practiced strokes sliced the remainder, peeling and all, of both potatoes into the pan along with the frying meat. Adding a pinch of salt, he stirred the contents of the pan. Scooping a handful of coffee from the tin, he dumped it into the boiling water of the coffeepot.

Joshua didn't resent having to do all the work around camp, he was used to working. In the swamps where he grew up there was always something that needed doing. Joshua was expected to pull his weight since he was knee-high to his papa.

Throwing a quick glance at the girl, he was relieved to see she hadn't moved. She still slumped motionless against the rock, seemingly unaware of anything going on around her.

"Hurry up with that food, boy!" his Uncle slurred loudly.

"It'll be ready in a minute."

Sure wish the Kid would get back soon, Joshua thought.

There ain't no telling what Uncle Zack might do when he gets good and drunk.

Using his knife, Joshua raked part of the salt pork and potatoes into a tin plate, then hurried over and handed it to his drunken Uncle. Without taking his glassy, bloodshot eyes off the girl, the big man used his dirty fingers to shove the food in his mouth.

Careful to leave half of the remaining food in the skillet for the Choctaw Kid, Josh raked the rest into another plate, poured a tin cup full of water from a molasses bucket, and walked over to squat beside the girl. She still sat motionless, staring off into space. She didn't seem to notice his presence.

"What's your name?" he asked softly.

If she heard him she didn't let on. Josh cut a quick glance at his Uncle, and tried again.

"I've got some food here. You need to eat something."

There was still no response. *What am I gonna do?* He wondered through mounting panic. *If I can't get her up and around, they'll kill her.*

Touching the cup to her dry lips he tried to get her to drink. The water ran from her mouth and down her chin, soaking the front of her dress. She made no effort to swallow.

Then he remembered. The woman from the swamps...

Neighbors found a woman wandering around in the swamps and brought her to pa's house. She looked half-dead at the time, just like this girl. Joshua heard his pa say she'd been raped. After trying and failing to get her to respond, his pa brought her around by hauling off and slapping the daylights out of her.

The thought made Josh sick to his stomach. He stared at the beautiful face in front of him. *I can't do it,* he thought. *How could I ever lay a hand on her? She's so innocent, so helpless, so beautiful. But what else can I do?* He knew deep inside himself what he had to do, it was the only chance to save her.

Glancing again at his drunken Uncle, he used every ounce of willpower he could muster to draw his open hand far back. For a long slice of eternity it hung suspended in the air, refusing to obey. More than he had ever wanted anything in his whole life he prayed for the strength to do what his heart screamed out for him not to do. Clamping his teeth tightly, his mouth narrowed, and his hand scribed an arc through the air.

The impact of his open palm against the girl's soft cheek sounded like the crack of a bullwhip in the stillness of a growing twilight. Her head snapped sideways.

Wide, tear-soaked eyes blinked with fear and looked at him for the first time. Her quivering lips opened in a sharp gasp of surprise and a look of shock swept across her face. Every drop of Josh's blood drained toward his feet.

Suddenly she was on him like a wildcat. Balled fists lashed at him, pummeled him. Clawing fingers stabbed and tore at his face. Her bare feet lashed out, kicking at him again and again. But Josh was so excited about bringing her back from the world of the walking dead he hardly felt the punishment she inflicted on him.

"Let me get ahold of that little gal," his Uncle's voice slurred from behind Joshua. "I like 'em when they fight."

Before Joshua could protest, a big hand swept him aside like a rag doll, sending him sprawling. His head hit a rock. The world spun. Bright pinpoints of light burst before his eyes. For a long moment he lay stunned, unable to move.

A terrified scream jerked him back to his senses. He looked quickly toward the sound.

His Uncle was already on the girl, his huge body completely covering her. A big hand held both of hers in a vice-like grip above her head. Josh saw his Uncle's other hand tearing at her flimsy dress, yanking it up around her waist, then prying her legs open.

The girl tried desperately to fight him off, but she was no match for the giant. Her screams, mixed with sobs, pierced the twilight. Her head rolled from side to side. Frantic eyes blazed from a contorted face. Suddenly her widened gaze fell on Josh. For only the briefest instant their eyes met, but in the girl's tear-blurry eyes he saw a desperate pleading for help.

Blind fury raced through him and found lodging in his mind. Outrage melded with anger and gave birth to tears. Unconsciously his hand grasped the stone his head had encountered and, scrambling to his feet, he covered the few steps to stand over his Uncle.

A cry tore from his throat and with every ounce of his strength, he brought the rock down on the back of his Uncle's head. The impact sounded like a pistol shot. His Uncle uttered a grunt, went limp, and collapsed on top of the girl.

Using both hands, Josh managed to roll the unconscious giant off of her and gather her into his arms. Great, wracking sobs shook her young body. She clung to him as if to life itself. For a long minute they remained locked in a comforting embrace. Josh's mind whirled, lost in a feeling of helplessness, guilt, and responsibility.

Just as quickly a more sinister thought sent fear racing up his spine. *We've got to get out of here before Uncle Zack wakes up, he'll skin us both alive! The Choctaw Kid will most likely return any minute, too.*

With a shaky breath he forced the words past the huge knot in his throat.

"We can't stay here," he told the girl, hoping he sounded calmer than he felt inside his stomach. "They'll kill us both."

Raising her head from his chest she looked directly into his eyes for a lingering moment. Tears scoured the rims of her lashes. She blinked them away, and in a quivery voice asked, "What are we going to do?"

"We've got to run for it. It's our only chance."

She took a shuddery breath and swiped away the tears with the back of a hand. Without another word she turned and ran toward the saddled horses.

Joshua took a quick step to follow, then spun around, taking time to yank his Uncle's pistol from its holster and jam it into the waistband of his pants. Then wheeling around, raced to where the horses were tied. The girl was already in the saddle. Joshua quickly mounted his own horse and gathered the reins.

"Follow me and stay close," he told her breathlessly.

Kicking the horse's flanks, Joshua whipped the reins along the animal's neck and felt it break into a full gallop. Twisting a look over his shoulder, he was pleased when he saw the girl's mount staying close to his.

Twilight was fading and darkness hovered close, hesitating briefly before cloaking the land under a shroud of night. A quarter moon offered enough light to help them avoid trees and large rocks that littered the area. Joshua gave no thought as to the direction they were riding, all he could think of was getting as far away from his Uncle and the Choctaw Kid as possible.

After what he figured was the better part of two hours, Joshua slowed his mount to a walk, giving the horses a much-needed breather. He knew his Uncle and the Kid would follow, but most likely not until daylight.

"Can we rest a while?" the girl pleaded from behind him.

"I reckon maybe for just a bit," he said over his shoulder. "The horses need some rest, too."

Reining up, Joshua climbed from the saddle, wrapped his reins around a sturdy bush, and reached to help the girl to the ground. A nearby log offered a welcome resting place. They both sat down and collapsed against it. For an awkward minute neither spoke.

"I don't even know your name," Joshua finally managed.

Shooter

"Cathy, my name is Cathy Buckner."

"I'm Joshua Thibodeaux," he said, clearing his throat in an effort to keep his voice steady. "My friends just call me Josh."

"That's an unusual name, your last one I mean. I never heard it before."

"Yeah, well, it's French. I'm mostly Cajun, I reckon you'd say. I'm from Louisiana."

"That's a long way away, isn't it? What are you doing way up here?"

"My ma and pa both died and I had to go live with my Uncle. Bad as I hate to say it, that's him back there. I'm really sorry for what he..." He bit down hard on what he'd intended to say.

"Oh," she replied.

It seemed they both ran out of words, and for long minutes, they sat in silence. The night lay quiet, only the sounds disturbed the silence: the never-ending chatter of crickets and tree frogs. Somewhere a whippoorwill called its lonesome sound, and a coyote barked...and the darkness deepened.

"Is...are my folks all...?"

He could hear the tears in her voice. He couldn't answer. The words backed up in his throat and refused to come further. *How can I tell her they're all dead? How can I ever convince her that I had nothing to do with it?* Not trusting his voice, he just nodded his head sadly.

Joshua heard the sob start deep inside Cathy's chest. It rolled and boiled and burst past her lips in a near scream. Her voice frayed and tears broke free. She buried her face in her open hands and wept uncontrollably.

Hearing her weeping tore at his heart. A lump crawled up the back of his throat and lodged there. Tears escaped the corners of his eyes. He swiped them away with a sleeve

Reaching out, he coiled his arm around Cathy's shoulders and pulled her to him. Her body shook as wave after wave of grief poured from her. Joshua heard the sounds of the girl's distress and tried to blink away his own unwelcome tears. Feelings of compassion, guilt, and responsibility twisted his insides.

It took a while for her to cry out the hurt. Finally, her agonizing subsided to a body-jerking snub.

"We need to get moving," he whispered.

She only nodded, swiped her tear-drenched face with her sleeve, and pushed herself up from the log.

"They'll come after us won't they?" she asked as he held a stirrup for her.

"Not until morning."

"Aren't you scared"? she asked, staring into his face.

Joshua turned his face away, unwilling for the girl to see the feelings he knew might be reflected there. The fear, the confusion, the feelings of helplessness. Finally, gaining control over his emotions, he turned back to look deep into her sparkling blue eyes, still blurred from her tears and lit by the moonlight. He didn't want to worry her, so he said, "Well, yeah. I reckon I am and I ain't. My pa always said being scared ain't always a bad thing. Sometimes it helps us do what's got to be done. I figure that's what we got to do."

"What will we do if they catch us?"

"Don't worry. It's going to be all right," he assured her, wishing in his heart he believed his own words.

Helping her into the saddle and climbing onto his own horse, they headed off into the night.

Chapter VII

Dawn brightened the eastern horizon. It was coming good day when Johnny and the boy drew rein on the crest of a low hill. They had ridden hard all night. Johnny's black gelding was winded and lathered. The boy's plow mule looked like it was about to drop in its tracks. For long minutes they sat their mounts and watched the Buckner cabin.

Fingers of red colored a bank of puffy clouds and set them ablaze. Light of a new day crept across the little valley and swallowed up the darkness. A slow minute crept by, then two. Nothing stirred. Still Johnny did not move. A silence followed, lengthening. The mule snorted. The far-off happy sound of a mockingbird belied the tragic scene below.

Lifting a look, Johnny's gaze followed two vultures as they drew lazy circles in the sky, dropping lower with each pass. The smell of death reached them from somewhere. Others would follow. He touched heels to the gelding's flanks and moved forward.

As they neared the cabin Johnny caught a quick mouthful of air against the stench of death and set his jaw angrily. He flicked a glance at the boy. Riley Buckner's face was set as if carved from stone. Purpled lips scrolled a tight line and pressed hard against clenched teeth. Tiny silver tears escaped the corners of his blue eyes, eyes that were fixed on the two bodies lying in the yard.

"Let me see to them, boy."

"No sir, they're my kin. It falls on me to do the burying."

The sun crept near noon-high. Johnny, hat in hand, stood beside the man-child who stood, staring through tears at three freshly covered graves. Peeled sticks lashed together formed crosses that stood at the head of each grave. Here, in this remote little valley, the remains of the Buckner family would rest for all eternity.

Their story was not a new one. They would join the ranks of unnumbered others who sought to follow their dream in an untamed land only to end up in a shallow grave on the edge of nowhere. Only the faces of the mourners changed.

What am I gonna do with the boy? Johnny asked himself for the hundredth time, still unable to find an answer. *It's too dangerous to take him with me. I'd lose another day if I took him back to town, and besides, I doubt he'd stay there anyway. I wouldn't, if it were me. I sure can't leave him here alone.*

Johnny watched the boy swallow back a sob and drop to both knees. Lacking flowers, he reverently placed a handful of mistletoe on each of the three graves. Then, digging a hand into his pocket, he slowly withdrew a shiny pocketknife. From the boy's expression, Johnny could tell it was clearly his most prized possession. For a long moment he stared lovingly at it, then, with tears escaping both eyes, he used a finger to gouge out a little trench in the black earth of his younger brother's grave and placed the knife inside. Smoothing it over, he paused a long minute before standing to his feet.

"I'm ready, mister," he said in a quivery voice, swiping tears from his face with the sleeve of a faded blue shirt.

Johnny looked into the face of the fifteen-year-old, but saw the eyes of a man. The tattered and patched bib overalls he wore hung by one strap. Worn-out and run over hand-me-down shoes were more off his feet than on. Yet, in the face of Riley Buckner, Johnny saw mirrored the same determination he himself felt after the Kimes brothers murdered his own parents.

A gun belt and holster belonging to the boy's pa was looped over Riley's head, across one shoulder, and dangled below his waist. The pistol was old, but the 1847 model .44 caliber Walker looked to be in workable condition. In his hand he grasped a twelve gauge double-barreled shotgun.

"What am I supposed to do with you, boy?" Johnny asked. "I can't take you with me."

Riley Buckner's face flushed red. His eyes flashed, went wide, then narrowed to thin slits. His jaw jutted out as he spat out the words like they tasted bad.

"Mister, my pa taught me to be respectful of my elders, and I'm shore obliged for what you've done, but I'm telling you straight out, I'm aiming to go after them that killed my folks and little brother. They took my sis and I aim to get her back. They got to pay for what they done. If you won't help me, I'll do it by myself."

A huge lump knotted in Johnny's throat. An overwhelming surge of pride swept through him. *The boy will do to ride with me,* he decided.

* * *

The killers were headed northwest. The trail was more than a day old, but Johnny and Riley Buckner had no trouble following it. They rode steady all afternoon, stopping only when it got too dark to follow the outlaws' tracks. A grassy spot with a fresh running creek nearby offered an inviting place for night camp. Johnny reined up and stepped from the saddle.

"It's too dark to see the trail," he told the boy. "We'll camp here for the night and get an early start in the morning. How about unsaddling and watering the stock while I get a fire going?"

"We're gonna catch up to them and get Cathy back, ain't we, Mister?" the boy queried with a shaky voice.

Johnny heard the desperation in the young voice.

"That we are, son," he tried to assure him, wishing he was as confident as his words. "We'll get your sister back."

By the time the boy had the horse and mule cared for, the fire licked toward a darkening night sky. Johnny dumped half a handful of coffee into the small pan of boiling water, then added a bit of cold water to settle the grounds. He sliced two potatoes, peeling and all, into the frying pan, and shaved several strips of salt bacon in on top. While supper was cooking, he cleared the rocks and sticks away and spread their blankets nearby.

The boy sat cross-legged near the fire, staring intently at the flames, watching the red-orange sparks lift into the dark sky. From the absent look on his face, Johnny figured the boy was wrapped in his own thoughts of sadness over the loss of his family as well as the fate of his sister. Johnny, squatting across the fire from the boy, thought to himself.... *It's a mighty big load for those small shoulders.*

Drawing the big hunting knife from his scabbard, Johnny cut a green stick and laid it across the top of the boiling coffee.

"What'd you do that for?" the boy asked.
"That green stick will keep the coffee from boiling over," Johnny told him.
"Really? I never knowed that. How'd you learn all them things"?
"My pa used to take me hunting with him from the time I could walk. Sometimes we stayed out for days at a time. He taught me how to hunt, and track, and do all kinds of things a boy needs to know."
"Is your folks...?"
"Yeah. They were murdered too, just like yours."
"Did they ever catch the ones who did it?"
For a minute Johnny didn't answer. His mind flashed back to when he found his folks. He remembered how he felt back then. He remembered how the hurt turned to hatred. The boy must be having those same feelings about now.
"Yeah, they paid for what they done, just like those that killed your folks will pay. I promise you, boy. They'll pay."

The Choctaw Kid needed only a quick glance to know something was wrong as he broke out of the trees into the little clearing where they'd set up camp. He was looking forward to some grub and a hot cup of coffee. Instead, he saw his grizzled companion unconscious, sprawled face down in the dirt. There was no sign of the boy or that girl they brought along. Both of their horses were missing.
A searching look around the camp told the story. Most likely that drunk tried to have his way with the girl and the boy somehow managed to knock him unconscious with the rock lying nearby. *Good enough for him, I told him not to mess with* her.

Sliding off his horse, the Kid used the toe of his boot to roll the giant over onto his back. Seeing a half-filled bucket of water nearby, he dumped it on his companion's face. Sputtering, moaning, and blinking his eyes, the big man sat upright. Lifting a hand to the huge knot on his head, he let out a stream of curses.

"I'll kill 'em!" he shouted. "I'll kill 'em both!"

"I ought to kill *you*," the Choctaw Kid told him. "I told you to leave the girl alone. Forget them, we've got to meet the other boys at the Horseshoe Trading Post on the Arkansas River by tomorrow."

"I ain't aimin' to forget 'em," the Cajun managed between curses. "That boy conked my noggin and I'm gonna cut his throat from ear to ear fer it."

"You'll do what I tell you or I'll kill you right now," the Kid said, matter-of-factly. "Besides, they're long gone by now, you can't track them in the dark."

"Come first light I'll run 'em down. I can catch up with you and the others in a couple of days."

"It's a waste of time. They ain't worth it. I told you not to bring the kid along in the first place."

"Nobody hits me over the head and lives to tell about it, kin or no kin."

"Have it your way then," the Choctaw Kid told him, turning and picking up the frying pan with the leftover food in it. "Right now I'm gonna eat and get some sleep."

"He took my gun too!" the big man hollered as he discovered his pistol missing. "That kid stole my gun. That's the thanks I git fer takin' him in and looking out fer him like I did. He stole my gun."

"You're a sorry excuse for a man," the Choctaw Kid mumbled around a mouthful of food. "Wish he'd shot you with it before he lit out."

"Come mornin' I'll make him wish he'd never been born. He's gonna die real slow, that kid is, stealing a man's gun like that. And after all I done fer him."

Joshua and Cathy rode slowly through the night, stopping from time to time to rest and give the horses a breather. Daylight struggled to life through heavy, low clouds. Flashes of lightning lit the dark and ugly bank of clouds that rolled toward them out of the west. They were in for a storm. He could smell the approaching rain on a stiff breeze. Joshua knew he had to find some kind of shelter, but where?

He glanced back and saw Cathy slumped in the saddle, struggling to stay awake. *She must be plumb tuckered out,* he thought, terrified at the overwhelming feeling of responsibility that swept over him. A ripple of dread shot up his spine. Somehow, he had to shield her, to protect her.

A low rumbling thunder and the sharp crack of lightning announced the storm's arrival. Black clouds rolled and churned and the wind picked up. Within minutes the clouds opened up and the rain started falling. Joshua knew he had run out of time, he needed to find shelter of some kind.

His searching gaze circled their surroundings. They were riding through a heavily wooded valley. Off to their right lay a line of low mountains. Pine and cedar trees fought for lodging among hulking gray rocks. House-size boulders jutted out of the earth and reached their scraggly fingers into the sky. It seemed to be the only possibility for shelter. He reined his horse in that direction.

Squinting through the driving rain, he spotted a large outcropping of rock in the side of the mountain with a hollowed out space underneath. *That will have to do.* Twisting a quick glanced over his shoulder he motioned for Cathy to follow.

Upon arriving, Joshua was pleased to discover the cavity was larger and deeper than he first thought. Swinging down, he lifted Cathy from the saddle, then led the horses as close to the shelter as he could and tied them to a low-hanging limb of a huge pine tree.

Joshua helped Cathy into the little alcove. At least it was dry. The big pine tree's shaggy branches partially shielded the entrance to their shelter, blocking some of the wind and driving rain.

"We'll rest here and wait out the storm," he told her. "You're soaked to the bone. I'll unsaddle the horses and we can use the saddle blankets to keep the chill off. Wish I had something to build a fire, but I left everything back at the camp."

Cathy hugged herself with both arms against the damp, chilly wind and nodded that she understood. Joshua hastened from the shelter and made short work of unsaddling their two horses. He piled the saddles against the trunk of the big pine and, taking both saddle blankets and his newly acquired rifle, made his way quickly back to the shelter of their little hideaway.

He found Cathy clutching herself tightly and shaking. Her lips quivered from the cold.

"You need to get out of those wet clothes before you catch your death," Josh told her.

She jerked a look at him and for an instant Josh saw fright and suspicion reflected there.

"It's okay. I'll turn my back. I won't look."

Her look softened.

He turned his back and closed his eyes, but he couldn't stop the picture his imagination was playing out in his mind. He had never seen a girl without her clothes on, but he had tried to imagine what one would look like many times.

"You can turn around now," she said softly.

She stood before him with a saddle blanket wrapped tightly around her. She clutched the top tightly against her throat. Her lips were blue and she shook from the cold.

"Let's sit back there in the corner away from the wind," he told her, reaching a hand to her shoulder and guiding her that direction.

Spreading the second blanket on the ground, he helped her sit down, then sat beside her and pulled the blanket tightly around them both. Her body quaked and her teeth chattered uncontrollably. He had to get her warm. Joshua encircled her shoulders with an arm and pulled her close. For a long time they huddled together. How long? He neither knew nor cared. Time seemed to cease. This was an eternity of its own with no beginning and no end. To him, this was the only thing that mattered, being here with her, being together. Her nearness filled his thoughts.

Finally her shaking stopped. He held her close. Her head rested on his shoulder. He listened to the pounding rain just beyond their shelter and her peaceful breathing. He could feel her warm breath on his neck.

The soothing sound of the rain outside their sanctuary and the distant thunder did its work. Joshua and Cathy clung to each other under the warm blankets and were soon fast asleep.

Johnny's eyes flicked open. It was still dark. A low rumbling off to the west told him what he didn't want to know. A storm was coming. It would wash the ground clean of any tracks and make following the Choctaw Kid, and his bunch, impossible. He cursed his luck and rolled out of his bedroll. He stoked last night's fire to life and set the leftover coffee over the flames before stomping his boots on.

He glanced at the boy. The kid lay curled up in his saddle blanket near the fire. His young face wore a peaceful look. His sandy eyelashes melded with his wind burned cheeks. His hair tumbled in disarray. He slept soundly. *May as well let him sleep awhile,* Johnny decided. *No point in rousting him out now. That storm is still a ways off. We'll have some coffee then find us a place to stay dry.*

He sure hated to have to tell the boy there was no use going on, but it would be a waste of time. The only thing left to do was head back to Fort Smith and get Riley settled in someplace, then wait to hear something about where the Choctaw Kid might be headed. He knew the idea wasn't going to set well with Riley Buckner.

Johnny poured some coffee into the tin cup and blew the steam away. He sipped slowly and watched the sleeping youngster. He couldn't get over how much the boy reminded him of himself when he was that age: same stubborn streak, same grim determination that, once his mind was made up, he would see it through come hell or high water.

Halfway through his second cup, the boy opened his eyes and sat upright. A deep gray started to tinge the eastern sky.

"Morning," Johnny said, eyeing Riley over the rim of his cup. "Want some coffee?"

"Is it gonna rain?"

"Sure looks like it."

"Hadn't we better get started?"

"No point. The rain will wash away their tracks. Finding them without a trail would be like looking for a needle in a haystack. There's a lot of country out there. They could be headed anywhere."

"Then what we gonna do, Mister Shooter?" the boy's voice sounded desperate. "We can't just give up! They've got my sister!"

"I know, son. Wish there was something we could do, but I don't know what it would be."

"I'm going on!" the boy said emphatically as he jumped to his feet and headed toward his mule. "I ain't gonna let a little rain stop me."

Johnny sat silent, staring into the dark depths of his coffee cup. *The boy's got a point,* he decided. *I wouldn't stop if it were my sister.*

"Okay, boy. You win. We'll play it out as far as we can. Let's break camp and get moving before that rain hits. Maybe we'll get lucky."

At the first crack of dawn, Zack Thibodeaux was already in the saddle. The Choctaw Kid had left soundlessly sometime during the night. Zack didn't care, his only concern right now was finding that no-good nephew of his and making him pay for busting his head and stealing his gun. Nobody stole his gun and got away with it. *After I take care of him, I'll take my time with the girl. Yes, sir. I'll take my good old sweet time with that little gal.*

He leaned far over in the saddle, squinting at the faint tracks of two horses. The low rumbling of an approaching storm jerked his big head up. *Better find them before the rain sets in,* he thought, kicking his horse into a short lope.

He rode for hours. Over the distant mountains lightening split the sky and stabbed the earth. When it did, the earth howled as if in pain and the ground shook and the thunder rolled like distant cannon fire. The driving rain soaked him to his skin.

Still he rode on. It was getting harder to see their tracks, but he refused to give up. Suddenly the tracks veered off to the right. Zack jerked his mount that way.

Peering through the gloomy thickness of the pouring rain he spotted their horses tied to a big tree. Reining up, he slid from his horse and tied its reins to a young sapling. At first he missed it, and then spotted the cave-like recess under the large outcropping of rock.

"I got ye now," he snarled out loud as he pulled his big Bowie from its scabbard and headed for the opening.

Some sixth sense, some awareness of a sinister presence tickled along his spine and awoke Joshua from a deep sleep. His eyes snapped open. What he saw brought his heart into his throat and sent shivers of fear ripping up his spine. His Uncle Zack loomed like a giant just inside their hideaway, not ten yards away. He held the big Bowie knife in his fist.

Joshua felt his eyes go wide. His heart thundered against the wall of his chest. His breath came in harsh and quivery gasps. For a brief moment he froze like a helpless rabbit hypnotized by a snake as he waited for the inevitable. He knew as sure as the sun rises, his Uncle was fixing to kill him.

Then he remembered Cathy. He knew without a doubt what fate awaited her after his Uncle finished with him. *No! I can't let that happen! I won't let that happen!*

In one lightning move, he threw his body to his left in a rolling motion. His hand grasped the rifle that leaned within reach against the rock wall. The action pulled the blankets loose and woke Cathy. An ear-splitting scream erupted from her throat and distracted his Uncle. Joshua rolled to his knees with the rifle in his hands.

Shooter

Zack stood frozen in his tracks, his wide-eyed stare fixed unmoving on the girl's nakedness. Joshua levered a shell into the rifle. The giant's massive head swiveled in Joshua's direction. An evil snarl spewed from his mouth as he charged toward him like a boar grizzly walking upright.

The rifle bucked in Joshua's hands. The bullet smacked into his Uncle's stomach like a hand striking bare flesh. The force of the impact slowed his charge, but failed to stop him. Joshua worked the lever again, and again he fired, this time at point-blank range. Zack staggered like a drunken man, regained his footing, and lunged at Joshua.

Something sharp and hot pierced his stomach. His eyes followed his hand to the spot. Red liquid spilled between his fingers. The world flared hot and bright before his eyes. Pain ripped aside sight and sense and consciousness. The last thing Joshua heard was the shattering terror of Cathy's scream.

Johnny heard the shots. Then he heard the screams.

"Let's go, boy!" he shouted over his shoulder through the pounding rain. "That's got to be your sister."

The black gelding leaped forward at the touch of Johnny's heels, breaking into a wind-splitting gallop within a half dozen strides. Riley's mule struggled gamely, but quickly fell far behind.

Spotting the horses up ahead, Johnny leaned far back in the saddle and slid the Winchester from its saddle boot even as he hauled back on the reins. Blackjack planted his hooves in the muddy ground and slid to stop. Johnny leaped from the saddle and levered a shell as he ran toward the opening under the big rock.

I can't just go charging in, he reasoned with himself as he ran. A thick pine tree with saddles piled at its base loomed ahead. He took cover behind it.

Inside, a girl's screams continued to shred the silence. The boy hurried up, out of breath and gasping for air.

"Does that sound like your sister?" Johnny asked anxiously.

He couldn't answer. He just nodded his head frantically.

"Stay here," Johnny told him, as he dashed forward into the semi-darkness of the overhang, his rifle at the ready.

He swept the cave with a quick look. The first thing he saw was the girl. She sat cowing against the rock wall, a saddle blanket clutched tightly around her. Between body-wracking sobs she screamed hysterically.

The apparent lifeless hulk of a huge man lay sprawled nearby. At first glance, Johnny overlooked the boy that was mostly covered by the body of the big man. Both appeared dead. A large Bowie knife protruded from the boy's belly.

"Cathy!" Riley Buckner yelled as he rushed into the cave and fell on his knees beside her. He gathered his sobbing sister in his arms and spoke comforting words. "It's all right now, sis. Hush crying. It's gonna be all right."

Chapter VIII

They buried Joshua Thibodeaux underneath the big pine tree near the entrance to the cave. Two sticks lashed together marked his final resting place. When the task was finished Johnny, Riley, and Cathy stood beside the grave. For a long minute all three were silent. Then the girl spoke.

"He saved my life, twice. I'll never forget him."

Nothing more was said nor needed to be.

Three days later the little procession loaded onto the ferry and crossed the Arkansas River to Fort Smith. Around the campfire at night, Cathy related all she could remember of the events leading to their escape and the killing of Joshua and his Uncle.

"I'm glad we left his body lying in the cave," Riley said bitterly. "He didn't deserve a Christian burial."

At the livery stable they sold Riley's mule and the three

extra horses for two hundred-fifty dollars. Zack's pistol rig and Bowie knife brought another eighty dollars at the Gun Shop.

"That's more money than I ever seen," Riley exclaimed as he stared wide-eyed at the handful of bills. "Here, sis. I think you ought to take care of it."

"Let's get on over to the boarding house and get you settled in like we talked about," Johnny suggested. "I betcha we can talk Miss Lila into rustling us up some supper. Whaddya say?"

Johnny led his black gelding and walked beside his two new friends.

He darted a quick glance at the brother and sister. He felt sorry for them, losing their family like they did, but it was more than sympathy. Responsibility. That was the feeling growing inside him, he felt responsible for them.

Johnny tied his horse out front and knocked before pushing the big front door open and ushering his two companions inside. Luckily, the guests were just sat down for supper. A wide smile broke across Libby's face and her eyes went wide when she looked up and saw Johnny.

"Well, lookee here!" Marshal Fagan said around a mouthful of food. "If you ain't a sight for sore eyes." He laid down his fork, scooted back his chair, and came forward with his hand extended.

"Howdy, Marshal, Mrs. Russell, Miss Libby," Johnny said. "I'd like you folks to meet two new friends of mine. This here is Cathy Buckner and Riley Buckner."

After the two youngsters were greeted warmly by all, Miss Lila waved all three newcomers toward empty chairs around the table.

"Land sakes, you all must be starved half to death. Libby, get three more plates for these folks."

Libby's gaze lingered on Johnny as she rose, then she turned and disappeared through the kitchen door.

"How was your trip?" the marshal asked as he sat back down at the table.

"I'll fill you in after supper," Johnny replied, his eyes glued on the door to the kitchen. *She's even more beautiful than I remembered.*

The kids squirmed uncomfortably in their chairs and gawked around the big room in wide-eyed wonder. Obviously they had never seen a home like this. Libby returned to the dining room with plates, silverware, and napkins for the new arrivals.

"There's plenty, so just eat your fill," Miss Lila said in her usual boisterous voice.

"Miss Lila, I was wondering if you might have room for Riley and Cathy for a while?" Johnny asked. "Their family was murdered and they need a place to stay. They've got a little money and can pay your regular rate if you have room."

"You poor dears. Of course we have room. We'll get you settled in right after supper."

After the youngsters ate all they could hold, which was considerable, Libby took them upstairs to show them their rooms.

Johnny, Marshal Fagan, and Miss Lila retired to the sitting room to enjoy another cup of coffee in front of the roaring fireplace. Johnny spent considerable time going over the whole story, laying it out in great detail. After he finished, the marshal leaned back in his chair and puffed on his pipe for a long moment before speaking.

"I think you need to give your report to the Judge, personally. It's past eight and he's likely already left his office for the day. He puts in long hours ,but he usually leaves about this time. I'll tell him you're back in town and that you'll be in his office at nine o'clock tomorrow night. Is that agreeable? That big fellow, what did you say his name was?"

"Thibodeaux, Zack Thibodeaux."

"Unusual name. Sounds familiar, too. I'm pretty sure I've heard that name before. It ain't a name you're likely to forget once you've heard it."

"What do you have in mind for the children?" Miss Lila asked.

"Got no idea," Johnny admitted. "I just know I feel responsible for them. They've lost all the family they had. They've got nobody left."

"What about their schooling?" the woman asked, leaning forward in her big wing-backed chair with a look of concern on her face. "There's a public school just a few blocks from here. There's also an excellent Catholic boarding school in Fort Smith.

"Libby seems to have hit it off with them already, after they settle in for a few days, maybe she could talk to them and see which they would prefer."

"They need some clothes, too," Johnny said. "All they've got to their name are the ones they're wearing. Reckon Miss Libby would have time to take them shopping? I'll give her the money."

"I'm sure she would love it," Miss Lila said, settling back in her chair.

"What would I love?" Libby asked, overhearing the last comment as she and the youngsters entered the room.

"The kids need some new clothes. I was saying that you would love to take Cathy and Riley shopping tomorrow."

"Of course I would. Would you have time to go with us, Mr. Shooter?"

"Don't see why not."

Cathy's face lit up and a smile widened her lips—the first one Johnny had seen.

Shooter

"What we gonna buy, Mr. Shooter?" Riley asked around a mouthful of hot biscuits with sorghum molasses. Everyone at the big table had finished their breakfast long ago. Marshal Fagan excused himself a few minutes ago and left. The boy was still eating. Johnny marveled at the youngster's appetite and wondered where he was putting it all.

"I've never been shopping before," Cathy confessed.

"You'll love it," Libby told the girl excitedly. "Ladies shop differently from men. Men just find what they want and buy it. Ladies take their time and look at everything that's available, then decide what they want to buy."

"When are we going?" Riley asked.

"Just as soon as you finish breakfast," Johnny told him, "but I'm beginning to think that might not happen until noon."

Everyone laughed and Riley's face turned red.

They walked together, side-by-side, Johnny and Libby, with Riley and Cathy hurrying along in front of them, talking excitedly.

"Thank you for taking time to help me with the shopping," Johnny said, glancing over at the beautiful lady by his side.

"I'm glad you asked me. No lady ever turns down an opportunity to go shopping. They seem like wonderful children. Cathy is really quite lovely."

"She's gone through an awful lot for a girl her age, with the kidnapping and all. It's a miracle she's still alive."

There was a long moment's silence before Libby's gaze locked with his. "I'm...I'm glad you're back."

Johnny was speechless. His mind raced. *Does she mean it the way it sounded or is she just being nice?*

"It's good to be back," he finally managed to say.

"Will you have to leave again?"

"Most likely."

"How long can you stay before you have to leave again?"

"No way of knowing."

"I know you work with Marshal Fagan somehow. Is it dangerous?"

"Could be I reckon. I can't really talk much about what I do."

"I see."

As they arrived in front of a large clothing store he withdrew a wad of bills and handed them to Libby.

"Here's fifty dollars in case we get separated. I'm sure you and Cathy will want to look around the ladies section. Buy her whatever she needs. If you need more money just let me know. Riley and I will be looking at men's clothes and stuff."

The boy's face beamed as he and Johnny headed toward the men and boys section of the huge store.

A short, bald-headed fellow in a gray business suit hurried up. "May I help you, sir?"

"This young man needs a couple of outfits, everything from the skin out. Whaddya you say we look for shoes first?" Johnny suggested."

"Mister Johnny, reckon I could have some boots like yours?"

"Well, mine have high heels and are made for riding. I reckon if the man has something made for walking, then I don't see why not."

"Have a seat over here and let's see what size you're going to need," the man said, smiling and motioning to a seat.

He produced a wooden slide with some marks and, slipping off the worn out work shoes, measured Riley's foot.

"Seven and a half. Let me see what we have in your size."

In no time the sales clerk returned with a pair of black boots similar to the ones Johnny wore. Riley's face lit up at first sight of the boots. The clerk helped the boy slip them on. He and Johnny watched as Riley walked around the area smiling from ear-to-ear.

"What do you think, son," Johnny asked. "How do they feel? Do they fit your feet?"

"They feel just fine," the young man said through a huge grin. "Them are the best boots I ever seen."

"Then I reckon that settles that," Johnny told the clerk. "Now he'll need pants, shirts, and a coat."

Finally, with Riley all decked out in a brand new outfit and both him and Johnny carrying the extra packages, they headed over to the ladies section of the store. Libby and Cathy had a pile of packages already and were still picking through the racks of dresses. It looked like they would be a while.

"We'll be back in the hardware section," Johnny told them. "Come on back when you ladies get finished."

"We won't be much longer," Libby told him, offering a beautiful smile when she said it.

Johnny spotted a display of knives as they were looking around and remembered the prized pocket knife Riley buried with his little brother. He decided the boy had earned another.

"I think you and me need us a good pocket knife," he told the boy. "I've been needing one for a long time."

They took their time and each selected one that suited his fancy. Just as they were paying for their purchases the girls walked up. Each one smiled over an armload of packages.

"All finished?" Johnny asked.

"Mr. Johnny, this is the best day of my whole life," Cathy told him, wrapping both arms around his neck and hugging him close. "Thank you for buying all those things for me."

"You're shore welcome. Both of you look mighty sharp in

your new duds. Say, I think I saw an ice cream shop just down the street. Would anybody like some ice cream?" He didn't have to ask twice, all three of his companions shouted, "Yes!"

The day passed all too quickly. Back at the boarding house the kids talked a blue streak, telling about their shopping spree and showing Miss Lila their new clothes. They were still talking excitedly over supper, but Riley slowed down enough to put away another big meal.

"Son, I swear to my time, you can put away more food than any grown man I've ever laid eyes on," Miss Lila laughed as she sipped an after dinner cup of coffee.

It was a fantastic day, maybe the best day Johnny could remember. Basking in the presence of the most beautiful girl he had ever seen, he stole frequent glances at her, only to encounter her steady gaze already fixed upon him. Their eyes were drawn to each other like a moth to a flame, holding for long moments, searching to the depths of the other's soul.

Now, sitting at the supper table, he felt her look upon him again. He glanced quickly at the marshal, then at Miss Lila, before swinging his look toward Libby. Their eyes met, and held, before a small smile lifted one corner of her beautiful lips and she lowered her gaze.

"The judge is expecting you at nine o'clock," Marshal Fagan commented.

"Yeah, reckon I better get a move on," Johnny said, scooting his chair back and rising. "Wouldn't want to keep him waiting."

"No, that wouldn't be a good idea. He's a stickler for promptness and expects it from others, too."

The yellowish street light outside the courthouse drew a jagged circle of light across the lonely ground. Eerie shadows danced just inside the edge of darkness. An uncomfortable feeling, an ominous presence tugged his attention to his left. Outlined against the faint light of a moonless sky stood the gallows.

He stopped. For long moments Johnny stood motionless, staring transfixed at the instrument of death. The thought of how close he had come to his own short drop into eternity sent shivers splaying along his spine. Slamming his eyes shut he closed off the past and turned away.

Light from a single second-story window served as a reminder of his appointment and quickened his pace. He climbed the concrete steps and pushed through the double doors. The hallway was dimly lit. His boots sounded unusually loud on the wooden stairs and echoed along the quietness of the empty building as he made his way up the long flight.

Finally he stood just outside the frosted-glass entrance to the judge's office. He paused for a moment, took a deep breath, and opened the door.

Judge Isaac C. Parker sat behind his big desk. His attention was concentrated on a stack of legal papers arranged neatly in front of him. Tiny, wire-rimmed glasses sat on the tip of his nose. For several long moments he seemed oblivious of Johnny's presence.

Johnny stopped in the same spot he'd stood during his first visit. He shifted his weight uncomfortably from one foot to the other. To say he was intimidated would have been an understatement. He glanced nervously around the room.

Johnny was so tired and nervous the last time he visited the judge he hadn't even noticed how large the office was. A red leather sofa, matching the chair behind the judge's desk, sat against one wall. Several copies of the Fort Smith Elevator newspaper lay on a small table beside the sofa. Two large windows behind the judge were covered with heavy drapes. The rest of the wall space was occupied with glass fronted cases filled with law books.

Finally, the judge's cold eyes glanced up over his spectacles at a large grandfather clock against the wall, then swung back to fix his guest with a stern look.

"It's seven minutes past nine, Mr. Shooter. You were to be here at nine o'clock."

"Yes, Sir."

"I will not tolerate slothfulness from one of my deputies. See that it doesn't happen again."

"Yes, sir."

"Now, Marshal Fagan informs me you have a report."

Johnny took a deep breath around the huge lump lodged in his throat that wouldn't budge. He cleared his throat, gave up and started talking. Slowly at first, then gaining confidence, he related the events just as they had happened, being particularly careful about every detail. It took awhile. During the telling the judge never wavered his gaze from Johnny's eyes. Finally, when it was finished Judge Parker leaned back in his chair and removed his glasses.

"Where are the children now?" he asked.

"They're staying at Miss Lila's boarding house."

"Good. Then you have no idea where the Choctaw Kid is headed?"

"No, sir. He disappeared without a trace. The rain wiped out any tracks."

"I'll have Marshal Fagan alert the other deputies. He'll turn up."

"Yes, sir, but seems like wherever he shows up innocent folks get killed."

"That's true, but about all we can do for now is wait. That was a good report, Johnny. Keep up the good work."

"Thank you, sir," Johnny said. Sensing the meeting was over he clamped his hat on his head and turned to leave.

"Oh, by the way. It turns out there were several warrants out for the arrest of that Thibodeaux fellow. There was a reward posted for him, too. We discussed it and decided the two hundred dollars should go to the children. Do you agree?"

"Yes, Sir," Johnny agreed. "That will help a lot."

"Very well. Keep me informed."

Chapter IX

The little community of Whitefield, in Indian Territory, was nothing more than a small, clapboard general store, a dirt floor saloon, and a few scattered farmhouses occupied by farmers trying to scratch out a meager existence from a stingy land.

The Choctaw Kid reined his pinto to a halt and slouched in his saddle for several minutes. His eyes squinted against the setting sun as he cast a sweeping gaze over the tiny community. Finally, he settled a hard stare on the store. He figured it was the most likely place to put his hands on some cash money.

A farm wagon was backed up to the porch in front of the store. Two slat-ribbed plow horses swatted at pesky horseflies with their long tails. The baldheaded old storekeeper and a lanky farmer in bib overalls loaded sacks of feed into the wagon. They were the only people in sight.

Four saddle horses were tied to a hitching rail across the street in front of the rundown saloon. They stood hipshot, like they'd been there a while.

He had been here before, several times in fact. He knew he

Shooter

would be recognized, but it didn't matter, he had to have some money. He'd spent the twelve dollars he took from the dirt farmer on a bottle and a whore at the trading post he stopped at the previous night. He was flat broke. Lifting the pistol in the holster tied low on his left hip, he resettled it lightly and touched heels to the pinto's flanks, urging his horse toward the store.

"Afternoon Kid," the short, elderly storekeeper said, glancing up at him with a look of recognition and shouldering the last sack of feed onto the wagon. He paused and sleeved sweat from his forehead. "It's been a while."

"That it has," the Kid replied, stepping down from his horse and slanting a lingering stare at the farmer.

"This here is Ed Freeman. Him and his family settled over in the bottoms awhile back. We just finished up with his load of feed. Ed, folks call this fellow the Choctaw Kid. Don't recollect ever hearing him called anything else. What is the name you was born with, Kid?"

"Reckon that'll do just fine."

"Howdy," the lanky farmer said, offering only a quick glance as he climbed up onto the flatboard wagon-seat and gathered the reins. "I better be getting on toward home. It'll be after dark before I can make it now."

"Much obliged, Ed," the storeowner called.

The Kid leaned against the hitching rail and watched the tired-looking horses lean into their load. The heavy wagon creaked and squeaked as it moved slowly down the road into a setting sun.

"What can I do for you today, Kid?"

"I need a couple of things," the Kid said as he pushed away from the rail and sauntered casually into the gathering dimness of the store.

"Make it snappy," the storekeeper said, "I was just about to close. The wife will be waiting supper"

"Fraid you're liable to be a little late," he said, lifting his pistol and raising it within inches of the man's nose. "Hate to do this old man, but I need all your money."

Fear registered in the storekeeper's rounded eyes. His mouth dropped open. His lips quivered uncontrollably.

"Take it, take the money," the old man stuttered. "Please, Kid, just don't hurt me."

"Where is it?"

"In the drawer. There, under the counter."

Keeping his gaze riveted on the old man, the Kid stepped behind the counter and jerked open the cash drawer. Scooping up a handful of bills and the hard money, he stuffed them into his pocket.

"Where's the rest of it?" he demanded.

Tears of fear escaped the old man's tired looking eyes. For an instant the Kid felt a tinge of sympathy for the old fellow but it was short lived. I got to take care of myself, he thought. This old geezer ain't nothing to me.

"The rest of your money!" he said, raising his voice and pushing the pistol close to the terrified man's face. "I know you got more than that hid around her someplace. Where is it?"

"That's all. That's all there is," the man said, near weeping.

The pistol lashed out, striking the storekeeper across his nose. The snap of bone cartilage was a sickening sound in the gathering darkness of the store. Blood splashed over the old man's dirty-white apron and he crumpled to the floor.

"Gonna ask you one more time, old man," the Kid snarled wickedly. "Last chance, where's the rest of the money?"

"Okay, it's in the coffee can on that shelf."

"Good choice. You just saved your life," he said, grabbing the can and scooping out the roll of bills inside.

"What's going on in here?" a voice from the doorway called out.

The Kid whirled and fired in one lightening motion. The .44 slug from his pistol struck the intruder square in the chest. The force of the bullet drove the man backward with staggering steps, through the open door and onto his back in the dusty street.

Gotta get outta here, the Kid's mind screamed at him. Wheeling, he sprinted for his horse with his pistol still clutched tightly in his fist. He found a stirrup with the toe of his boot and swung into the saddle even as his sweeping gaze caught sight of several men pouring from the small saloon.

"He's done shot Jake!" somebody hollered.

"Get him!" another bellowed angrily.

He bent over and hugged low in the saddle as he jammed heels into the pinto's flanks. In two jumps his pinto ran flat out and belly to the ground. Swinging a look, the Kid saw three fiery flowers of red and orange blossom in the darkness. Bullets singed the air around him and hissed at him with the deadly purpose of a rattlesnake.

Realizing he still held the pistol, he twisted in the saddle and snapped off two quick shots, hoping only to discourage his attackers, but felt satisfaction when he heard a man scream out and saw him double over and crumble into the dirt.

Darkness swallowed him up. He felt certain they would follow, but also knew his trail would be quickly lost in the moonless night. He soon slowed his pace, settling the pinto into an easy short lope. *I'll put some tracks behind me tonight, just in case I'm followed. I outta make it to Tahlequah by sometime late tomorrow.*

* * *

The next few days went by in a whirlwind of activity for Johnny. Marshal Fagan sent him on several short trips to pick up petty criminals and serve summons, but other than that, his days were mostly his own. He borrowed a horse and saddle rig from the livery for the boy, and he and Riley went riding a couple of times. Once they went fishing in the river and brought home a nice stringer of trout, which Miss Lila quickly converted into their supper.

Libby really took Cathy under her wing. The two went shopping most every day, at least that's what they called it, but mostly, about all they did was look. The two were becoming very close. When they weren't off somewhere together they were laughing and giggling around the house.

"We're having a pie supper and cake walk at the church Saturday night," Libby announced at the supper table on Monday, looking straight at Johnny. "Cathy and I are baking pies to take. Would you and Marshal Fagan like to come?"

"If I'm around I'd shore like that," the marshal said, looking up from his coffee. "I've got to ride down to Danville with one of my Deputies. We're leaving early tomorrow morning."

"What about you, Johnny?" she asked, a mischievous smile spreading across her face.

"Sounds like fun. What about it, Riley, want to try your luck buying some pretty girl's pie?"

Riley stopped chewing long enough to answer around a mouthful of peach cobbler. "I ain't spending my money buying some dumb girl's pie."

"Wonder how long it will take him to change his mind about that?" the marshal laughed.

"Probably only until he sees all the pretty girls that will be there," Miss Lila said.

"We're raising money to put a new steeple on the church," Libby explained.

"Sounds like a good cause," Marshal Fagan said. "Like I say, if I'm back in time I'll be there, but I'll chip in ten dollars toward the project in any case."

"That's *wonderful*. Thank you, Marshal, that's awfully generous of you." Libby said. "Pastor Sullivan will be happy for your donation."

"What kind of pie will you be taking?" Johnny asked, bending his head to take a sip of hot coffee but still gazing at Libby's beautiful face over his coffee cup.

"Oh, I don't know, I haven't decided yet, what's your favorite?"

"Apple, I guess. My ma use to bake the best apple pies I ever tasted."

"Then apple it will be, but don't expect it to be as good as your mother's. Of course that means you have to buy it."

"I reckon I can handle that."

Libby flashed those big eyes at him and lingered for a moment longer than necessary. One corner of her lips lifted in a tantalizing smile that melted his heart and caused it to skip a beat.

"Let's take our coffee into the sitting room," Miss Lila said, pushing back from the table. "There's a fire going and you men can enjoy a smoke with your coffee."

Johnny reluctantly tore his gaze away from Libby's magnetic face and unfolded from his chair.

"I'll help with the dishes, Miss Libby," Cathy volunteered anxiously. "Riley, you best go on and get your bath, we start to school tomorrow."

"Aw, sis, it's too early to be taking a bath."

"The men folk will be needing the bathroom later on, and don't forget to scrub behind your ears," she called after her brother as he sulked from the room.

Libby and Cathy gathered up the dirty dishes as Johnny followed Miss Lila and the marshal into the sitting room. A fire crackled in the fireplace. Golden flames licked around split logs and lifted toward the chimney. Johnny settled into a comfortable upholstered chair, watched the flames, and sipped his coffee. Somehow it reminded him of the times he and his folks sat around the old pot-bellied stove back home.

"Got a little job for you tomorrow," Marshal Fagan said, "I talked to Judge Parker and he recommended I send you after this fellow." The Marshal withdrew a legal-looking paper from his pocket and handed it to Johnny, then settled back in his chair to pack his pipe with tobacco.

"That's a warrant for a jasper named Otis Talbot. We shipped him off to prison up in Illinois for a couple of years for stealing horses. He was released a few months ago. Now it seems he's back to his old ways. He was seen taking a half dozen head a week or so ago from the Sunrise Ranch up in the Boston Mountains.

"See if you can locate the stolen horses and return them to their owner, and bring Talbot in. I'm plumb tired messing with him. Do you understand? Be careful though, this fellow's meaner than a timber rattler."

"Got any idea where he might be holed up?"

"He use to have a rundown little shack on Dutch Mills Creek up near Siloam Springs. His place is about a mile or so from the state line. If it was me, I'd start by looking there."

"Don't reckon you've heard anything about the Choctaw Kid?"

"Nope, not a word. He'll turn up though. Fellow like him can't stay outta trouble long."

"I'll ride out first thing in the morning," Johnny said, folding the arrest warrant and slipping it into his pocket.

Shooter

* * *

Long after the others went to bed, Johnny sat in the swing on the porch. It was a crisp, clear October night. A chill filled the night air. A million stars hung like sparkling diamonds in a velvety-black sky. The moon was full and close, seemingly only an arm's length away. Glancing up, he judged it to be near midnight, yet he wasn't the least bit sleepy.

His mood was heavy with memories: memories of the little farm house where he grew up, memories of his father and mother. Memories of the good times and the bad.

What a turn my life has taken. Just a short time ago I was only hours from the hanging, now here I am a United States Deputy Marshal, with good friends, a nice place to live, and more money than I've ever had in my whole life. Life sure does have some twists and turns.

A slight scraping sound behind him turned his head. Libby slipped quietly through the partially open door and closed it softly behind her. She wore a blue house-robe and clutched a white crocheted shawl around her shoulders. Her long, auburn hair cascaded loosely about her shoulders. For a long moment she stood motionless, staring up at the stars.

"They're beautiful, aren't they?"

"Sure are," he murmured, his eyes drinking in her breathtaking beauty.

"I couldn't sleep. Mother told me you were leaving again in the morning."

"Yeah, the marshal has a job he wants me to do."

"How long will you be gone?"

"It shouldn't take long, maybe a few days."

"Will you be back in time for the pie supper at the church?"

"Sure hope so. I'd hate to think some other fellow got to eat my apple pie. Would you like to sit down?"

"Yes, I'd like that. It's such a beautiful evening."

Johnny scooted over to make room for her, but not too far over. He could feel the warmth of her presence. He felt the brush of her leg against his as she folded gently into the porch swing beside him. His breath caught. His heartbeat flickered and picked up speed. Her nearness set off ripples of awareness in him, just as it always did. An awkward silence stretched into the night.

"The job you'll be doing, will it be dangerous?"

"I reckon it could be, but not likely. I'm supposed to find a horse thief, arrest him, and return the horses he stole to their rightful owner."

"Johnny," she said, her soft fingers gently touching his arm, her voice suddenly breathy and low with concern, "you will be careful, won't you?"

"Yes, ma'am, like I said, I'm looking forward to that apple pie."

His answer brought a smile to her face and a slight squeeze from her hand that remained on his arm. Her single touch felt like a red-hot branding iron. The heat from it raced all the way to his heart.

His look flicked to her face. She was staring at him. Their gazes locked, and held for an eternity. She seemed to be probing the very depths of his soul with those soft, green eyes. Searching, questioning, and begging for an answer to unasked questions.

His left hand settled gently over hers, lingered for a moment, then crept slowly along her arm, past her shoulder, and found itself entwined in those long, soft, flowing auburn curls of her hair.

Libby's face flushed. Her heart skipped a beat, pounding inside her chest like it was about to explode. A sense of anticipation washed over her, so wondrous and sweet, so exciting it took her breath away. Her breath came in short, labored gasps.

In his eyes she saw her own yearning mirrored there. She felt his hand in her hair, touching the back of her neck, gently urging her face toward his. She yielded willingly, completely, surrendering to her long restrained inner longings.

A sharp gasp filled her chest. She felt the honey-sweet mingling of their breaths, the coming together of their hungry mouths, a low moan escaped from somewhere deep inside her as his lips found hers. His lips were soft and smooth and moist, and she liked the way he tasted, the way his strong arms made her feel safe and womanly and good. He kissed her with a simmering intensity that made her head spin and her bones dissolve. Her eyes closed. The world spun crazily as she soared on wings of love into a paradise she never knew existed.

Johnny tugged his sheepskin coat tighter around his neck and bowed his head into the wind as he rode north. The sun's first rays struggled through the trees to make an appearance, but were barely visible through an overcast sky. He'd been riding for more than an hour.

The rolling, humpbacked hills he rode through were like a stairway to the Boston Mountains that lay in front of him. The narrow, rutted road wound like a restless snake through heavy forests of sycamore, white oak, and cedar. A mountain stream fought its way over polished rocks along a nearby valley as it rushed toward the Arkansas River behind him.

Again and again his mind replayed the events of the night before. It seemed like a dream. He still found it impossible to believe that a beautiful girl like Libby would be interested in a nobody like him. The memory of their time together on the porch sent a shiver of vitality surging through him like a flooding river. For the first time since discovering the mutilated bodies of his aged parents, he had hopes for a future that amounted to something. He had someone who loved him.

The day was half spent when Johnny topped a rise and reined his horse to a stop. The road before him angled steeply downward into a wide valley. A thin tendril of smoke rose from the rock chimney of a small, rough-board farmhouse and bent sharply in the wind. A fresh running mountain stream hugged a low hill and flowed directly behind the house. A woman in a pink bonnet, wearing a long work dress covered from the waist down with a white apron, was busy hanging freshly washed clothes on a clothesline. Children ran and played nearby. It was a peaceful scene.

In a partially cleared field near the road a lean-looking farmer labored with a long pry bar to dislodge a stubborn stump. Tied around the waist of his bib overalls were the long reins to a team of mules. The big mules were straining mightily at the heavy log chain tied to the stump. It didn't appear the farmer was making a whole lot of progress. Johnny reined Blackjack to a stop nearby.

"Morning," Johnny greeted, swinging a leg over his saddle and stepping to the ground.

"Howdy-do," the farmer breathed heavily, stopping to sleeve beads of sweat from his forehead.

Johnny picked up a double-bladed ax lying nearby and stepped down into the large hole surrounding the stump. He swung the ax skillfully in several powerful attacks of the thick root.

"Get up in there, Jake!" the farmer shouted loudly, popping the reins against the mule's rumps and throwing his weight against the pry bar.

The big Missouri browns dug their rear hooves deep into the ground. Their muscles bulged as they labored against their trace chains. With a loud snap the root gave way. The mules dragged the stump from the hole.

"Whoa, mules," the farmer called, pulling them to a stop and wrapping the long reins around the stump.

For the first time the farmer turned to look at Johnny.

"I'm obliged for your help, mister," the man said. "I'm Chester Phillips."

"Don't mention it. I've cleared more'n my share of stumps. Name's Johnny Shooter."

"Well, no telling how long that job would've took if you hadn't come along. Where you be headed?"

"Place called Siloam Springs. Is this the right road?"

"Sure is. 'Bout a half day's ride northwest. Maybe less on that fine looking horse you're riding. You won't find much when you get there, though, ain't nothing but a small store and a few scattered farmhouses."

"Ever hear of a place called, Dutch Mills Creek?"

"Reckon so. If you take the left fork about three miles up the road, you'll run right into it."

"You're a big help. I'm obliged for the information."

"Is that a Marshal's badge I see peeking out from under your coat?"

"Matter of fact it is. I work for Judge Isaac Parker down in Fort Smith."

"Pleased to make your acquaintance. I was just about to knock off for lunch, would you sit and eat a bite with us, Mr. Shooter?"

"Don't mind if I do, if you have enough. I left before first light this morning and missed out on breakfast. Feels like my belt buckle is rubbing my backbone."

"I know the feeling. Likely won't be more than beans and cornbread, but there'll be plenty. Walk on down to the house with me. Mind me asking who you're looking for?"

"Fellow named Otis Talbot. He's supposed to have a little place on Dutch Mills Creek. Ever hear tell of him?"

"Shore have. He rode by here a few weeks back leading a string of ponies. I figured at the time they were stolen."

"Seems so."

"Might want to watch yourself if you're going after that fella. He's a bad'un."

"So I've been told."

As they approached the house the children stopped and stared at Johnny.

"Wife, this here is Mr. Shooter, a deputy marshal out of Fort Smith. He'll be sitting to lunch with us."

"Howdy do, Mr. Shooter. We'd be pleased to have you join us."

"You can wash up over yonder," Phillips told him, motioning toward a bench beside the house with a wash pan on it. "I'll fetch a bucket of fresh water."

The farmer scooped up a water bucket and headed for the nearby stream behind the house.

"Nice place you folks got here," Johnny said, as the woman headed toward the house to prepare lunch.

"Thank you. We enjoy living here. We're from Illinois. We've been here going on six years now. It's good ground. Chester is a good farmer and a hard worker. Say you're a deputy marshal?"

"Yes ma'am."

"You work for that judge, the one they call the hanging judge."

"Yes, ma'am."

"I suppose he only hangs the ones that need hanging."

"He's seems to be a fair-minded man."

"Well, if you'll excuse me I'll go check on the beans and see if the corn bread's about done. Make yourself to home, Mr. Shooter."

"Thank you, ma'am."

The two children were still standing nearby, still staring wide-eyed at Johnny. One was a blonde girl that looked to be five or six. Her older brother was a tow headed boy of probably eight. Johnny flashed them a broad smile.

"Is there any fish in that creek," he asked.

"Yes, sir," the boy spoke up. "I catch 'em all the time. I caught a bass the other day that was this long," he held out his hands a good foot apart.

"You must be quite a fisherman. I bet that was good eating."

"Yes, Sir. Ma cooked it and we had it for supper. Shore was good."

"You're a strong looking boy for your age. I bet you help your Pa with the farming, too?"

"Yes, sir."

"That's good. You gonna be a farmer like your pa when you grow up?"

"I reckon. Pa says I'm good help."

"What's he filling your head with?" Phillips asked jokingly as he walked up and sat the bucket of water on the bench. "That boy will talk your leg off if you let him."

"He was telling me about a big fish he caught."

"Yeah, it was a nice one, sure enough. He'd be sitting on the creek bank from daylight to dark if we'd let him. Let's sit in the shade till the beans are ready," the farmer said, pointing to two woven willow chairs near a big Oak tree.

"You been a law man long?"

"No, not long."

"I reckon it's pretty dangerous work. I hear they've been losing lots of deputies lately."

"Yeah, I think so."

"I'll stick to being a farmer. My pa and his pa before him were all farmers. It's all I ever knowed how to do. Besides, not likely to get shot at following a plow. Now you take that Talbot fella. They say he's meaner than a snake. They say he's spent time in prison up in Illinois."

"Yeah, that's a fact."

"You gonna take him in, huh?"

"That's my job."

"Well, like I say, better watch yourself, he's not above back shooting a fella."

"You said earlier that he passed with a string of horses, did you notice how many?"

"Counted six. Fine looking stock. Looked plumb funny though, the nag he was riding looked like she was on her last leg."

"You men come on in and sit up to the table," Mrs. Phillips called from the doorway.

"You know, marshal, I just thought about it. There's a little hidden valley about two miles or so downstream of Talbot's place by a steep bluff. I stumbled on it one time a while back. The only way into it is a cutback that's mostly hid. Sure would be a good place to hide them stolen horses."

"I'll check it out. Much obliged for your help."

Chapter X

Libby awoke slowly. She snuggled deeper into the large feather pillow and relished the comfort of her warm, cozy bed. Her mind gave birth to half consciousness. The memory of the previous night immediately washed over her, consumed her, and swept her helplessly along in a flood of unbridled contentment. She never knew one could be so wondrously happy.

The first rays of sun filtered silently through the window at the head of her bed and spread across the room. She knew she should already be up and dressed and helping her mother prepare breakfast. *Just another minute,* she thought, clinging intensely to the memory that she never wanted to go away.

A soft tap on her door scattered her thoughts.

"I'm awake, Mother. I'll be right there."

Flinging back the covers, she extended her legs over the edge of her bed. Her bare feet touched the multi-colored crocheted rug beside her bed. Reaching her arms toward the ceiling in an elaborate stretch she sat motionless for a long moment in silent contemplation. Where would Johnny be this morning? Would he be thinking of her?

Even the thin material of her flannel nightgown had a sensual softness against her body as she pulled it over her head and rose to dress quickly.

The coffee was boiling and breakfast was almost cooked when she hurried into the kitchen.

"I'm sorry, Mother, I must have overslept."

"It's no wonder, as late as it was before you came in."

Her mother's statement brought a sharp gasp of surprise. She jerked a look to examine her mother's face. How did she know? What did she know?

"I...it was such a beautiful night. We were just talking."

"I was young once, too, you know."

"He's...he's a very unusual man, not at all like anyone I've ever met."

"Just be sure you know what you're doing. Now check the biscuits and then get the children up. They need a good breakfast before they go to school."

Libby moved through her daily routine in a trance. Her hands kept busy making beds, carrying out dirty bath water and replacing it with clean, sweeping, moping, dusting, but her mind was far from her chores.

A thousand times or more she replayed the events of the night before: the manly aroma of his nearness, the excitement of his touch, the thrill of his kiss. Who was he, this gentle giant, this stranger that had taken control of her mind? What miracle had brought him to her? Fate somehow opened the door to this new and exciting life and welcomed her inside.

What does Johnny see when he looks at me? A tall girl with red hair and wide green eyes? Slowly her hand lifted to stroke her burning cheek. Her skin flushed as she remembered his hand tracing the curve of her throat, drifting softly along the ridge of her collarbone. Her mouth went dry. It seemed she had never lived inside this body until Johnny helped her discover herself last night. There was more he could teach her, more she wanted to learn, needed to learn, about herself.

It was near sundown. The great ball of red was being swallowed up by the western horizon when Johnny reined up at the edge of Dutch Mills Creek. He slackened the reins and allowed Blackjack to slake his thirst.

As his horse drank, Johnny let his slow gaze crawl slowly over the face of the one hundred-foot high bluff across the creek that shouldered up against the water and formed a seemingly solid wall of rock. Scraggly scrub cedar clung precariously to cracks and crevices along its face but, otherwise, he saw no opening whatsoever.

Johnny shucked his hat and sleeved sweat from his forehead while he studied the bluff again.

This looks like the place the farmer described, but I shore don't see no opening in that bluff.

Then his gaze detected a darker green in the depths of a large cluster of cedar bushes. *Those don't look exactly right.*

Touching his heels to the horse's flanks, he urged Blackjack down the creek bank. As he waded across the wide pool of water and approached the far bank, he suddenly spotted the opening.

Hidden from view by the cedars, it would go unnoticed to the casual observer.

Ducking his head, Johnny urged his mount through the thick cedars and into the opening. A tunnel-like crack opened into a small valley. A tiny pond nestled in one corner and a half dozen horses grazed peacefully on the lush green grass.

This is the perfect place to hide a string of stolen horses. I would never have found them if the farmer hadn't told me about this place.

Leaving the heavy limb that served as a barrier to keep the horses inside, Johnny turned his horse and retraced his steps back through the opening.

It was dusky-dark when he approached the small, rundown cabin. The orange glow of lamplight spilled through the single window and settled on the porch.

"Hello the house!" he called loudly, hooking a thumb in his gun belt near his pistol.

A long moment of silence made Johnny uneasy. The lamp inside the cabin went out. He waited.

"Who are you and what you want?" A gruff voice inside the cabin, called.

"I'm Deputy United States Marshal Johnny Shooter from Fort Smith. I need to ask you a couple of questions."

"Yeah, like what?"

"Step outside and we'll talk about it."

Johnny watched the window carefully, half expecting the nose of a rifle to appear. Instead, the door creaked open and a large, burly man appeared. He held a rifle cradled in the crook of his arm.

"You Otis Talbot?" Johnny asked, keeping his voice calm.

"Yeah, what about it? What kind of questions you got?"

"I've got a warrant for your arrest."

"Arrest, what for? I ain't done nothing."

"Horse stealing. You were seen taking a half dozen horses from the Sunrise Ranch up the mountain a ways. Just put that rifle down and come along peacefully. I don't want no trouble."

"Ain't stole no horses. All I got is that bag of bones in the corral, yonder."

"What about that string in the little valley up the creek a ways, know anything about them?"

The horse thief's eyes went wide. Johnny saw Talbot's mouth set in a hard line and his eyes blaze. The nose of the man's rifle arched upward.

"Don't do it, Talbot!" Johnny shouted as he threw himself sideways in his saddle, at the same time clearing leather with his Colt Peacemaker.

A ball of red blossomed from the mouth of the Winchester in the horse thief's hands. Hot lead sizzled within inches of Johnny's chest. The pistol in his hand bucked and belched fire. Once, twice.

The horse thief rose high on his toes and stumbled backward. His rifle slipped from his fingers and clattered to the porch. Johnny's .44 caliber slugs nailed Talbot against the front wall of the cabin. He hung there for a long moment before his lifeless body slid slowly to the porch.

A heavy fog shrouded the mountains. A cold, misty rain soaked the winding, worn road up the mountainside and made progress slow. He rode steadily through the shank of the day. Now, at mid-afternoon he was cold and wet and tired.

He'd spent a restless night after the shooting. He'd covered the horse thief's lifeless body with a horse blanket and spread his own bedroll on a bed of soft hay in the barn, but sleep eluded him. Finally, sometime before first light, he saddled up and hit the trail.

The six stolen horses plodded along behind, strung out on a long lead fashioned by a lariat taken from the horse thief's cabin. He draped Talbot's body belly-down across his saddle, his hands and feet tied to the stirrups. The reins to his horse were looped around Johnny's saddle horn.

Up ahead the steep road flattened to a large plateau. A carved sign hung above the road suspended by two upright poles, SUNRISE RANCH.

Off in the distance a sprawling cluster of buildings nestled against the backdrop of a sheer bluff that reached at least three hundred feet into the thick fog. A split rail fence surrounded a large log ranch house. Several barns with sturdy corrals stood nearby. A large herd of horses grazed peacefully on the fetlock-high grass. It was a peaceful scene.

As Johnny drew near the main house several curious wranglers stopped their work and gathered close. The front door opened. A tall, wide shouldered man with weathered skin, gray hair and dark, piercing, whiskey-clouded eyes stepped onto the porch. His long, uncertain strides brought him to the edge of the porch.

"You the owner?" Johnny called out, reining up near the fence.

"Yep, Ben Stoker is the name. Who might you be?"

"I'm Johnny Shooter, Deputy Unites States Marshal out of Fort Smith. I understand these horses belong to you."

"I reckon. How'd you come by them?"

"Jasper by the name of Otis Talbot had 'em. Thought I'd return them to where they belong."

"I'm guessing that would be him slung across the saddle?"

"That's him."

Shooter

"I'm obliged, Mr. Shooter. Come on in the house. Boys, take our horses and put 'em in the corral and see to the deputy's horses, too"

Johnny followed the Rancher through the door into a spacious hallway. They turned right into a large den with a rock fireplace that stretched from floor to ceiling. A leather sofa and chairs faced a roaring fire.

"Have a seat, deputy," he said, motioning to the sofa and taking time to pour himself a stiff drink before taking a seat in a nearby chair. "Care for a drink to warm your insides?

"No thanks."

Shooter, huh? I thought I knew most of Marshal Fagan's deputies. You must be new?"

"Yeah, guess you could say that."

"Where you hail from, son?"

"Scott County, down near Mena."

"We'll be having supper in a bit, I'd take it kindly if you'd stay and eat a bite with us?"

"I reckon I need to be getting on back."

"Nonsense. I won't hear of you setting out on a night like this. We've got a spare bedroom and you're welcome to it. You look like you could use a good night's sleep."

"I appreciate the offer, Mr. Stoker. Truth is, I could use some shut eye."

"Then it's settled. Supper will be on the table in a bit. Meantime, tell me about the shooting. How'd it happen?"

Johnny spent the next half-hour relating the details surrounding the recovery of the rancher's horses, avoiding talking about the actual shooting.

Ben Stoker listened intently, examining Johnny's eyes, and gulping the drink in his hand.

"What about Talbot? How'd that happen?

"Reckon he didn't cotton to going back to prison."

"Well, no big loss. He was a no-good anyway. He's been nothing but trouble around these parts for years. I would've hung him myself if I'd caught him with my horses."

"You've got a nice place here. Are horses all you raise?"

"Oh, no. We run a couple hundred head of cattle, but horses are my bread and butter. I've got some of the finest quarter horses west of the Mississippi. Speaking of good horses, that black gelding you're riding is as good looking a horse as I ever seen. Mind telling me where you found an animal like that?"

"Bought him at the livery in Fort Smith. The hosteler said he came from Kentucky. He's a runner shore enough, and the smoothest ride I ever seen."

"Don't suppose you'd be interested in selling him?"

"No, reckon not."

"Can't say as I blame you."

The tinkling sound of a small bell brought the rancher struggling to his feet.

"Sounds like supper is on. Let's see what the ladies have set for us."

The rancher guided Johnny across the hallway into a spacious dining room. A long table was crowded with ten high-backed upholstered chairs and covered with a spotless, white tablecloth. Steaming bowls of fried potatoes, corn on the cob, and fresh bread were scattered along the center of the table. A pile of thick, juicy-looking beefsteaks sizzled on a huge platter. The aroma of fresh coffee tickled Johnny's nose. It was truly a supper fit for a king.

"Johnny, these are my two boys, Charley and Booger. Boys, this is Johnny Shooter. He's a U. S. Deputy Marshal out of Fort Smith. He recovered our stolen horses and brought Otis Talbot in belly down across his saddle."

The one called Charley set his coffee cup down and pushed back from the table. Like his father, the eldest son was a big man. His broad shoulders stretched the denim shirt tight across his barrel chest. A sandy-colored mustache tilted upward as an easy smile broke across his weathered face.

"The hands told us about you when we rode in a little bit ago. They said you was one mean-looking hombre. Can't say they stretched the truth any. Pleased to meet you, Johnny."

A hand the size of a side of beef extended toward Johnny. He took it, and quickly wished he hadn't. The strength of the big man's handshake nearly crushed Johnny's knuckles.

The younger son looked to be in his late teens. He didn't bother to stand. He slouched back in his chair and pinned Johnny with a critical look. A smirk curled the corner of his lips.

"Shooter, huh?" the boy said sarcastically. "Kind of odd name for a deputy, ain't it?"

The obvious insult furrowed Johnny's brow. He lingered a long gaze at the boy, trying to decide whether to let it pass. After all, he was a guest in Mr. Stoker's house. But the challenge was too obvious to let it slide.

"No more than, Booger, I reckon," he said evenly, returning the boy's fixed stare.

The big rancher interrupted the tense mood quickly. "Johnny, this is my wife, Henrietta."

Johnny swung a look at the beautiful lady who was just entering the room. Her long, black hair cascaded loosely over her shoulders and fell down her back to near her waist. She wore a floor length, wine-colored dress. She moved across the room so gracefully that her feet seemed to barely touch the floor. Elegance, Johnny thought, but young, not nearly old enough to be the mother of the two boys.

Her black eyes fixed on his and held his gaze as she approached and stopped directly in front of him. Something in those eyes set off warning bells in his head. A slow, tantalizing smile lifted one corner of her full lips. Johnny suddenly felt very uncomfortable.

She extended a hand, palm down. He took it and bent at the waist to gently brush the back of it with his lips.

"Honey, this is Johnny Shooter, a Deputy Marshall out of Fort Smith," the rancher said. "I've asked him to spend the night."

"Mr. Shooter," she said in a soft voice barely above a whisper, her unblinking gaze never wavering from his, "Welcome to our home. We don't get many visitors up here."

"Thank you for having me," he said in a shaky voice, suddenly realizing he still held her hand. He quickly released it as if he had touched a red-hot stove. The taunting smile on her lips widened.

They took their places at the table. Ben Stoker sat at one end of the long table and his wife at the far end. The two brothers sat on one side with Johnny directly across from them.

Two heavy-set Indian women brought cups and filled them with steaming coffee.

"Mr. Shooter recovered and returned our stolen horses," the rancher explained to those around the table, the alcohol beginning to slur his words.

"I could'da got them back if you hadn't stopped me," the cocky younger son said loudly. "I told you all the time that no-good saddle tramp was the one that took 'em. We should'da stretched his neck a long time ago."

"We don't go around hanging people just because we think they might have stole our horses," the old rancher told his son.

Johnny forked a steak from the platter to his plate when they were passed around. Soon his plate was piled high with food. A vague uneasiness gnawed at him. Between bites he glanced quickly toward the end of the table. The rancher's wife

was staring unashamedly at him, seemingly with little regard of her husband and stepsons' presence.
"You must be pretty salty with that pistol," the smart mouthed son said, gazing over the lip of his coffee cup at Johnny.
"I've managed to stay alive so far," Johnny answered.
"Betcha I could take you, easy," the boy said. "Some of the boys said the horse thief was shot twice but they didn't say if he was shot in the front or the back."
"That's enough!" The old rancher shouted, slamming his fork onto the table. "Keep a civil tongue in your head. This man is a guest in our house. I won't stand for you talking to him in that tone. You hear me?"
The boy just crinkled a thin grin and went back to eating his steak. Johnny was fuming. He couldn't decide whether to get up and leave or confront the young hothead openly. He decided on the latter.
"Mr. Stoker, I'm a guest in your home so just this once I'm gonna chalk that accusation up as coming from a kid that don't know better. Any grown man says that to me and I'd kill him before he got it out of his mouth."
"Booger, leave the table! I'll deal with you later!"
The boy slammed his cup onto the table so hard it sloshed coffee all over the white tablecloth. He pushed slowly to his feet, kicked his chair over backwards, and nailed Johnny with a poisonous look.
"We'll meet again, mister, you got my word on it!"
Wheeling, the young loudmouth stalked from the room.
"Mr. Shooter, please accept my apologies," the big rancher slurred. "I'm afraid I've lost control of that boy."
"Maybe I better just leave. I don't want to cause trouble."
"You'll do nothing of the kind. You are our guest and I won't hear of you leaving. I just don't know what to do. He won't listen to anyone. I don't know why he can't be more like

Charley here. He never give me a minute's trouble his whole life."

"Booger don't mean half of what he says," the oldest son said around a mouthful of steak. "He mostly just talks to hear hisself rattle."

"It don't matter. You don't call a man a back shooter. That kind of talk will get you killed. Finish your dinner, Mr. Shooter. Then we'll go into the den and have a drink."

Throughout the entire affair Mrs. Stoker hadn't said a word. She sat silently, picking at her food, and openly stealing long glances at Johnny.

"Think I'll go sit in on the poker game in the bunkhouse," the oldest son said, pushing back from the table. "Stop by again sometime, Mr. Shooter."

After Charley left, Ben Stoker and Johnny headed for the den.

"Mind if I join you?" the rancher's wife asked.

"By all means, my dear."

They made themselves comfortable in front of the fireplace. The Indian house girl brought fresh coffee. Ben Stoker strode to the nearby cabinet and took out a bottle.

"Sure you won't join me in an after dinner drink, Mr. Shooter?"

"No, thanks. Think I'll pass."

Johnny watched as the rancher poured a full glass of the golden liquid, downed the entire amount and poured another before returning to his seat next to his wife. *At the rate that fellow is downing that whiskey, he'll be out cold before long.*

"How long have you been a lawman?" Henrietta Stoker asked, ignoring her husband and leveling her gaze at Johnny.

"Not long."

"It must be an exciting job."

"Yes ma'am, it can get that way at times."

"I'm sorry you had to see that outburst at dinner."

"It's okay. I just didn't want to cause problems."

"If it hadn't been you it would have been something else. Things are not always as they seem."

Johnny didn't like the way the conversation was going and glanced quickly at Ben Stoker. The rancher's head was resting against the back of the chair and his eyes were closed.

"Oh, don't worry about him," Mrs. Stoker assured him, "He's out for the evening, as usual."

"Maybe I better turn in, too," Johnny said, pushing up from the chair.

"I'll show you to your room," Henrietta told him, rising and leading the way up the stairway.

Johnny had no choice but to follow. Her long dress swayed smoothly from side to side with each exaggerated step she took up the stair.

At the top of the stairs she turned left down a hallway. At the first door she paused long enough to push the door open and step inside.

This will be your room," she said in a low, tantalizing voice. "My room is right next door."

Her dark, flashing eyes suggested more than the words. Stepping toward him, she lifted a hand, and let the back of her fingers feather slowly, temptingly, along his cheek, all the while holding his gaze with hers.

"If you need anything, anything at all, just tap on the wall."

Johnny couldn't believe what was happening. The rancher's wife was making her meaning abundantly clear. A surge of hot blood raced through him and flushed his face. He was a man, and she was a beautiful woman, *very much a woman.*

His body told him to reach out and take her in his arms and have his way with her. But his mind told him that would be against everything his ma and pa taught him. She was a married woman. Her husband entrusted him and took him into his home. Besides, a picture of Libby flashed into his mind, a woman he already knew he loved. He swallowed hard and then again before he could push the words past the lump in his throat.

"Thank you, ma'am, but it's been a long day. I reckon I won't have any trouble sleeping."

Chapter XI

An afternoon sun played hide-and-go-seek behind puffy, white clouds as Johnny rode down the main street of Fort Smith. His black gelding's hooves made muffled sounds on the thick dusty street. An approaching team and wagon swung wide to make room for him and his body-laden lead horse to pass. Bustling shoppers stopped on the boardwalk to gawk and whisper to one another.

Up ahead the local news photographer hurried to set up his bulky camera in the street. The powder in the flashpan ignited, and another headline was born. By tomorrow his picture would be plastered all over Fort Smith. The news media had already painted Parker as a cold, heartless judge hell bent on hanging everyone that appeared before him. The nickname they gave him had stuck. Now they referred to him openly as the hanging judge.

Johnny ignored the newsman's shouted questions and rode on up the street toward the Undertaker's Office. The sooner he got rid of Otis Talbot's body, the better he would feel.

The dealer in death was a gangly fellow with a long neck and a hawk nose. His eyes set deep in his head giving him a ghostly appearance. He glanced up briefly at Johnny before stepping forward and taking the reins to Talbot's horse.

"Who you got there, Marshal"? Someone shouted.

"Horse thief," Johnny replied as he reined Blackjack around.

He was glad to see Marshal Fagan's red bay tied to the hitching rail in front of the Marshal's office. He swung a leg over his saddle and stepped to the ground.

James Fagan glanced up from a stack of papers as Johnny pushed through the door.

"Glad to see you back, kid. Somebody told me you rode in with a man belly down across the saddle. I take it that would be Otis Talbot"?

"For a fact."

Johnny spun a straight-back chair and straddled it.

"What happened?" The marshal asked as he leaned back in his chair and pulled out his ever present pipe.

"He drew down on me. He gave me no choice. I had to shoot him."

Fagan put fire to his pipe full of tobacco and tugged open a squeaky desk drawer. Pulling out a paper, he pushed it across the desk.

"Write it all down just like it happened. Don't leave nothing out."

Johnny hated paperwork. He looked on it as a waste of time but knew it was part of the job, so he scooted his chair closer to the desk, touched the pencil lead to his tongue, and started writing.

The marshal leaned back in his chair and puffed on his pipe as Johnny wrote out his report. No words were spoken, but Johnny could feel his friend's gaze like a man can tell when another is looking at him.

It took a while, but finally he laid down the pencil and pushed the paper back across the desk. Fagan picked up the paper and took his time reading it, all the while letting the blue smoke escape from the corner of his mouth and trail lazily toward the ceiling.

"Good report," he finally said. "You forgot to sign it."

Johnny pushed from his chair, bent over the desk, and scribbled his name at the bottom of the paper.

"By the way," the marshal said casually. "News came in about the Choctaw Kid. Seems he shot up a store over in the territory a few days back, place called Whitefield. Killed a couple fellows and got away.

"Then just today we got word somebody saw him and his gang at a watering hole just outside Tahlequah. Place called Sadie's. It's a real den of rattlers. It's a whorehouse, saloon and gambling dive where life is cheap and pleasure is almighty expensive. Talk is, the Kid's sweet on a little Indian gal that works there name of Little Star, I think it is. Thought you'd want to check it out.

"Don't know how many he's got with him, but at least two of his bunch was seen. A gun slick named Jack Monday and a sickly looking kid with snow-white hair they call Whitey. They've both been running from the law for years. Here are their wanted posters and a warrant for their arrest. They're worth five hundred apiece, dead or alive. Reward on the Choctaw Kid is up to a thousand now.

"Monday is right handy with his pistols, so don't take any chances. He's a natty dresser. He wears a black hat with a rattlesnake hatband. Of the two, though, Whitey might just be the most dangerous. Don't let his looks fool you. He looks like a snot nosed kid but he's a cold-blooded killer. He's mad dog crazy and his wagon is a few bricks shy of a full load.

"They raided a farmhouse awhile back. Whitey chopped the farmer's arms and legs off with an ax. They made the man watch while the whole gang took turns with his wife. When they got through with her Whitey chopped her head off just for fun. We caught one of their gang not long after that little party and he bragged about it like he was proud of it. Course he changed his tune just before we hung him."

"Sounds like a bunch of snakes that needs stomped. Reckon I'll ride out first thing in the morning," Johnny said, turning toward the door.

"Just one more thing," the marshal said, drawing in a deep inhale from his pipe and letting it out slowly before speaking again. "Right good job with Talbot."

Johnny raised a hand before pushing through the door.

He dreaded having to tell Libby that he had to leave again in the morning. He had really been looking forward to that pie supper at the church. But a man's gotta do what a man's gotta do, he figured.

The closer he got to the boarding house the more nervous he got. *I'd sooner face a man in a standup gunfight than to face Miss Libby and tell her what I gotta say.*

Johnny reined up at the small stable behind the house and swung down. Stripping the saddle and bridle from Blackjack, he turned him into a stall. He hung his saddle from a rope dangling from the ceiling and was about to pour a bucket of oats into the feed trough when Libby hurried into the stable and stopped just inside the door. He swung a look over his shoulder.

She wore a mixture of excitement and expectancy on her face but with a hint of uncertainty. Her green eyes danced in the dim light of the stable.

He's home! she thought, jerking a nervous look over her shoulder toward the house before breaching the slight distance between them in a run. A sob worked its way up her throat as she threw herself into his open arms. For a long moment they held one another, savoring the closeness, filling her very soul with indescribable joy. She clung tightly to him, afraid if she let go he might somehow slip away from her.

"I'm so glad you are home safe," she whispered from the hollow of his shoulder. "I was so worried about you."

"It's good to be back," his hesitant voice replied.

He lifted his left hand to her cheek, feathered his knuckles along her jaw, and gently raised her face to his. His strong right hand found the small of her back and gathered her in. She arched instinctively into his embrace. His touch sent delight spinning through her. She closed her eyes as their mouths sought and found each other. His lips came soft and full on hers, his tenderness belying his obvious strength. Their kiss was long and searching, igniting a yearning deep inside her. She tingled from head to toe. She opened her mouth, drinking him in, seeking to quench a thirst she never before knew existed.

She was quivering when Johnny finally raised his head. For a long moment they just stared at one another. She could see that he was every bit as affected by the kisses as she had been. His face was flushed and he was breathing almost as hard as she was.

"Libby," he said hoarsely, cleared his throat, and tried again. "There's something I need to tell you but..."

She raised her head to stare into his eyes with a look of concern. "But what"?

She saw him swallow hard, seemingly trying to force words past a lump in his throat.

"I have to leave again at first light in the morning."

Her eyes went wide. A feeling of near panic surged over her.

"Leave? So soon? But why?"

"It's my job. It's what I do."

"Why do you have to leave? Couldn't it wait another day or two?"

"No, I'm afraid not. I have to go."

"But, but you'll miss the pie supper at the church."

"Yeah, I know. I'm sorry."

Libby was silent for a space of time, her gaze on the toe of her shoe raking straw on the floor. Johnny waited.

"Then I'll just have to bake that apple pie for supper tonight," she suddenly said cheerfully, reaching a hand and poking him in the ribs. "But you, Johnny Shooter, have to help me peel the apples."

"I reckon I can manage that," he grinned.

Chapter XII

A brassy, mid-morning sun filtered through an open grimy window, past the faded curtains, and crept silently across the small room. Millions of dust particles, like tiny living things, drifted lazily along the beam's path. The warmth of its rays came to rest on the bed and the two motionless figures lying there.

Little Star blinked her eyes open, frowned, and swung her legs over the side of the rickety bed. She had a pounding headache. She glanced casually over her shoulder at her companion. He was still fully dressed right down to his boots, lying on his stomach, exactly as he had fallen last night when she helped him to bed.

For a long moment she stared at him. Most folks knew him as the Choctaw Kid, but she knew him as Billy. She knew he was wanted by the law. She'd heard the stories about him. They said that he killed many men. But what did she care? She knew he was sweet on her, but to her, he was just another in a long line of customers. A very long line. She was sick to death of the life she lived, but knew she would never change.

She started whoring when she was fourteen, right after her ma died. That was five years ago. She never knew who her pa was. Her ma never talked about it. Probably ma didn't even know. As far back as Little Star could remember, there had been a steady stream of men that beat a path to their door, so it could be anybody.

She got to her feet and winced at the pounding in her head. Staggering on wobbly feet to the dresser, she cupped a handful of water from the white basin and splashed it over her face. When she rose up she caught a glimpse of the face staring back at her from the mirror. She was nineteen years old and fifty years wise.

She was nineteen, but the face in the mirror looked forty. Turkey-track lines creased her skin from the corners of both eyes. Dark, puffy areas below both eyes spoke of too much whiskey and too many men on too many nights. She looked and felt awful. She needed a cup of coffee.

She pulled a thin white housecoat over her naked body as she headed for the door. Old Sam would have the coffeepot on downstairs in the kitchen. It was too early for customers. She padded barefooted down the stairs.

"Mornin', little darlin'," the big barkeep said in his usual bullfrog voice. He stopped sweeping long enough to let his stare crawl hungrily over the brown skin showing where the flimsy housecoat gaped in front. Little Star felt his gaze, but ignored him. "You and the Kid shore nuff tied one on last night."

"My head is reminding me," she mumbled as she stumbled toward the kitchen. "You got some fresh coffee made?"

"Shore do. Made it fresh jest last night."

She made her way into the cluttered and filthy kitchen, found a tin cup that wasn't too dirty and wiped it out before

pouring it full of the thick black liquid. She blew the steam away, took a sip and wrinkled her face as she stumbled back into the saloon.
"How do you drink this awful stuff?" she complained.
"It might be a tad weak, shore enough."
"Weak? This stuff would make good axle grease. Is Sadie up yet?"
"Lordy, no. You know she never gets up till the middle of the afternoon. Besides, you better be glad she ain't up. She's mighty put out with that fella of yourn."
"He ain't my fella. What's she mad at him for?"
"Cause he's laid up there in your room fer more'n three weeks and hadn't paid a red penny fer you or the room, either. Besides that, he's drank up fifty dollars worth of her best whiskey on the credit. Sadie said his credit jest run out."
"Glad it ain't left to me to collect from him. He gets mighty riled if you wake him before noon."
"I'll wake him and I'll collect from him, too. I ain't scared of that half-breed."
"Think I'll be someplace else when that happens."
The batwing doors pushed inward to allow three tough-looking Cherokee to enter. The last one was a giant of a man; his shoulders near brushed both sides of the door.
The one in front was the obvious leader. He wore his black hair loose, hanging down his back to near his waist. His face was hard. His eyes were cold and expressionless. At his waist he wore a pearl handled Colt in a belly holster.
The three looked like they had come a far piece on a dusty road. They swept the saloon with a searching gaze that lingered long on Little Star's flimsy attire. She clutched her housecoat close. They sauntered over to the table where she sat, scraped out chairs and sat down without saying a word.

"Mornin', Gents," Sam bellowed out in his friendliest voice from behind the bar. "What'll it be?"

"Whiskey," the hard-looking one snarled, "and a glass for the little lady."

"I'm obliged, but I'm drinking coffee," she said, pushing up from her chair. "Besides, I've got to be going."

A hand shot out and grabbed her arm, jerking her roughly back into her chair. "Sit down!" the leader ordered. "I said we was gonna have a drink. Then you and me are gonna go upstairs and get to know one another better."

Little Star skewed her eyebrows and raked the man from head to toe with a look of contempt.

"I told you I'm not having a drink with you. I'm off-duty. Besides, from the looks of you three, you couldn't come up with five dollars between you."

For a moment the man was speechless. Then, jerking open his shirt he yanked a leather pouch from around his neck and dumped its contents on top of the table.

She felt her eyes go wide. A large double handful of shiny new gold double-eagles scattered across the table. Sam arrived with a bottle and four glasses. He, too, stood speechless while staring wide-eyed at the pile of money. Little Star had never in her whole life seen that much cash money at one time. She swallowed hard.

"Okay, so you got the money. I still can't go upstairs with you. I'm spoken for."

"Yeah," the man snarled. "By who?"

"By me," said a cold voice from the area near the foot of the stairs. Every gaze in the saloon swung toward the voice. The Choctaw Kid stood with his hand only a hair's breath from his pistol.

By instinct and experience, both Little Star and Sam melted away from the table leaving the three Indian no-goods sitting there in their chairs. For an instant no one moved. Then, without warning, catching the Cherokee completely off-guard, the Kid's hand swept his pistol from its holster in one fluid motion, and began firing.

His first shot struck the leader square in the center of his chest, knocking him over backwards and killing him instantly. The next shot took out the man to the leader's right. The only remaining Indian was the huge giant of a man. He sat motionless, his hand suspended in mid-air halfway to his pistol. Calmly, the Choctaw Kid walked slowly over to stand only a few feet away from the trembling survivor.

"Never did have any use for Cherokee," he snarled as he raised his pistol and fired point-blank into the Indian's face, blowing the man out of his chair.

Little Star stood in shock. A hand covered her mouth in disbelief. In her years working the saloons she had seen many shootings, but she'd never before witnessed anyone brutally shot down in cold blood. The sight sickened her.

The killer snatched the bottle Sam had just brought from the table and turned it up to his lips and took several long swallows of the golden liquid. Wiping his mouth with a sleeve he eyed the pile of double-eagles.

"Reckon that won't do them much good where they're going," he said, scooping up the money and stuffing it in his pocket. Striding over to the bar, he counted out ten double eagles and slammed them onto the bar top, then flipped an extra gold coin to the bar keep. "Settle up with Sadie for me and have somebody get that scum out of my sight and stick 'em in a hole."

* * *

It took two days of hard riding for Johnny to reach Tahlequah. It was near sundown when he drew rein at the livery stable. He flipped the Indian boy a dollar and told him to put Blackjack into a stall by himself and give him a double ration of grain. The young boy only nodded and went about his chore.

He had seen the hotel down the street when he rode in and headed that way. In the short walk he passed three saloons already going full blast. Must have a passel of thirsty Indians in these parts, he thought as he stepped through the front door of the Tahlequah Hotel.

A short, fat, bald fellow glanced up from the dime novel he was reading and peered over the top of his horn-rim glasses.

"Yes, sir," he greeted cheerfully. "How can I help you?"

Johnny laid both of his sawed-off double barrel Greeners on the counter. The desk clerk's eyes bugged wide and he licked his lips.

"Need a room, upstairs in the front. I want clean sheets and a bath brought up. How much?"

"Clean sheets will cost you extra. We only change the beds once a week."

"How much?"

"With the bath that will be four dollars."

Johnny pitched four silver dollars onto the counter and scribbled his name in the book.

"Where's a decent café a fellow can get a good meal?"

"Right down the street. Place called the Arrowhead Café. They dish up mighty fine vittles."

"Looking for a place called Sadie's," he said, scooping up the key the desk clerk laid on the counter.

"Bad place, mister. I'd think twice before I went there. There's lots of good saloons in town."

"You gonna tell me where to find Sadie's or preach me a sermon?"

"No skin off my back. Two miles west out of town."

"I'm obliged."

By the time he stowed his saddlebags and pried off his boots, two Indian women arrived with a large bathtub. After a half-dozen trips they had the tub brimming with steaming-hot water. Johnny shucked his clothes and lowered himself carefully into the hot water. It took a while, but the soap, bristle brush, and hot water finally loosened the trail dirt and soothed his tired muscles. He lazed in the tub and thought about Libby.

After a good hour in the tub and another devouring the thick steak, fried potatoes, turnip greens and corn bread, he almost felt like a new man.

"Think I got just enough room left for a slab of that apple pie I see over yonder," he told the pretty Indian waitress.

He took his time with the pie and another cup of coffee. He was in no hurry. He figured to give the Kid and his bunch time to get liquored up before he went calling.

The clock in the café said it was half past nine when Johnny paid for his supper and left the pretty Indian girl a generous tip.

Johnny walked to the livery and saddled up his horse, telling the boy he was going for a ride and would be back in a bit. As he rode west he opened both of his double-barreled Greeners and thumbed in four loads of buckshot.

He heard the noise from the saloon before he saw it. A tinny piano and drunken laughter carried on the still night air. Johnny shifted in his saddle and swallowed hard. He checked his pistol to make sure it was fully loaded for the third time He didn't know what lay before him, but he was determined to face it head-on. *Reckon I'm as ready as I'll ever be.*

More than twenty saddled horses stood hipshot, tied to hitching posts in front of the large building. A whitewashed sign hung attached to the balcony along the front. Lamplight from four upstairs windows spilled into the dusty road. Most likely the whores' rooms, he figured.

Johnny paused just outside the batwing doors. His height allowed him to peer over their top and sweep the large room with a searching gaze. The stench of the place was overwhelming. The smell of stale whiskey, sweat, body odor, and cigarette smoke engulfed him like a shroud and burned his nose.

The room was large. A long bar occupied most of the lefthand wall. A huge barman poured drinks for the six Indians bending their elbows. A door at the far end of the bar opened into what appeared to be a kitchen. A stairway to upstairs hugged the wall directly across the room from where Johnny stood. A skinny little fellow played an upright piano that badly needed tuning and to which no one was listening.

Several tables were occupied by an assortment of Indians and barflies. There were two green-topped poker tables in the room. One was empty. Four men sat at the other one. Two of the men were Jack Monday and Whitey. Most likely at least one, maybe both, of the other two were part of the Choctaw Kid's bunch. But the Kid was nowhere in sight. Most likely he was upstairs with his girl. A hard-looking house whore sat draped all over the gun slick. A large woman in a bright red dress sipped a drink and watched the game. Johnny took her to be Sadie.

Swallowing the lump that lodged somewhere just above his Adam's apple, Johnny took a deep breath, pulled back the hammers of his sawed-off Greeners, and stepped inside.

He held both shotguns hidden behind his legs as he strode casually toward the poker players. Sadie glanced up and at the sight of Johnny her eyes went wide. She touched the shoulder of the other girl and motioned with her head. They both melted quickly away from the table. The piano player jerked a nervous

look and stopped in the middle of his tune. An unwelcome hush settled over the room.
 Johnny stopped ten feet or so from the table and raised both shotguns to waist level.
 "I've got two sawed-off double barrels pointed at you boys. Don't want to kill you, but will if I have to. First hombre that moves is a dead man."
 For the space of several seconds it was as if the men at the table were frozen solid. Finally Jack Monday looked up right into the nose of Johnny's shotguns. The muzzle of those Greeners must have looked like the double gates of hell.
 "Who are you? What do you want with us?"
 I'm United States Deputy Marshal Johnny Shooter. I have a warrant for your arrest. Got one here for you too, Whitey."
 Monday went for his pistol. The last mistake of his life. The blast from Johnny's shotgun sounded like a stick of dynamite going off in the confines of the room. The single load of double-aught buckshot tore the gunfighter's head from his shoulders. It exploded like a ripe watermelon in a stomach-wrenching mixture of blood, bone, and brain tissue.
 Johnny's second barrel blew two of the men near in half, knocking the one called Whitey out of his chair. The killer rolled on the floor, bloodied all over from the buckshot but he still clawed for his pistol. Johnny raised his second shotgun and feathered a trigger. The blast chewed up the outlaw something terrible. Even his mother wouldn't have recognized what was left. It all happened in the space of a handful of heartbeats.
 A sweeping glance around the room revealed no one looking to take a part. Johnny walked over and kicked the weapons aside and checked to see if any of them were still alive.
 They weren't.
 "You the owner?" he asked of the lady in the red dress.
 She nodded.

"Where's The Choctaw Kid?"

She didn't say a word, but her gaze flicked upstairs. Johnny took the stairs two at a time in a long-legged run. The sound of glass crashing told him someone or something had gone through the window in the second room. He kicked the door in then ducked back behind the doorjamb, half expecting a shot from the room. There was none.

Chancing a look he swept the room with a quick glance. A Indian girl he took to be Little Star sat upright in bed clutching a bed sheet to her nakedness. The remains of a torn window curtain fluttered in the breeze where a window, use to be.

Wheeling, he ran back down the stairs and burst through the batwings in time to see the backside of the Choctaw Kid hightailing it out of town on his Pinto. All he could do was stand and watch the killer disappear as darkness swallowed him. Johnny knew his chances of trailing the Indian in the dark were slim and none. By morning the outlaw would lose himself in the vast woodlands of the Indian Territory, a land he knew like the back of his hand.

Dejected, Johnny went back inside to load up the four he had killed. It would be a long ride back to Fort Smith knowing he'd came so close to the Kid, but would once again return empty-handed.

The news of Johnny and his little caravan of corpses reached Fort Smith before he did. Travelers he met on the road grabbed their nose and gave him a wide berth.

As he led his body laden horses onto the gerry, the ferry captain wrinkled his nose and pulled his bandana up to cover it. "Heaven sakes, man, them fellows should have been in the ground days ago."

"Yeah, they got a little ripe on me, I reckon."
"Ripe ain't the word for the way they smell. Lead them horses to the far end of the ferry."
"Reckon what all the fuss is about over on the far bank?" he asked the ferry boat operator.
"It's them news people. Word got here before you did. They're out to get Judge Parker. You boys are supplying them the ammunition by bringing back folks across the saddle instead of in it. But I reckon them boys needed killing and it shore looks like you done a good job of that. Never seen men tore up so bad. We're living in sorry times, son, and getting sorrier every day."

As the ferry approached the dock the crowd continued to grow. Folks ran from every direction to witness the occasion. News photographers set up their cameras, ready to record the event. Men and women pointed and whispered.

The ferry tied and the ramp lowered, Johnny led Blackjack off, followed by four horses tied bridle to tail bearing the dead outlaws. Women took one look at what was left of the outlaws, which wasn't much, gasped, and turned away. Grown men lost their breakfast. Cameras flashed, news people shouted questions, but Johnny ignored them and hurriedly led his little caravan up the street to the Marshal's Office. James Fagan stood on the boardwalk leaning against a post and smoking his pipe as Johnny approached.

"Well, well," he said, exhaling a cloud of blue smoke around a crooked grin. "I was beginning to worry about you. Who you got there?"

"Jack Monday, Billy Spears, Ike Wheaton, and the one called Whitey."

"Whew! Smells like they done spoiled on you. All those boys have posters on 'em. You tallied up a right tidy sum this trip. See any sign of the Choctaw Kid?"

"Yeah, I saw his backside as he was high tailing it out of town."

"Well, come on in the office and fill out your report. I'll have one of the boys take these gents over to the undertaker and get them planted."

"Doing paperwork is my favorite part of this job," Johnny mumbled as he headed into the office.

"Yeah, I know, mine too, but the judge is a stickler for having a complete report."

Johnny spent the next hour putting it all down on paper, exactly like it happened. When he finished he pitched the report across the desk with an exasperated sigh. The marshal picked it up and read it slowly, puffing on his pipe.

"Good report, Johnny, them was mighty stiff odds though, taking on four killers face up."

"I was just lucky to get the drop on them. Having those two scatterguns helped even up the odds a mite. Think I'll mosey down to Miss Lila's and scrub some trail dust off me before suppertime."

A thin grin wrinkled the corner of the marshal's mouth. "Yeah, most likely Miss Libby will be right glad to see you, too."

"You coming for supper?" Johnny asked over his shoulder as he opened the door.

"I'll be there. I make it a point of being right close when Miss Lila sets a table."

Johnny closed the door, toed a stirrup and swung into the saddle. He reined Blackjack around, ignoring the wad of men gathered outside the marshal's office. He was aware of the whispered comments and finger pointing as he rode slowly down the street.

Chapter XIII

The Choctaw Kid lashed his pinto with the long reins and rode through the night. He knew fear for the first time in his life. *Who was that fellow?* he wondered, angry at himself for letting anyone get the drop on him like that. *How'd he get by Jack and the boys? Sounded like he was using a shotgun. This fellow must be one tough hombre to take on all four of my boys like that. They must all be dead or they never would have let him come up those stairs. Maybe I better lay low for awhile. Think I'll ride up to Belle's hideout in the mountains, there ain't no law dog can find me there.*

Two days later he rode cautiously along a mountain stream that snaked between two mountains thirty miles south of Whitefield. He eyed the craggy rocks along the mountaintops wearily, knowing there would be lookouts guarding the most notorious hideout in the Indian Territory.

He was there, once before, a couple of years or so ago. At that time there were more than a dozen men enjoying the safety of the spacious cave. It was the safest place for a man on the run.

Folks said Belle Starr herself visited frequently, and offered her favors to them that had the money, but Sam Starr, her sometimes husband, was the only one the Kid had ever saw at the hideout. He'd never met Belle and wouldn't know her if he met her face-to-face.

He picked his way slowly along the creek. He knew he was being watched. He just hoped whoever it was didn't shoot first and ask questions later. Up ahead, the stream took a sharp dogleg to the right as it passed through a narrow gap in the steep rocks. He figured that's where the lookout was located. He reined up and kept his hands well away from his pistol.

"Just hold up right there!" A gruff voice from the top of the rocks shouted. "Who are you and what you doing out here?"

"I'm called the Choctaw Kid. I'm looking for Sam Starr."

"Just sit easy and keep them hands where I can see 'em."

Hearing a sound behind him, he jerked his head around. Two tough looking hombres with rifles trained square on him emerged from a clump of trees. Two more blocked his way from behind a huge boulder in front of him. He slowly raised his hands. One of the riders in his path spurred his mount forward.

"You say you're the Choctaw Kid, huh? Well, we'll see about that. In the meantime I'll relieve you of those guns."

"Nobody takes my guns."

"I'll either take your guns or the boys will blow you clean outta your saddle. Your choice."

"I want to see Sam Starr."

"All in due time. Right now I need them guns. I won't ask again."

The Kid knew he had no choice. He carefully lifted his pistol with thumb and forefinger and handed it to the man.

"The rifle, too."

Withdrawing his rifle from the saddle boot, he handed it over.

"Now follow me. We'll go see what Sam has to say. You better hope he knows you."

Sandwiched between four riders they picked their way between large boulders and up a narrow draw, emerging near the mouth of a large cave—Robber's Cave.

A large Indian, dressed in white man's clothes and smoking a cigar, strode casually from the opening. The Kid recognized the man as Sam Starr. Sam wasn't a big man, at least in height, but his wide shoulders and heavily muscled arms witnessed to his strength. His hair was long and straight, tied at the back with a leather thong. An ugly knife scar started at the edge of his mouth and ended along his temple.

"This fellow claims to be the Choctaw Kid. He asked to see you. You know him?"

Sam Starr puffed on his cigar and gave the newcomer a long, dark-eyed stare as if searching his memory. Finally a fake looking smile broke the stony look the Indian normally wore.

"I know. You got money, Kid?"

"Some. How much?"

"I hear much about you. Cost you two hundred dollars a month. Pay now."

"That's pretty steep."

"Up to you. Pay or ride."

"Reckon I'll hang around a while," the Kid said, digging out the roll of bills from the Whitefield robbery and counting out two hundred dollars.

Reaching out and taking the money, the big Indian flashed a wide smile exposing rotting, yellow teeth.

"Light down. Supper's almost ready."

The Kid climbed from his mount and led it to the nearby rope corral. He unsaddled and turned his horse in with a dozen others. As he returned to the cave he glanced around at the collection of ten hard-looking men lounging around a camp fire. They were a scroungy bunch. He recognized Shorty Ferguson and Jake Stallings. They rode together on a bank job up in Missouri a while back. The rest he had never seen before.

He found an empty tin cup and poured himself some coffee from the blackened pot sitting on a flat rock. A kettle of stew simmered over the fire. He sat down on a big log near the campfire.

"So you call yourself the Choctaw Kid, huh?" one of the men asked.

The Kid slanted a look at the one who spoke. He was a big man, big and mean looking and ugly. He had a full scraggly beard and mustache that hid his face. Only his gray eyes were visible below a wide-brimmed hat. They looked bleary and whiskey soaked.

"Some call me that."

"Who you running from, Kid?" the man asked sarcastically.

"I don't run from no man."

"You supposed to be tough or something?"

"I manage to stay alive."

"You fast with that pistol you were wearing?"

"Like I said, I manage to stay alive."

"Leave him be, Ed," Sam said, strolling up and hearing the conversation. "Why he's here ain't none of your business."

"I just might make it my business. I don't like the fellow's looks. Besides, you don't tell me what I can say and can't say."

Without a word Sam Starr drew his pistol and shot the big mouth right between the eyes. His head exploded and his body tumbled backwards off the rock where he sat.

"Now let's eat. That rabbit stew is ready," Sam muttered, slipping his pistol back into his belly holster.

***

News of Johnny's arrival in town must have already reached Libby because she was waiting on the porch for him. He was still a block away when he saw her.

She wore a light blue skirt and white, button-up-the-front, blouse that was open at the neck. She also wore a white half-apron tied around her waist. A big smile covered most of her face as she lifted high on tiptoes and waved a happy welcome.

She shore is a sight to behold. He returned her wave. Makes a man want to stay close to home.

Libby left the porch at a run, one hand holding her skirt off the ground, her feet flying down the street to meet him. Swinging to the ground, he opened his arms. She filled them. Her arms encircled his neck. Her lips found his.

"Maybe I need to go away more often," he mumbled between kisses. "What will the neighbors think?"

"Who cares what they think? I'm just happy you're home."

"That makes two of us," he said, as they walked side by side down the street toward the stable. Riley burst from the door and ran to meet Johnny, smiling from ear to ear.

"Glad you're home, Mr. Johnny."

"Looks like Miss Lila's cooking's agreeing with you. I bet you've put on ten pounds."

"Yes, sir. Her and Miss Libby shore cooks good. Want me to take Blackjack and stable him for you?"

"Thanks, be sure to give him some corn, he's had a long ride."

"I'll take care of it," the boy said, taking the horse's reins and heading toward the stable.

"Supper's almost ready. Mother and I were just finishing up. I've got a surprise for you."

"Hope it's one of those apple pies of yours."

"How'd you know?" She said, wrinkling her forehead in surprise.

"Cause I could smell it two blocks down the street," he laughed. "Marshal Fagan said he'd be along for supper, too. I need to wash up."

"Yes, he sent word that you were back and said he'd be here for supper. That's how I knew you were coming. I'll run and help Mother finish up. Hurry, so we can talk."

Johnny watched her as she ran ahead into the house. Once she glanced back over her shoulder and saw him watching her. She smiled and swayed her way into the house.

He paused before entering the screened-in porch to swat the dust from his clothes with his hat.

The aroma of home cooking wafted through the air. *Shore smells good,* he thought, as he poured water in the pan to wash up. Marshal Fagan rode up and stabled his horse, then he and Riley walked together to the house and pushed through the screen door as Johnny was drying his face and hands with a towel.

"Is that apple pie I'm smelling," the Marshal asked, "or is my nose lying to my stomach?"

"Libby said she cooked me and Riley one apiece, don't know if she cooked one for you or not."

"How come I'm eating better since you moved in? Oh, by the way, I told the judge you was back. He wants to see you tonight at nine o'clock."

"Got any idea what it's about?"

"Yeah, some, but I reckon I'll wait and let him tell you. I figured up what those boys you brought in was worth. You got sixteen hundred dollars coming. That's more than I make in a whole year. Maybe I ought to quit my job and start riding with you."

"Be glad to have you. Most likely wouldn't be much help but might be good to have someone to talk to," Johnny kidded.

Miss Lila pushed open the door and stuck her head out. "You men folk gonna stand out there jawing all night? Supper's on the table and getting cold."

"That's just what I was telling him," the marshal said, winking at Johnny and heading for the door.

Supper was a wonderful time. It was one of those memories that lodges somewhere in a special place in a man's mind and just pops out now and again. Laughter, joking with one another, closeness, family. Exactly. It felt like family.

Johnny thought that to say Riley and Cathy had adjusted would be a big understatement. They were the center of attention. He was halfway through the big steak in front of him before Riley finished telling how somebody—he wouldn't say exactly who—put a frog in Mrs. Hofstadter's desk drawer at school. Everyone at the table laughed so hard they could scarcely eat.

After the meal, James, Johnny, and Miss Lila took their coffee into the sitting room and settled into comfortable chairs in front the fireplace. Riley and Cathy helped Libby clear the table and do the dishes.

"I hear your arrival back in Fort Smith caused quite a stir, Johnny," Miss Lila said.

"Reckon folks got to talk about something."

"I hear you brought in four dead men. Is that true?"

"Johnny brought in four cold-blooded killers, Miss Lila," Marshal Fagan added quickly. "They murdered whole families just for the enjoyment of seeing them suffer, men, women, and even children. When Johnny tried to arrest them they tried to kill him. He had no choice but to do what he did. That's his job."

"There's just so much violence these days."

"Yes, ma'am, these are violent times, but our job is to bring those that do violence to justice."

"I know, and I appreciate the work that you men do. If we didn't have the law to protect decent folks I don't know what we would do."

"Johnny's a fine deputy marshal, one of the best I've got."

"You never told me that," Johnny kidded.

"I'm telling you now, but don't let it go to your head."

"How are the kids doing in school, Miss Lila?" Johnny asked.

"Remarkably well not having any previous formal education. They are exceptional children. Riley is all boy, of course, but that is to be expected. He minds well and does his chores without complaining. Cathy and Libby are like sisters. Where one is the other won't be far away."

"Will you be going out again soon," Lila asked Johnny.

"Can't say for sure."

They sipped their coffee and watched the flames in silence for a few moments. *Feels kinda like when we use to sit around that old pot-belly stove at home,* Johnny remembered. *Peaceful, comfortable, safe.*

"Don't mean to rush you, Johnny," the marshal said, glancing at the big grandfather clock standing nearby, "but it's half past eight."

"Yeah, I better get a move on," he said, pushing from the chair. "Don't want to keep the judge waiting. Shore was a fine supper, Miss Lila. Tell Libby I don't know how long I'll be. Tell her I'll see her in the morning."

Johnny purposefully avoided going by the kitchen, knowing he would have to explain about his meeting with Judge Parker. He hurried to the stable, saddled Blackjack, and swung into the saddle.

It was a short ride to the courthouse and he arrived several minutes early. He'd rather be early as late for a meeting with the judge. He tied his mount to the hitching rail in front of the courthouse and took the steps two at a time. Arriving at the door to the judge's office, he tapped quietly.

"Yes, come in," he heard the judge's voice from inside. Johnny pushed open the door.

Judge Parker rose from his desk and crossed the room to meet him with an outstretched hand and a smile on his face. It was the first time Johnny ever saw the judge smile. Johnny stood in his regular place in front of the Judge's desk.

"Welcome back, Deputy Shooter. Marshal Fagan tells me you had a successful trip."

"Well, yes, sir. I suppose you could say that, even though I didn't get the Choctaw Kid."

"You will. I have no doubt of that. Care for a cigar?"

"No, thank you. I never cared much for smoking."

"Wise choice. I limit myself to one a day. I've found after a fourteen-hour day, a glass of brandy and a good cigar does wonders for my disposition and helps me rest better. Do you indulge in alcoholic spirits, Mr. Shooter?"

"No, sir."

"I read your report. Excellent, I must say, you seem to be working out even better than I had hoped."

"Thank you, sir."

Opening a desk drawer the judge withdrew a large envelope containing more money than Johnny had ever seen before in his life and handed it across the desk.

"You did pretty well for yourself this trip. There's sixteen hundred dollars. What will you do with that much money?"

"Salt it away for a rainy day, I reckon."

"You're an intelligent young man, Mr. Shooter. I understand

there's a certain young lady in your life now. That won't interfere with your duties will it?"

"No, sir."

"Splendid. I have another assignment for you. There's a family called, Pike. The father is a self-appointed preacher, or at least he claims to be, named Rufus. He has four sons, but counting his sons and relatives this Pike gang numbers as many as twelve. Together they make up one of the worst gangs to come along in a while. They've robbed trains and stage coaches as far away as Missouri and Kansas. They've stolen horses and cattle and hung anyone that dared get in their way. We just found the last three deputies we sent after them hanging from a cottonwood tree.

"They live in a communal settlement of kinfolk they call Pikeville. It's about three or four days ride southwest of here on the southern side of the Winding Stair Mountain Range. Their village is near the headwaters of the Kiamichi River.

"When they hung my deputies, that was the last straw. Take as many men as you feel you need to get the job done. Marshal Fagan has already been briefed and will provide as much manpower and supplies as you need. I want these murderers dealt with severely. They must be made an example of. Do you understand?"

"Yes, sir. I understand."

"You will be in complete charge of the operation. Here are the warrants. I've thrown in an extra half-dozen John Doe warrants just in case you need them. Considering the distance, it won't be necessary to bring back—and shall I say—anyone that resists to Fort Smith. Unless, of course, they choose to surrender. I will take your word for the outcome. It shouldn't take more than a day or two to put your posse together. I will expect a full report upon your return."

The judge stood and extended a hand. "Good luck, Deputy Shooter."

"Thank you, sir, I'll do my best," Johnny said, pushing to his feet.

"Without a doubt."

After seaving the courthouse, Johnny untied his horse and led it behind him as he walked slowly toward the Arkansas River. He had some mighty deep thinking to do. He found a grassy spot on Belle Point near the old fort and sat down.

It was late. Most of Fort Smith's residents were home with their families except the night people who frequented the local saloons. The faint sound of a piano drifted on a cold November wind. The quiet ripples of the river and the call of night birds gave the place an almost reverent feeling.

Seems like I shore got me a mouthful to chew this time. I don't know beans about heading up a posse, but the judge give me the job to do. Like my pa always said, "A man's got to do what a man's got to do." Reckon I'll learn. Just don't want to get anyone killed while I'm learning.

The judge said I could take all the help I needed. Wonder how many I should ask for, or who, for that matter? I've heard the names of a few and heard stories about some of the better known, but for the most part I don't even know most of the deputies.

Think I'll ask Marshal Fagan which ones I should take with me, after all, he hired them all and knows them better than anyone. If he's still up I'll talk to him when I get home, if not, first thing in the morning. The judge said I ought to have everything ready to go in two days. It'll be a busy couple of days getting everything together. Guess I better try to catch the marshal before he goes to bed.

***

The light in the parlor was still on when Johnny finished taking care of Blackjack and pushed through the back door. Someone was still up. It was Marshal Fagan. He sat sipping coffee and staring into the dwindling fire.

"What are you doing up so late, Marshal? It's past midnight."

"Waiting on you, kind of felt like you might need to talk. Pour yourself a cup and have a seat. Did the judge fill you in?"

Johnny poured himself a steaming cup of coffee and eased into a large chair in front of the fireplace before he replied.

"He filled me in. Seems I got myself a lot to chew on."

"Yeah, I'll say you have. Any idea how you're gonna handle it?"

"I was hoping you might have a suggestion or two. He said you would furnish all the manpower and supplies I would need."

"You decided how many men you need?"

"I've been considering that. Here's how I'm seeing it. I'm leaning toward taking just a few. Maybe three or four of the very best you can let me have. Travel light. Take no more than we can carry on a couple of packhorses. I figure if a whole passel went charging in there, Pike and his boys would just light out and we'd end up chasing them all over tarnation."

"Sounds like good thinking. Anyone in particular you want to take with you?"

"You know who your best deputies are. Who would you take on a job like this?"

Marshal Fagan sipped on his coffee and stared into the leaping flames in the fireplace for a few long minutes, obviously in deep thought, going over his deputies, considering their strengths and shortcomings. Finally he looked up at Johnny and spoke.

"Lobo."

"Come again?" Johnny said.

"Lobo. That's what he's called. His real name is Henry Whitehorse, but I don't reckon anybody but me knows his given name, everybody just calls him, Lobo."

"Without a doubt he's the best tracker I've ever seen. He loves a good fight. There ain't a better man living with a knife. He can pin a fly to the wall from fifty feet away. I've seen him do it. Just keep the whiskey away from him and he's one of the best men I've got."

"He sounds like a man I could sure use. Is he available right now?"

"So happens he's between assignments. I had him working with the Choctaw Lighthorse police over around Tuskahoma until a week or so ago, but he's free to go with you if you want him."

"I'd like to talk to him."

"Bass Reeves is a man you ought to look at. He's near forty, but you'd never know it. He's been a deputy almost two years now and he's proved himself to be one of my best men. He's black. He speaks the Creek language fluently, but can converse reasonably well in any Indian dialect. He's a master with any firearm you want to name. In the two years he's been a deputy he's already killed seven men."

"Count him in," Johnny said.

"I've got a young hothead I could send with you if you want him. He's a dead shot with a rifle. He's absolutely fearless. In that regard he's a lot like you. Don't reckon he ever backed down from a fight in his whole life."

"What's his name?"

"Smokey Seymour. He ain't but twenty. If he don't get himself killed with his recklessness he'll make a good lawman some day."

"Can I talk to him?"

"I'll have them all in my office in the morning by ten."

"I'll be there."

"We better get some sleep. You're likely to come up short on that for the next few weeks. Good luck to you, Johnny. It's a mighty big job you're taking on."

"Reckon so, marshal. Goodnight and thanks."

Marshal Fagan and three strangers to Johnny sipped coffee and chatted quietly in the marshal's office when Johnny arrived.

"Morning," James Fagan said, raising his cup in welcome. "Pour yourself a cup."

Johnny nodded to them and poured a cup of thick muddy coffee from the blackened pot on the stove.

"I reckon none of you have met. Men, this is Deputy United States Marshal Johnny Shooter. Johnny, say howdy to Bass Reeves."

Johnny swung a gaze at the big black man as he unfolded from his chair and extended a hand. He would stand as tall as Johnny, well over six feet, deep chested with shoulders the breadth of a double tree. Even through his threadbare work shirt and wool jacket you could see the strength of his arm muscles.

His black hair was streaked with a hint of gray. His thick lips were shrouded by a heavy moustache. Piercing dark eyes were intense and all business. He wore a Smith & Wesson in a worn holster. The man's handshake was vice-like. *He will do to ride with,* Johnny decided immediately.

"Howdy, Mr. Reeves."

"If'n we's gonna be riding together you needs to call me, Bass."

"Then Bass it will be," Johnny said, withdrawing his hand from the crushing handshake and liking the big fellow right off.

"Johnny, this is Lobo. Like I told you, he's the best tracker I've ever seen, and nobody's better with a knife. He's deadly with that sawed-off shotgun there beside him, too."

The Indian was short, and heavily muscled. A well used Colt Richards Conversion pistol poked out of a belly holster near the middle of his stomach and two large knives hung on either side of his hips in fringed leather sheaths. His long black hair hung loose down his back. He wore heavy woolen britches tucked into near knee-high boots, a blue work shirt and a worn vest buttoned to the top. He wore a red bandana knotted loosely around his neck, and a floppy hat sat square on his head. His coppery skin stretched tight over high cheekbones. His black eyes raked Johnny slowly from head to toe and back again.

The Indian took Johnny's offered hand and shook it like he was pumping water from a well.

"Good to meet you, Lobo."

The Indian just stared at Johnny, not saying a word. Finally, he looked Johnny square in the eyes and nodded once. They broke the handshake and Lobo sat down again.

The third man looked more like a schoolboy than a deputy marshal. He was cocked back in his straight-backed chair balanced on two legs, sipping coffee and chewing on a matchstick.

He wore two pearl handled Colt Peacemakers in tied-down holsters, and a black hat tilted forward about as far as his chair was backwards. The kid Marshal Fagan called Smokey Seymour looked bored with the whole thing.

"Howdy, Smokey."

The man didn't even look up or acknowledge Johnny's greeting. Johnny decided he had to get the kid's attention if they were going to watch one another's back. He took a step forward and hooked his toe behind the leg of the tilted chair and jerked. The boy hit the floor like he had been cold-cocked with a sledge hammer. Leaping to his feet with fire in his blue eyes he went for his guns only to stare face-to-face into the noses of Johnny's two pistols before his cleared leather.

"When I speak to a man I expect a reply," Johnny said quietly, meeting the boy's angry stare squarely. "If you don't want to make this trip, just say so right now and you're out."

For a full minute their gazes locked in a battle of wills. Johnny knew their future relationship would be determined in the next few heartbeats. Finally a thin grin crooked its way across the boy's handsome face. He lifted his hands away from his holstered pistols in an exaggerated move.

"You're fast, mister. You're real fast," the boy said, reaching a hand. "I'm Smokey Seymour. So you're Shooter? Seems you're as bad as they say."

"And you're as reckless as they say. Moves like that are liable to get you killed."

"There's worse things than dying. If a man ain't willing to live, he's already as good as dead."

Interrupting, Marshal Fagan spoke as he rose and poured himself another cup of coffee.

"I've asked Johnny to lay this one out for you men. No getting around it, this is a tough assignment, that's why it's strictly a voluntary mission. The last three deputies we sent after this bunch, we found hanging from a cottonwood. After Johnny fills you in, any man who wants to walk out the door is free to do so. I want to make one thing clear, though, Johnny Shooter is in complete charge. Anything he says is the same as me saying it. Any man got a problem with that is free to leave right now. Go ahead, Johnny, tell them what this is all about."

Johnny swept a slow gaze around the room, making eye contact with each of the deputies. He could see he had their attention.

"There's a gang over around the Winding Stair Mountains that's got too big for their britches. Reports are they put as many as a dozen men in the saddle. They specialize in robbing trains, banks, and stage coaches as far away as Missouri and Kansas. They don't hesitate to gun down anybody that gets in their way. This is a family operation. The head of the family and the leader is a self-anointed preacher named Rufus Pike. He and his four sons rule the little commune called Pikeville. Seems nobody lives there but family members, so we can't expect any help.

Like the Marshal said earlier, we just found three of our fellow deputies that Pike and his gang hung. Our job is to eliminate this whole gang one way or another. We'll use whatever means necessary to do that. Anybody got any questions?

Smokey slipped up a half-raised hand. "Does that mean what it sounded like it meant?"

"I mean just what I said."

"Then count me in."

"I'm in," Bass Reeves said in his deep bullfrog voice.

A quick nod from the Indian made it unanimous.

"Then I guess we've got our posse. Bass, how about you and Lobo arranging for a couple of pack mules from the livery. See they are loaded and ready to go by first light tomorrow with enough supplies for a month on the trail.

"Smokey, see the supply clerk and draw an extra rifle and plenty of ammunition for each man, we don't want to run short in case this comes to an all out fight. Oh, while you're at it, pack a dozen extra ropes."

All three of the deputies pushed up from their chairs and headed out the door. Johnny and the marshal watched them go.

"Good job, Johnny. So you're leaving in the morning, huh? You just might get to liking this law business."

"Don't plan on it," he said as he drained his cup and headed for the door.

Johnny and Libby went for a walk after supper. She threaded his arm with hers as they strolled silently along the dimly lit street toward downtown. He'd already explained that he must leave early the next morning, though he didn't go into the purpose or danger of his trip; undoubtedly that had something to do with her silence.

"Do you have to go?" She finally asked.

"Yeah, I do."

"How long will you be gone?"

"With any luck maybe a couple of weeks or so. Could be longer, though."

"That means you might not be back in time for Christmas?"

"Hope it's not that long. But just in case it is, here's some money. Would you mind getting something nice for Riley and Cathy? Pick up something for Miss Lila and the Marshal for me, too, will you?"

"Of course I will."

"Here, I picked up something for you today, just in case I wasn't back in time to give it to you for Christmas."

Reaching into a pocket he withdrew a blue, velvet covered jewelry box and handed it to Libby. She looked at it, then up at him, and slowly opened the top—and gasped.

A gold, heart shaped locket stared back at her. A sparkling diamond was mounted in the very center of the heart.

"Oh, Johnny, it's the most beautiful locket I have ever seen! Thank you so very much! This must have cost a fortune. Can I wear it? Would you put it around my neck, please?"

He was all thumbs as he fumbled with the tiny clasp on the golden chain. Finally he got it open and placed it around her beautiful, soft neck and closed the hook.

"Thank you," she said as surrounded his neck with her arms and tiptoed to find his lips with hers in a long, searching kiss. His strong arms pulled her against him and held her close in a warm embrace.

"What would you like to have for Christmas?" Libby asked, pulling her lips from his and searching his eyes.

"What I would like to have I don't reckon is possible right now."

She stared with a questioning look for a moment. "What would that be?"

"We'll talk more on it when I get some things worked out."

Chapter XIV

It was a cold November morning. A stiff wind whistling in from the north sent shivers down Johnny's backbone. He pulled the collar to his heavy wool coat tighter. The eastern sky began to show a tinge of grayness. A heavy frost covered the ground almost like snow.

Three horses and two pack mules stood outside the Marshal's office as Johnny rode up. Little puffs of steam rose from the animals' nostrils with each breath *This is shaping up to be one God-awful trip,* he thought as he glanced quickly at the heavy packs lashed securely on the mule's backs.

Stamping his feet he pushed open the door to the office and stepped inside. He saw four men huddled around the big potbelly stove sipping coffee.

"About time you showed up," Smokey said, lifting his cup in a welcome. "We was about to leave without you"

"Morning. You boys ready to take a little ride?"

"Can't this trip wait until spring?" Smokey joked.

"Fraid not. Did you pack some extra rifles and ammunition?"

"Sure did. I brought along eight brand new Winchesters model 73 fifteen shot, with a twenty-four inch barrel for longer distance. I packed enough ammunition to start a young war. I also packed six boxes of double-aught buckshot for your shotguns."

"Good. How about you, Bass? Looks like you got two pack horses loaded and ready."

"Shore do, Mister Johnny. Got us enough trail supplies for at least a month."

"Then we better be lighting a shuck, we're burning daylight. Be seeing you, Marshal."

"You boys ride careful, you hear?"

"Don't be wasting your worry on us, Marshal," Smokey said. "It's that Pike gang you ought to be concerning yourself about."

The morning broke cloudy and cold. Gunmetal clouds hung low and heavy, like it was going to start pouring any minute. The wind lashed at the little caravan as it turned south on a small, rutted road that followed the Poteau River.

Johnny rode in front, followed by Smokey and Bass, both leading a pack mule apiece. Lobo brought up the rear. They rode at a steady walk, not pushing their animals. Around noon Johnny found a sloping access to the river and reined Blackjack down to the water's edge.

"Let's water the animals."

The other fellows swung to the ground and topped off their canteens. Smokey munched on a strip of beef jerky and appeared to admire the Winchester 76 he slipped from his saddle boot.

"This is the finest piece of shooting machine I've ever seen."

"You reckon you can hit anything with it?" Bass Reeves asked the boy.

"I can hit what I'm shooting at."

The big negro glanced at the river. "See that turtle down yonder swimming across the river. Think you could get close enough to scare it?"

The boy squinted and peered in the direction Bass was pointing. Lifting the rifle to his shoulder, he closed one eye and sighted along the barrel for an instant. He feathered the trigger and the rifle cracked. In the distance the turtle's head exploded.

Johnny couldn't believe his eyes. *That turtle must have been eighty yards away.* He looked at Smokey with a new respect. "That was some shot," he told the boy.

"Woo-hoo!" Bass exclaimed. "That was some kind of shootin'!"

"Where'd you learn to shoot like that?" Johnny asked.

"Guess it just kind of comes natural. Back home I used to practice shooting at crows in my pa's corn field."

"Well, it's good to know. That kind of shooting might come in real handy before this trip is over."

Once the horses slaked their thirst, Johnny and his little posse mounted and continued south. About mid-afternoon the skies finally opened up and began to rain. Wind blew relentlessly, making for a miserable ride. The river veered west, but Johnny chose to continue south.

They found a likely place for night camp near a small community called Poteau. It was still too early to stop for the night, but with the weather so bad, he figured it would be a wise decision. They found an old abandoned farm with part of the barn still standing. Half the roof was gone, but at least they would have some protection from the rain.

While Smokey and the Indian tended the horses and pack

mules, Bass and Johnny scrounged up enough dry wood to get a fire going and coffee boiling. Bass fried some salt pork then sliced several potatoes into the pan and opened a tin of beans.

After a good meal they all huddled around the fire in their rain slickers and sipped coffee. No one even mentioned the task that lay before them. Each man sat with his head down sipping on the steaming-hot coffee, lost in his own thoughts.

The wind finally died down and the rain settled to a steady downpour that looked set in for the night.

"Reckon we better turn in," Johnny said, draining the last swallow from his cup. "We've got a long ride ahead of us tomorrow."

They spread their ground sheets around the fire and rolled out their bedrolls. Johnny checked the load in his Colt Peacemaker, laid it on his stomach as he always did when he was on the trail, pulled his blanket up around his neck, and listened to the pounding rain on the sheet-iron roof of the barn. He took the image of Libby from the shelves of his memory and loved her until sleep wrapped its peaceful arms around him.

Libby suddenly awoke and sat upright. Light filtering in through the window beside her bed told her Johnny would already be gone. They said their goodbyes the night before, a heart-wrenching time. She always worried when he rode away, but somehow, this time was different. She struggled with a frightening feeling that this assignment wasn't like the others.

There was no doubt in her mind that she had fallen in love with Johnny Shooter. Although neither of them put their feelings into words, yet, she was certain he felt the same way about her. *Wonder what he meant when he said we would talk when he got some things worked out? What things?* Did she dare to hope he was going to tell her how he felt about her? A month, he'd said, a whole month? How could she stand him being gone that long?

She clung to her pillow for another few minutes before forcing herself from the warm bed. There was breakfast to prepare and she must get the kids off to school. Then a hundred other chores awaited her.

The sky was dark; the black-dark that comes just before dawn. A slight scraping sound jolted Johnny awake. His hand tightened on the pistol in his fist. His eyes snapped open, his mind instantly alert. He saw Lobo stoking the fire. Bass and Smokey were still snoring. The fire leaped to life as Lobo emptied the contents of a canteen into the coffee pot and dumped in a handful of coffee.

Johnny crawled from his bedroll, shook out his boots and put them on. He replaced the pistol in its holster and swung the gun belt around his waist.

"Looks like it stopped raining," Johnny commented, squatting near the fire. The Indian only nodded.

"It rain again tomorrow," Lobo said. It was one of the few times Johnny had ever heard the indian speak.

Bass rousted out and joined Johnny near the fire. "Where you from?" Johnny asked him.

"I was born a slave and belonged to Colonel George Reeves of Grayson County, Texas. I grew up near Paris, Texas."

"Are you a married man?"

"Shore is, got the sweetest little woman that ever lived. We got seven children, so far."

"What made you decide to become a Deputy Marshal?"

"I reckon as how it's always been in my blood. Besides, it

Shooter 157

pays better than farming. Seems like I spent most of my life working one patch of ground or another from dark to dark."

While Reeves talked he rustled up breakfast. Before long, with the smell of bacon frying in the pan, Smokey rousted from his bedroll.

By good daylight they'd finished breakfast, broke camp, and mounted their horses. All day they picked their way along a southerly road when one was available. When there wasn't a southerly route they weaved their way through thick groves of sycamore, white oak, and blackjack trees. Several times they forded the Poteau River as it snaked its way through the wooded countryside.

Mostly they rode in silence, except for Smokey. He kept up a steady stream of discussion about something. The subject didn't seem to matter. For a while Johnny tried to listen to the boy, but finally gave up and let his endless rambling go in one ear and out the other.

By sundown they reached the foothills of the Winding Stair Mountains. They found a little mountain stream of fresh water and decided to make camp for the night.

"We'll tackle those mountains in the morning," Johnny told them.

Everyone busied themselves tending the animals and setting up camp. Johnny was pleased at the way his men worked together. Bass turned out to be quite a cook and seemed to accept this role as part of his contribution to the group.

"I figure it will take us most of tomorrow to cross the mountains," Johnny commented during supper. "According to reports, Pikesville is on the southern slope near the headwaters of the Kiamichi River. Word is these boys are no tenderfoots. They've captured and hung three deputies already. I ain't hankering to add to that number. Here's the way I'm thinking.

We find us a likely spot and set up a base camp. Lobo, I'd like for you to take as much time as you need and scout the layout and report back to us. Then we'll put our heads together and decide the best way to take this bunch down. Anybody got a problem with that?"

All of his men nodded agreement. "Then we better hit the sack. Wind's picking up and it's getting cold fast."

Bass propped a couple more logs on the fire before everybody turned in.

A heavy fog shrouded the mountains. A man could barely see a few feet in front of him through the soupy, gray mass. The wind blew from the north and the temperature was near freezing when Johnny set up in his bedroll and scratched his bare head. Bass was already up and had a fire going and coffee boiling.

"Gonna be mighty slow going, picking our way over the mountain in this fog, Mr. Johnny."

Johnny crawled from his bedroll and pulled his boots on. "Yeah, but we got it to do. Let's skip breakfast and make do with coffee this morning."

Johnny threw a cup of cold water into the coffee pot to settle the grounds and poured himself a steaming cup of the thick liquid. He kicked Smokey's feet through his bedroll. "Better crawl out and get yourself a cup of coffee before I drink it all," he told the youngster. "Where's Lobo?"

"He was up and gone before I woke up," Bass said. "I reckon he's out doing what you told him to do."

"I judge him to be a good man to have on our side, but he sure don't talk much. That how you read him?"

"Shore do."

After they all finished their coffee, they broke camp and climbed into their saddles. Even with the wind to their backs it cut through them like a knife. Johnny pulled his collar tight and hunkered down in the saddle.

The fog-moistened outcroppings of rock hugged the mountainside and made footing uncertain for the horses. They spent considerable time circling impassable rock slides but climbed steadily upward.

By noon the fog lift and the wind resumed. Johnny judged they weren't far from the top of the mountain. Suddenly Bass called out over his shoulder.

"Mr. Johnny, you might want to ride up here and take a look."

Johnny dug his heels into the big gelding's flanks and urged him on to the little half-acre plateau where Bass sat his saddle.

"What you got?" he asked, reining up beside the big fellow.

"Appears to me to be the home away from home we looking fer. Right nice little plateau with grass for the horses. Little mountain stream right over yonder a ways and what looks like could be a cave back there on the other side of them big pine trees. Want me to check it out?"

"Yeah, come on, we'll both take a looksee."

They made their way through the pine trees to near the entrance of the cave and climbed down. The opening was no more than a crack in the side of a bluff, the entrance no wider than a man's shoulders and about eight feet high. Bass examined the ground around the entrance carefully for recent animal tracks but found none. Nonetheless, he jacked a shell into the chamber of his Winchester and crept slowly forward. Johnny did likewise.

Through the dimness of the cave's interior they saw that it was ready-made for their use. The cavern was tall enough for a man to stand upright and about twenty-feet deep. The remains of several long-ago campfires told them they were not the first travelers to seek shelter here.

"This will do just fine," Johnny told his companion.

"What did you fellows find in there?" Smokey called from outside.

"Unsaddle the horses and pack mules," Johnny replied. "We'll bring the packs inside and set up housekeeping. Looks like we may be here a while."

It didn't take long before they converted the small cave into a livable shelter. The horses were hobbled so they could graze. Johnny and his companions spent most of the day cleaning and oiling their weapons and preparing for the encounter with the Pike gang.

Bass improvised a rabbit trap, and by sundown, he sat stirring a pot of rabbit stew. The aroma sure smelled good. Johnny poured himself a third cup of coffee and lounged near the toasty campfire.

"How long you reckon it will take Lobo to scout out that place?" Smokey asked.

"Got no idea. It'll take whatever it takes. No matter how long, we'll wait."

"But what if they spot him? We could be holed up here forever."

"Lobo's an Indian. Out in the bush you don't see an indian unless he wants you to see him and by then it's usually already too late to save your skin. I got a notion Lobo can take care of himself."

"You're building yourself quite a reputation among the other deputies," Smokey said. "They're calling you the Man Killer. But nobody seems to know anything about you. Mind me asking where you're from and how you got the job as a Unites States Deputy Marshal."

"Yeah, I mind," Johnny bristled.

"Forget I asked."

"Stew's ready," Bass said hastily.

After supper they lit the lantern and played poker for a couple of hours. Bass Reeves turned out to be a shrewd poker player.

"Where'd you learn to play poker so good?" Smokey asked.

"Not much else for slaves to do after working in the fields all day, besides, you can learn a lot about a man by playing poker with him."

"Is that right? What did you learn about me just now?"

"Well, I learned that you get a little twitch in the muscle under your left eye when you're bluffin'."

"I do? I never knew that. Are you sure?"

"Count your money then count mine and that ought to answer your question."

"Well, if that don't beat all. Somehow that don't seem quite fair."

"Nothing fair about takin' another man's money."

"What did you learn about me?" Johnny asked, staring at Bass over the rim of his tin cup.

"Aw, now. You's a different story. I figure you fer a deep thinker. You the kind that figure all the angles before you set your mind on something. But once your mind's made up, you stick with it come hell or high water."

Without commenting on his partner's observations Johnny drained the last swig from his cup, rose, and shook out his bedroll. "Smokey, how about you taking the first watch? Wake me around midnight and I'll take it from there. Bass, you won't draw watch tonight. We'll rotate so each will get a full night's sleep every third night."

* * *

Near sundown the next day, Lobo came riding into camp. He slid from the saddle and poured a cup of coffee before saying a word. The others gathered around and waited patiently.

"Village six miles south in little valley. Two guards stand watch night and day. One on both sides of valley. I count a dozen houses, all made of logs and built in a square, like fort. They have a herd of cattle, maybe fifty or sixty head, and half that many horses. Most of men must be off on raid. Not counting women and little ones, only fourteen in village, half of them young boys and old men.

"The valley has good graze for stock. Mountain stream cuts through valley."

"So you think most of their gang is gone, huh?" Johnny asked.

Lobo nodded.

"Any way we could take out their fighting men while the gang's away and have a little welcome home surprise waiting for them when they get back?"

Again the indian nodded.

"Not counting the boys and old men, how many you figure they got there now?"

"Six."

"Okay, then here's what we'll do. Bass has supper started so we'll get a good night's rest and hit them before first light. We'll leave our camp here and travel light. Pack all of our extra weapons and the ammunition on one of the mules.

"Bass, you and Lobo take out the two guards. Maybe if we can get into the village without causing a ruckus we can do this without hurting anybody we don't have to. Anybody got any questions?"

"What if they start shooting?" Smokey asked.

"Then shoot back, but let's be careful not to hit women or children. We're here for the Pike gang, not the womenfolk."

After supper, Johnny and the others huddled around the campfire cleaning their weapons and preparing for their raid on the outlaw stronghold.

Chapter XV

The night grew dark—dark and cold and deathly quiet. The only sound invading the predawn was a bone-chilling north wind that whistled through the small grove of pine trees where Johnny and Smokey squatted on their boot heels and waited more than an hour.

"Sure would hate to have that indian or black man coming for me in the dark," Smokey whispered.

Johnny didn't reply. His mind busied itself weighing all the possible things that could go wrong, some likely would.

Bass Reeve's fingers curved tight and sure around the long-bladed knife in his hand. It had taken him awhile to locate the guard, but now he lay belly flat and motionless behind a low bush not ten feet from the lookout.

Bass stared unblinking at the dim silhouette, leaning with his back to a large boulder and clutching a blanket tightly around his shoulders. His frequent movement told Bass that the guard wasn't asleep. To try to rush him would risk his ability to get off a shot from the rifle that lay across his outstretched legs. All the lawman could do was wait.

After a long wait, finally the lookout climbed stiffly to his feet, turned his back, fumbled with his britches and began relieving himself. That's when Bass made his move. Bunching his strong legs under him like a mountain cougar, he pushed quickly to his feet.

Three silent steps and he stood directly behind the unsuspecting guard. A quick left hand over the man's mouth jerked his head back. Bass's long knife raked across the soft skin of the neck. A muffled, gurgling scream died as quickly as the outlaw.

Lobo returned to the small clearing before Bass arrived to join the others. Neither Bass nor Lobo mentioned what happened to the two guards and nobody asked. Without a word the four mounted and urged their mounts along the trail that led along the crease between the two mountains. Lobo led the way.

Grayness tinged the eastern horizon as the village came into view at the far end of the box valley. Orange lamplight escaped from several windows set into the solidly built, log structures. A tall watch tower built of logs stood like a sentinel overlooking the gathering of buildings clustered in a square.

Lobo raised a hand and moved it to the right and the left. The four riders split up and melted into the pine trees on either side of the valley. Johnny and Lobo swung to the right of the trail and guided their mounts through the pine grove until they were within a half-quarter from the nearest structure before dismounting. Tying their horses securely, they slid their rifles from the saddle scabbards and crept through the scattering of pine saplings to within hearing distance of a large barn.

Day broke to a frosty morning. The village appeared to be coming alive. Thin tendrils of smoke rose from chimneys and trailed lazily into a cold, blue sky.

Movement and male voices from inside the log barn told Lobo that at least two men were going about their morning chores. In an adjoining corral, several milk cows with heavy bags milled about waiting to be milked. Several horses in another corral munched on fresh hay.

Lobo pressed his back to the wall of the barn and inched cautiously toward the open double door in the end. Johnny did likewise. He glanced quickly across the square and spotted Bass and Smoky creeping up on two log houses.

Nearing the corner of the barn, Lobo stopped and stood motionless. From inside they could hear the conversation between the two men.

"Looks like the weather's clearing," One of the voices said.

"None too soon for my likin'," the other man replied. "Never did cotton to cold weather."

"Glad it wasn't my turn to stand guard last night, bet Jacob and Ezra near froze out there."

"Where's Ben and Shorty? They're supposed to relieve the guards at daylight."

"Aw, you know Shorty. He'll be late for his own funeral. They're most likely still eatin' breakfast."

"Good thing the preacher ain't here, he'd tan ol' Shorty's hide. You know what a stickler he is for discipline."

"Yeah, a mite too much for my likin'. I didn't go along with him tying Ezra to the stake and using that strap on him."

"Ezra knowed better than to use a cuss word in front of the preacher."

"Just the same, it ain't right. Saying a cuss word ain't no reason to whip a man like that. Don't care if he is my uncle. Who made *him* God?"

"Best be careful with talk like that, Walter, you might find yourself tied to that stake."

"When you reckon they will be back?"

"No way of telling, but by my figurin' they should have already been back."

"You reckon they run into trouble with that bank job up in Springfield?"

"Hope not."

Johnny decided he'd heard enough. He tapped Lobo on the shoulder, nodded his head, and levered a shell into his Winchester.

"What was that?" one of the men inside the barn asked. "Sounded like a rifle being levered."

"I didn't hear nothing'"

"You couldn't hear it thunder. Think I'll take a look."

Just as the outlaw stepped around the corner of the barn Johnny stuck the nose of his rifle in the man's face and crossed his lips with a finger. The man's eyes walled white in fright.

Lobo stepped around the corner and through the open double doors. The second outlaw was sitting on a three-legged stool, milking a cow. He took one look, dropped the half-filled bucket, and made a dash for the doors at the far end of the barn. He didn't make it. A lightning fast flick of Lobo's wrist sent a long-bladed knife squarely between the man's shoulder blades. A loud moan breeched his lips. He clawed for the knife in his back, stumbled forward a few more steps and fell on his face in the cow dung that littered the barn floor.

Johnny backed the remaining outlaw ahead of him into the barn. "Will the other two come here to saddle their horses?"

The frightened man couldn't take his eyes off the nose of Johnny's rifle and managed only a weak nod of his head.

"If you want to live to eat breakfast don't make a sound, understand?"

Again, the outlaw nodded, this time more vigorously.

"Lobo, cut off a piece of that rope over yonder and tie this gent in that horse stall. While you're at it, stick a gag in his mouth. We don't want him warning his friends."

They didn't have to wait long. A door slammed and a quick look told Johnny that the two remaining men in the outlaw camp were on their way to the barn to saddle up. Johnny ducked inside a horse stall and squatted behind the railings. Lobo stepped inside a feed room on the opposite side of the open double doors.

The man they called Ben was a big man. His baggy britches and shirt made him look even bigger. He wore a full beard that hung down near to his waist. Shorty lived up to his name. He was a small man, but walked with a swagger as they approached.

"Hey, Walter!" The big outlaw called out as they strode into the barn. "Ain't you and Edward done milking yet?"

Johnny rose up from behind the horse stall boards and leveled his rifle.

"You boys just stand easy and raise your hands. I'm a Deputy United States Marshal. You're both under arrest."

Both men went for their pistols at the same time. Johnny shot the big man square in the heart and Lobo stepped from the feed room and shot the one called Shorty. Their side arms never cleared leather.

"Those shots will alert everybody in the village," Johnny told the indian. "We better get up to them houses and see if Bass and Smokey need help rounding everyone up."

In the houses, the few older men, youngsters, and womenfolk offered no resistance as they herded them into a large room in the main house. They stood in frightened silence, huddled together in little bunches. Small children clutched at their mother's skirt tails. The older men glared in open defiance, their dislike for lawmen obvious on every face.

"We're United States Deputy Marshals from Fort Smith, Arkansas. Do as you are told and no harm will come to you. We have warrants for each member of the Pike gang for acts of murder, robbery, and theft of property.

"We can do this the easy way or the hard way. If they surrender, they will be taken back to Fort Smith for trial. If they resist, they will be dealt with accordingly. The choice is up to them.

All of you will remain here in this room for your own protection. Anyone who attempts to leave will be arrested as an accessory."

One of the two older men stepped forward. "How long you aiming to hold us here?"

"Until this is over, however long that takes," Johnny answered. "Like I said, don't give us any trouble and you won't get hurt. Bass, how about staying here with these folks? The rest of us will take care of things outside."

Bass scooted a chair near the door and sat down in it. "I'll see to it," he said.

Johnny, Smokey, and Lobo left the big house and headed back toward the barn.

"Don't know when the gang will return, but we've got to be ready when they do. Lobo, take that fellow we've got tied in the barn up to one of the lookout spots and tie him to a tree or something that makes him look like he's on guard. Put a gag in his mouth so he can't yell or anything. Put on a fellow's coat and hat, then station yourself on the hill on the other side of the entrance so you can wave when they ride through. If they don't see guards they will know something is wrong.

"After they ride through you can come in behind them. The rest of us will be waiting up here. Maybe we can catch them in a cross-fire before they know what hit 'em."

Nodding, the indian hurried ahead toward the barn.

"Fetch our horses and the pack mule and put them in the barn, will you, Smokey? I'm gonna nose around a bit."

Johnny headed for the watch tower attached to one of the houses. The only entrance to it was from inside the house. He climbed the ladder to the platform. Gun ports had been cut into all four sides so a man inside could fire in any direction and be protected by the heavy log walls.

He climbed back down the ladder and hurried to the barn where Smokey worked at putting their horses in stalls and feeding them.

"When you get through there, I want to show you something" Johnny told the young deputy. In a moment Smokey joined him at the open doors.

"See that tower, yonder?" Johnny asked pointing. "I want you to take three of our Winchesters, plenty of ammunition, and make yourself at home up there. As good a shot as you are it ought to be like shooting ducks on a pond. When the shooting starts I want you to empty as many saddles as you can, as fast as you can, understand?"

A wide grin broke across the young deputy's face. One would have thought Johnny had just handed Smokey a Christmas present or something.

"I can shore handle that, boss," he answered, wheeling to gather up his weapons and ammunition.

Rufus Pike twisted in his saddle and swung a look at his men strung out behind him. It had been a long ride. They were

Shooter 171

gone the better part of two weeks. He was bone tired and anxious to get back home. Doing the Good Lord's work shore was tiring. The men rode slumped in their saddles. Weariness showed clearly in their faces. Each man led a string of horses stolen from farms along the trip home—nearly fifty in all. He deemed it a successful trip.

The bank in Springfield, Missouri was ripe for pickin and they shore picked it clean. More'n twelve thousand dollars, if his figurin was right. But he'd slipped away from the others the night before and hid half the money, just as he'd done several other times. By now he had a pretty sizable nest egg in case things went sour.

His gaze settled on his four sons who rode directly behind him. They were good boys, for the most part. He had to strap them now and again, but they generally minded what he said.

Jacob, his firstborn, was a big boy. He stood over six feet and was as strong as a bull. *Going on thirty now, I reckon. He'll take over the family when I'm gone. He'll be right good at it too. He's strict like me. They're all like a bunch of children you've got to keep in line.*

Esau was next in line. Like his namesake, he was a hunter. He spent half his life off in the woods somewhere. He was a crack shot with either rifle or pistols and a good man to have along on a raid. He was ruthless and loved to kill just for the sake of killing. He shot down a farmer up in the boot heel of Missouri. "I didn't like the way he looked," was the only reason he offered.

Joseph rode next. He was a mama's boy, always had been, always would be. He was the only son Henrietta ever bore. She was the second of Rufus's three wives. Rufus found wives generally more trouble than they were worth, except at bedtime, of course. That's about all they were good for.

David was different. He was Rufus's pride and joy. Like the David of old, a man after his father's own heart. He rode straight and tall in the saddle and lifted a hand when he saw his pa staring at him.

Nearing the entrance to their valley, Rufus glanced up to the hilltop where the lookout should be. He saw the man slouching against a tree with a rifle in the crook of his arm. It was too far for him to tell which of his followers it was. Swinging a look across to the mountaintop on the opposite side he saw the other guard raise his rifle and wave the all clear. He relaxed and dug his heels into his horse's flanks, pushing him into a short lope. He was anxious for a hot breakfast. They rode nonstop all night to get home.

A shrill whistle from Smokey in the guard tower alerted both Johnny and Bass. The outlaw gang was coming. Bass herded the villagers into a smaller, windowless room and dropped a bar in place, locking the door from the outside. Then he sprinted to a shuttered window, swung one side open, and peered out.

Off in the distance, at the far end of the valley, he saw a large bunch of horses. *Heavens to Betsy,* he thought, *there must be fifty or sixty in that bunch. We in a heap of trouble.* Then, as the riders drew closer he counted with some relief only a dozen or so riders, each leading a string of horses. He levered one of the two Winchesters, leaned it against the wall, and levered the other one.

* * *

Johnny jacked a shell into the chamber of his Winchester and propped it against the wall of the barn just inside the double doors. He removed the traveling loops from his two pistols and thumbed back all four hammers on his double-barreled shotguns.

"You boys put them spare horses in the corral," Johnny heard the leader command. "We'll work the brands over in the morning."

Johnny took a deep breath and stepped out from behind the wall of the barn.

"Hold it right there! The first man that moves is a dead man."

Several of the gang members swung legs over their saddles, dismounting as Johnny spoke. They froze in place.

Rufus Pike settled back down into his saddle and took measure of the stranger with the two shotguns. He was a big man, maybe bigger than his own firstborn, but thin around the waist. He had a hard set jaw and cold eyes. His hands lookedsteady. *This is a hard man.*

"Who might you be, stranger?" he demanded.

"I'm Deputy United States Marshal, Johnny Shooter and you're all under arrest. Throw down your weapons."

"What's this all about? We ain't done nothing. We've been on a trip buying up a few horses."

"I've got warrants for your arrest from Judge Isaac C. Parker in Fort Smith for hanging two of his marshals. I've asked you once to throw down your guns. I won't be asking again."

"Well now, you've got sand in your craw, I'll give you that. You figuring on taking us all on all by yourself? That's mighty big talk for just one man."

"I've got all the help I need right here in my hands."

"You might get some of us, but you can't get us all."

"Maybe so, but you and your four boys there will be the first ones to go. Whatever happens you're a dead man. You might want to chew on that for the next few heartbeats, cause that's how long you got to decide."

For a long moment, which seemed like an eternity, time seemed to stand still. Johnny swept the wad of men and horses with a gaze, watching for the move that was sure to come. When it came it wasn't what he expected.

Rufus jammed spurs into his horse's flanks and jerked back sharply on the reins. The frightened animal reared high on his hind legs, lost balance, and fell over backwards, pinning its rider underneath.

At their leader's action his men went for their guns. Johnny's shotgun bucked in his hand. The force of the heavy pellets swept Pike's two son's from their saddles like a giant hand.

The second barrel exploded. Men screamed. Horses bellowed and whinnied, their frightened pleas drowned out by the steady sound of gunfire. The double-aught buck shot tore into the bunched gang of outlaws like an angry swarm of hornets. Several were blown completely from their saddles. Blood splayed like driving rain through the air. A wounded horse lunged toward him trailing a broken latigo, snorting wildly as it charged past and away from the melee.

A pistol barked from one of the outlaws that still had control of his mount. Johnny ducked quickly behind the safety of the wall of the barn as a bullet chewed a chip from a log within inches of his head.

Above the screams he heard the steady crack of rifles. He knew that his men were doing their deadly work. Caught out in the open, Pike's men had nowhere to run, nowhere to hide.

A blood-curdling scream pierced the air. One of the outlaws staggered through the open barn doors on foot, clutching his stomach with a bloody hand, his eyes walled white with pain and fear. A long string of red saliva drooped from his mouth. A pistol dangled from his other hand. Johnny fired. The force of the blast literally lifted the outlaw off the ground and propelled him several feet backwards.

Chancing a quick look around the edge of the barn door Johnny saw two riders spurring their horses away from the killing field in a frantic attempt to escape. A short distance away, Lobo stepped from behind a large pine, bringing his Winchester to his shoulder, then fired. A puff of gun smoke reeled away on the wind. One of the outlaws did a backward somersault out of his saddle as Lobo's bullet plowed into him. His body bounced along the ground and finally came to a stop.

The indian fired again, and the second rider twisted from his saddle, dead before he hit the ground.

From somewhere near, two shots banged out. Hot lead whistled overhead, knifing into the wall. Another pistol barked. A bullet whispered near, caressing Johnny's cheek. He swung the remaining shotgun in the direction of the sound and fired both barrels. The thunderous explosion rocked Johnny back on his heels. Twenty feet away one of Pike sons, the big one, a pistol in each fist, took the twin loads of buckshot squarely in the face. A strangled cry escaped his snarling lips, above the echo of the shotgun blast as the pellets plowed into him. Blood, bone fragments, and chunks of flesh flew through the air.

A huge hole appeared where his Adams apple should have been. The man dropped his pistols and grabbed his throat with both hands and let out a gurgling sound, but nothing could stop the gush of blood. The outlaw staggered around and around, drowning in his own blood before collapsing in a gory heap.

As suddenly as the battle began, it ended. The battleground lay littered with the dead and dying. The stench of gun smoke, blood, and death drifted away on the wind. Riderless horses galloped to and fro. Cries and moans from dying men wrenched at Johnny's heart.

Lobo emerged from the trees, rifle still at the ready. Bass and Smokey walked cautiously toward the carnage their rifles meted out, alert for anyone who still had a stomach for a fight.

"Better check them out," Johnny called to his men. "See if there's any that can be patched up enough to make the ride to Fort Smith."

Laying his empty shotguns aside, he slipped a pistol from its holster and stepped around Pike's dead horse. The leader lay sprawled on his side with one leg pinned underneath his horse. His eyes were closed as if he was dead but he grasped a big Walker Colt in his right hand. Johnny kicked the pistol away.

"Open your eyes, Pike. You ain't dead, at least not yet." Johnny said as he thumbed back the hammer of his pistol and pointed it squarely between the outlaw's eyes.

The gang leader's eyes snapped open wide and fixed on Johnny's. A cruel snarl lifted one corner of the outlaw's mouth. His face twisted in an expression of fear and hate.

"You gonna shoot me, law dog?"

"Not hardly. That's too quick and easy. You're gonna die like those two marshals you hung, except slower. Bass, get everyone out here and bring them down by the barn. Lobo, toss a rope over one of them log beams sticking out from the roof of the barn."

"What a mess," Smokey said, walking up and pushing a wounded outlaw in front of him. "There's enough blood around here to paint a barn."

"Gather the wounded over there in front of the barn," Johnny told them.

When they made the tally there were nine dead gang members and three wounded, not including Pike who, miraculously, didn't have a scratch on him except for a broken leg where his horse fell on him.

"Smokey, gather up all their weapons and pile them in the feed room. While you're in there bring back a sack of feed."

By the time Bass returned with the people of the village, Lobo, following Johnny's instructions, had dropped a loop around the outlaw leader's ankles and hoisted him, upside down, high into the air.

A hangman's noose, fashioned from a short piece of rope and drawn tight, encircled Pike's neck. The other end of the short rope was tied around a large sack of feed, which was then placed in the outlaw's hands.

"You can't do this!" the outlaw protested loudly. "It just ain't right. This ain't no way for a man to die."

Johnny thought about his fellow lawmen Pike hung not long ago, showing them no mercy. He remembered the judge's instructions that this man was to be made an example of, all but telling him that he didn't want the outlaw leader returned to Fort Smith for trial.

"As long as you hold onto that sack you ain't gonna die," Johnny told him. "Wonder how long you can keep from dropping it?"

Some of the women and kids were crying. The women rushed to their dead loved ones, several cradling their husband's and son's head in their arms and wailing uncontrollably.

When the crying died down a bit, Johnny lifted his voice so he could be heard.

"Folks, we've got no quarrel with the rest of you. After we leave, you can go on with your lives as long as you don't break the law.

"These men murdered innocent folks, robbed, and stole what wasn't theirs. Before any of you think about riding the outlaw trail, I want you to take a long look and remember what you saw here today. These three wounded will be taken back to Fort Smith for trial.

"Most of the blame falls on Pike. He led you down the wrong trail. He hung two of our deputies. For that he's gonna hang. But I want him to think on what he's done before he drops that sack. You're welcome to watch or go on back to the house, it's up to you."

No one stayed around to watch, not even Pike's three wives. He grunted and clawed frantically to hold onto the heavy sack of feed. Great drops of sweat popped out on his forehead and dripped to the ground below. He cursed. He begged. He prayed. Gradually though, his strength gave out. The bag dropped. Pike's neck snapped.

Chapter XVI

The weather and the three wounded outlaws slowed them down. They spent their first night on their trip home in the little cave. It started raining sometime during the night. Thunder rolled across the mountains like cannon fire. Lightning split the sky and stabbed around them, lighting the darkness like it was day. Icy north winds howled outside their warm and cozy cave.

One of the outlaws died the second day out. They buried him on a hill overlooking the Poteau River. The hour was late on the fifth day before Johnny and his party rode into Fort Smith on December 24th, 1875.

"I'd about given up on you boys making it back before Christmas," Marshal Fagan said around his pipe as Johnny, Smokey, and Lobo pushed open the door and hunkered close to the pot-belly stove.

"Outlaw chasing ought to be limited to the summertime," Smokey complained, holding his gloved hands near the stove.

"Saw you ride in. Looks like you dropped off a couple of fellows over at the Doctor's office."

"Yeah," Johnny said, shucking his gloves and straddling a chair. "Left Bass with them until they get patched up and deposited behind bars."

"What happened to Pike and the rest of his gang?" Fagan asked.

"They couldn't make it."

"Dead?"

"Dead as a fence post," Smokey interjected proudly.

The Marshal gave the young gunman a critical look with a half-turned head. "I'll need your report."

"Figured you would," Johnny said, sliding a glance at the marshal then at Smokey. "Smokey volunteered to do the paperwork."

"I what?"

"Start at the beginning and don't leave nothing out," the Marshal told him, pushing a paper and pen toward Smokey. "What about Pike?"

"He hung himself," Johnny said, stretching himself up from the chair and heading for the door. "Merry Christmas."

The light rain that steadily dogged them for the entire trip home suddenly turned to snow. The white flakes were as large as a thumbnail, and by the time Johnny climbed the steps to Miss Lila's, nearly an inch or more covered everything in sight. It would be a white Christmas.

Light and happy laughter filtered through the door and Johnny paused to drink it in. The sweet aroma of hot apple cider wafted from the kitchen. It's good to be home, Johnny thought as he pushed the door open and stepped inside.

They were all in the sitting room. Miss Lila sat in her usual comfortable chair near the fireplace, sipping a cup of cider. Libby sat with Riley and Cathy on the floor at the foot of a large Christmas tree, inspecting the huge pile of presents. Riley was the first to spot Johnny and leaped to his feet.

"Mister Johnny's home!" he shouted, and made a bee-line to meet him. Cathy and Libby weren't far behind.

After hugging both youngsters and exchanging greetings, Johnny's gaze found Libby who stood a little ways off, waiting none too patiently. Their eyes met and held for several very long heartbeats. He opened his arms and in three running steps she quickly filled them.

"It's good to be home," he whispered.

"It's good to have you home," she replied into the crook of his shoulder. "I missed you something terrible. I'm glad you made it in time for Christmas."

She lifted her face and stared into his eyes. Johnny had an irresistible urge to kiss her. So he did. Right there in front of God and everybody.

This was truly the best Christmas Johnny ever remembered.

His days were filled with laughter, long walks in the snow, and quiet times just sitting in front of the fireplace holding hands with Libby. But the days slid by all too quickly.

"Judge wants to see you, Johnny," the Marshal told him one night after supper, while they enjoyed their usual second cup of coffee in front of the fireplace.

"I've been wondering when this vacation would end."

"I reckon it just did. He'll be waiting for you at nine o'clock."
"Then I better get a move on, it's after eight now."

A cold, blustery wind out of the north cut like a knife and sent chill bumps dancing up and down Johnny's spine as he rode slowly toward the courthouse. A single light in the upstairs window drew a yellowish square in the snow.

He swung down from the saddle and looped Blackjack's reins around the hitching post. His boots made crunching sounds in the snow as he trudged up the steps and went inside.

His footsteps on the stairs echoed along the long, empty hallway. He remembered those sounds from his first visit. He tapped lightly on the door.

"Come in,"

Johnny pushed open the door and stepped inside. The office felt cold.

Judge Parker sat bundled up in a heavy wool sweater. Johnny thought it was most likely one he got for Christmas.

"Good evening, Deputy. I trust you had an enjoyable holiday?"

"Yes, sir, and you?

"It was nice to have a day off. I have a job for you."

"Kind of figured you might," Johnny said, cracking a small smile.

"You ever hear of a strip of land over in the Territory called the *Neutral Strip?* Some are starting to call it No Man's Land because it belongs to no one."

"Some."

"It's a narrow strip of land about fifty-eight miles wide and two hundred-twenty or so miles long. It's bordered on the north by both Kansas and The Colorado Territory, on the east by the Indian Territory, on the south by Texas, and on the west by the New Mexico Territory.

"Due to some bureaucratic bungling when the politicians in Washington drew up the maps dividing the Territories, they overlooked this strip of land. As a result, it got forgotten.

"Most would call it a worthless land. Farmers ignore it, saying it won't grow anything but rocks and sand. A few ranchers tried unsuccessfully to run cattle on it from time to time. Law enforcement is nonexistent and so it has become a Haven to every outlaw and no-good in the country.

"One particular gang is the worst. It's led by a man that calls himself Colonel Marcus Solesby. As far as I have been able to ascertain, he was never a Colonel in any recognized military. He rode with Quantrill's Raiders during the war. He's nothing but a bloodthirsty killer.

"This, so-called colonel has managed to literally take over No Man's Land. He rules it with an iron fist and a fast gun, and a small ragtag army he's assembled made up of the rejects of society. My information says they have a hideout somewhere west of the Beaver Creek Trading Post. No one seems to know or is willing to divulge just where.

"This Solesby fellow has been a thorn in our side for far too long. He and his gang conduct raids in the neighboring territories then flee back to No Man's Land and disappear. Recently they are reported to have taken entire herds of cattle passing through the Indian Territory on their way to market in Kansas.

"It's a long trip and an extremely dangerous assignment, Mr. Shooter. In fact of the matter, you will be the very first law enforcement officer to venture into this area, but I'm convinced you are the man for the job.

"There is an army camp called Camp Supply somewhere east of this strip. If you wish, I can wire General Phillip Sheridan in Washington—he's a friend of mine—and request assistance from his troops. I want this so called colonel and his entire gang dealt with. Do you understand?"

"Yes, sir, I understand."

"There's a sizable bounty on this man, not to mention the other members of his bunch. You have a free rein. Take as many men with you as you need and as long as it takes to get the job done. Marshal Fagan will provide whatever assistance or supplies you might need. Here are the warrants. Good luck."

Johnny pocketed the stack of warrants, donned his hat, and left the office. Outside the judge's door he paused and let out a long sigh. Sounds like an impossible job, he thought. From the way the judge described the setup, this would be a job for the army. Well, no one said this job would be easy.

The light was still on in the sitting room and Johnny knew the marshal would be waiting. Sure enough, Marshal Fagan was sitting in front of the fireplace, sipping coffee and smoking his pipe.

Johnny hung his hat on the hall tree and poured himself a cup. He folded wearily onto the sofa. For a space of time neither man broke the thickness of silence. Johnny sipped the steaming coffee, stared absently into the cup, and drew lazy circles around the rim of it with a finger.

"This is a godawful assignment, son. No doubt about it, it's the worst one he's given you yet. I feel bad about it," the marshal finally said sadly.

"I reckon it could be worse," Johnny said.

"'Don't rightly see how," the marshal said, his gaze fixed on the leaping flames in the fireplace. "Several months ago, right after the judge arrived in Fort Smith, I suggested that we send in a whole company of marshals to clean out that mess, but he was afraid our losses would be unacceptable and the politicians would scream all the way to Washington. Apparently he changed his mind."

"Seems so."

"It's a big job, Johnny, and a dangerous one. From the information I've received, this man who calls himself a colonel has assembled quite a little army. I'll let you have all the deputies I can spare. Give me a few days and I can most likely put together a hundred or so."

"Could I have the same crew I took out last time?"

"You mean as part of the hundred."

"No, just them."

"I hope you ain't thinking what I think you're thinking."

"Don't mean to be putting down your other deputies, but I'll put those three men up against a hundred any day of the week and twice on Sunday. They're the best I've ever seen. If the four of us can't get the job done, a hundred more wouldn't make a lick of difference."

"They're good, I'll give you that, but you're gonna be facing odds of ten to one, maybe more."

" Do you reckon I could meet with my crew first thing in the morning?"

"I'll see they are in my office by coffee time."

"Good. Then I'm gonna hit the sack."

Marshal Fagan had long since left for his office, Riley and Cathy were off to school after their long break for the holidays, and the other two boarders already left for work. Johnny, Miss Lila, and Libby sat at the big breakfast table, sipping coffee. Johnny stared into his cup for a long, silent minute.

"You're leaving for another trip, aren't you?" Libby asked quietly.

Johnny nodded his head, still not diverting his gaze.

"When will you be leaving?"

"Next day or two, most likely."

"How long will you be gone?"

"No way of knowing, two, maybe three months, could be longer."

He glanced up into her searching eyes. The look he saw there tore at his heart. Disappointment, concern, and fear scored lines in her beautiful face.

"I'll clear the table while you two talk," Miss Lila said, quickly gathering the dirty dishes and heading for the kitchen.

"Two or three months?" Libby's pleading voice couldn't disguise the alarm it contained.

"My assignment is clear the other side of the Indian Territory in a part they call No Man's Land. It's a long ride."

"I'd be lying if I said I don't worry about you when you're gone on one of these assignments."

"I know, Libby, that's why I can't tell you right now what kind of feelings I have for you. Maybe if things work out, some day I can. I reckon it feels kinda good to know someone's worrying about me. Haven't had that in awhile."

"I will miss you something awful."

"I'll miss you, too, Libby. The thoughts of you take up most of my spare time when I'm gone."

"I'll think of you every minute while you're away," she said, reaching a hand to place it softly on his.

"Reckon I better be going. I'm supposed to meet Marshal Fagan and some of the boys. Suppose we could take a walk tonight after supper?"

"I'll look forward to it."

Johnny smelled the coffee even before he opened the door to the marshal's office. Bass, Smokey, and Lobo huddled themselves around the big pot-belly stove sipping coffee from tin cups. Marshal Fagan sat propped back in his chair, behind his desk, puffing leisurely on his pipe. Clouds of blue, sweet-smelling smoke hung like a cloud near the ceiling.

"You boys have a good Christmas?" Johnny asked, pouring himself a cup of steaming coffee from the blackened pot.

"Yeah, I went down home to see my ma," Smokey said. "Pa died a few years back. She was glad to see me."

"Where you call home, Smokey?" Bass asked in his deep, bullfrog voice.

"Half-day's ride south, near Waldron. My sister lives with ma and looks out after her, she's getting on up in years. Where do you live, Bass?"

"Got me a little farm down in the river bottoms, maybe ten miles or so south of Van Buren."

"Johnny has something he wants to talk with you boys about," Marshal Fagan told them.

"You boys up for another trip?" Johnny asked, twirling a straight back chair, straddling it, then propping his arms on its back.

"What'cha got going?" Smokey asked.

Johnny took his time laying it all out, just like it had been told to him. After the telling there was a long silence in the room. Johnny waited.

"Can't speak for nobody but me," Bass finally said, "I been hearing 'bout this bunch for more'n awhile. Time somebody read to them from the book."

"Is there bounty on any of these jay birds?" Smokey asked.

"Yep," the marshal answered, "lots of it. Most of the boys in the colonel's bunch decorate wanted posters in one place or another."

"Then when are we leaving?" Smokey asked, swallowing the last of his coffee. "I made more money on our last trip than

I could have made in a year doing regular law work."

"Before you boys go spending any of that bounty money, you ought to know that this is a very dangerous assignment." James Fagan warned them. "Don't underestimate this Colonel Solesby, he's as mean as they come and most of the ones that follow him are as bad as he is. I won't think less of any of you that don't want to tackle this one. Some of you, more likely none of you, won't make it back.

"As before, Johnny will be in complete charge of this assignment. What he says goes."

Johnny took a long minute to allow his slow gaze to fall and rest on each man's face. He searched for the slightest hint of doubt. He found none, only grim determination.

"Then my orders are to leave when I'm ready and I'm ready. We'll pull out at first light in the morning. Bass, I want an extra mount for each man. Pick the best you can find. Lobo, I want four pack mules and supplies for a month. We'll have to find a trading post to replenish our supplies somewhere up the trail. Smokey, you ever fire one of those Sharp .52 caliber buffalo guns?"

"If it shoots I can hit what I aim at with any kind of gun they make."

"Then find one for each of us at the supply depot and take them with us. Take plenty of ammunition, too. I want every man to carry two sawed off double-barrel shotguns on his saddle as well as his two rifles and side arms. One more thing, I want to take along a case of dynamite and plenty of fuse wire."

"Sounds like we're going loaded for bear," Smokey grinned.

"It ain't bear we're going after," Johnny assured him. "Anybody got questions?"

Johnny slid a slow gaze around the room.

"Then let's do it," he said.

His three partners turned on their heels and left to take care of their assigned chores.

"You got one salty crew there," the marshal said.

"That's a fact," Johnny told him, pushing up to leave. "I best get around, got a lot to do and a short time to get it done. Daylight will be here before we know it."

On the way home he stopped by the general store and picked out a heavy, fleece-lined coat, some extra longhandle underwear, and a couple of extra wool blankets. It's liable to get cold where we're going, he thought.

He stopped by the ice cream parlor and asked the proprietor what time they closed.

"We're open until nine o'clock."

"Good, thanks."

As they all assembled around the big table in the dining room for supper, a festive atmosphere filed the air. Even the two boarders were laughing and joining in the celebration.

"Johnny will be gone for quite a spell," Miss Lila announced over the excited conversation and laughter, "so we decided to give him a little going away party."

Libby and Miss Lila had pulled out all the stops: thick, juicy-looking beef steaks, baked potatoes, baked beans, home-made bread, and apple pies, were set in the middle of the table and everyone dug in.

As usual, Riley was the center of most of the conversation. His enthusiastic and animated stories about events at his school kept everyone laughing until their sides hurt.

He told how he and one of his buddies spent hours capturing a dozen mice from Mr. Potter's barn and taking them to school in Riley's lunch box.

"You should have seen the teacher and all the girls when we turned them loose during class," he laughed. "The teacher climbed up on top of her desk and all the girls were running and screaming their heads off."

"And don't forget to tell them how you had to stand in the corner with your nose in the circle for the rest of the day because of it, too," Cathy scolded.

"Yeah, but it was worth it," Riley laughed. "Could I have another piece of that pie?"

After supper was over and the dishes cleared from the table, Johnny asked, "Thought I'd take a stroll down to the Ice Cream Shoppe, anybody like to come with me?"

"You bet!" Riley spoke up quickly.

"Didn't figure you would have room for ice cream after the supper you put away," Johnny said.

"I always got room for ice cream."

"What about you, Cathy, you and Libby like to tag along with us menfolk?"

"I'd like that," Libby said, flashing a beautiful smile in Johnny's direction.

"Me, too," Cathy agreed.

Dim streetlights drew orange circles of flickering light into the darkened street as Johnny, Libby, Cathy and Riley made their way casually toward the downtown area. Shop keepers were busy closing for the day and a few stragglers hurried along making their way homeward.

More than thirty saloons did a booming business along Main Street from dark until the wee hours of the morning. It was near impossible to go anywhere in Fort Smith without passing several such establishments.

As they neared a noisy saloon called the Double-Eagle, the swinging doors slammed open. Lights from the inside bled out into the street and three young cowboys staggered onto the boardwalk, laughing loudly. They were still thirty feet away, so Johnny thought little of it until one of them shouted in a gruff voice.

"Well, would you looky what we got here. If it ain't the back shooter himself."

Johnny swept the three with a single glance and settled his gaze on the speaker. It was the young hot head he had the run-in with from the horse ranch in the Boston Mountains.

"Let's cross the street," Johnny whispered to Libby. "I don't want any trouble and those three have trouble written all over them."

Johnny and his little group stepped off the boardwalk and angled across the dusty street, hoping to avoid the encounter that he felt sure was about to take place.

"Hey, you! Back Shooter! Don't walk away from me when I'm talking to you!"

"Just keep walking," Johnny told Libby and the youngsters, ignoring the troublemakers.

Out of the corner of his eye, Johnny saw the loudmouth and one of his buddies step off the boardwalk into the street. The third followed reluctantly.

Johnny's right hand unbuttoned his coat and pushed it aside. He thumbed the traveling thongs from the hammers of his Peacemakers. As he did, light from a nearby street lamp reflected off the badge pinned to his vest.

"What'cha doing, Booger?" the reluctant one asked under his breath, "that fella's wearing a badge. He's the law."

"I don't care who he is. He bad mouthed me in front of my family. I don't take that from no man alive. I'm fixing to kill me a law dog."

Johnny knew the fight was unavoidable. He stopped in his tracks.

"Libby, you and the kids walk on down the street. I'll be along directly."

Libby's eyes swung and met his. Johnny could see concern reflected there, concern and fear.

"It's all right, just go on down the street and wait for me."

Turning, she took hold of the children's hands and hurried across to the boardwalk across the street.

Johnny turned to face the three men and brushed aside his coat flaps, revealing the twin, bone-handled Colt Peace Makers strapped low on his hips in tied-down, Slim Jim holsters.

A wad of spectators poured from the saloon onto the boardwalk. The sound of the tinny piano inside fell silent.

The chill of the night tightened around Johnny and the three gunmen, but the words that came from Johnny's lips were colder than an outhouse in dead winter.

"I don't want trouble. You boys can still walk away from this."

"Ain't nobody walking away from nothing!" The young hot-head shouted. "I asked around town about you. Folks say you got a reputation of being fast with those guns, but I say I'm faster. We're fixing to find out."

"You boys taking a hand in this?" Johnny asked the other two.

"We'll side our saddle Pard," the big man beside Booger said. The third man looked nervous and said nothing.

"Your choice," Johnny said softly, hardly above a whisper.

"Booger's hand streaked downward. His pistol cleared leather and started its journey level. That's when Johnny's Colt bucked in his hand and spat a .44 slug square into the middle of the loud mouth's chest. The would-be gunman's pistol spun from his hand as he clutched his chest. Blood squirted between his fingers as his boots did a backward dance of death.

In a single heartbeat, the nose of Johnny's pistol swung to cover the big man at Booger's side. The man's weapon was already up and firing. Red flames blossomed from the nose of his pistol. Johnny felt the heat from a bullet as it sizzled past his cheek only inches away. His own Colt belched a hot nugget of death. Once. Twice. The impact of Johnny's two shots spun the big man around in a staggering struggle to stay upright. He lost the battle and crumpled into the dusty street.

"Don't shoot!" the third man yelled. "For God's sake, don't shoot!"

He had both hands stretched above his head and was slowly backing away.

"Somebody go get the city marshal," Johnny said.

While they waited for the local lawman to arrive, Johnny walked down to where Libby and the children waited. All three of them looked stunned.

"I'm sorry you had to see that," he told Libby.

"Why did that man hate you so much?"

"Part of it was whiskey talk. His papa owns a horse ranch up in the Boston Mountains. We had a run-in a while back when I took their stolen horses back to them. He accused me of shooting the horse thief in the back."

"That is so crazy. It sounded like he just wanted to prove he could outdraw you."

"That was part of it, too. He was hungry for a reputation. Some men want it so bad they are willing to risk their life to get it."

"What will happen now?"

"The City Marshal will interview the witnesses and make a finding. Let's go on down to the ice cream parlor. I told them that's where I would be."

* * *

They just finished their ice cream sundaes when a big lawman in uniform pushed through the door and walked over to their table.

"I'm City Marshal Sam Reines. You'd be US Marshal Johnny Shooter?"

"That's right. Nice to meet you, marshal."

"Same here. I talked to several witnesses to the shooting. They all agreed it was clearly self-defense. Even the deceased's own partner said it wasn't your fault. I'll fill out a report and there will have to be an inquest, of course, but it is just a formality."

"I was leaving at first light on an assignment over in the territory, will that be a problem?"

"Not at all, there's no need for you to be present at the inquest."

"I'm obliged."

"Have a good trip."

When the Marshal left, Johnny pushed back his chair and stood.

"Reckon we better be getting back. Miss Lila might be getting worried."

Taking a different route back to the boarding house, they arrived without incident. Miss Lila and Marshal Fagan were sipping coffee in front of the fireplace. Libby went to tuck the kids into bed, and Johnny poured himself a cup and took a seat near the fire. He explained what happened.

"Oh, Heavens," Miss Lila exclaimed when he finished the telling, "I'm thankful none of you were injured. The children must have been terrified."

"They've seen more than their share of violence in their young lives," Johnny said. "I expect they will be okay."

"You still aiming to pull out in the morning?" Marshal Fagan asked.

"Yep."

"The other boys meeting you in my office?"

"That's the plan."

"Then I think I'll turn in. These old bones need more rest than they use to."

"It's past my bedtime, too," Miss Lila said. "You have a safe trip and hurry back to us, Johnny."

"Thank you, ma'am."

After both Miss Lila and the marshal left, Johnny sat alone staring into the fire. He was tired but wasn't sleepy. He sipped slowly on his coffee.

"The children were asleep almost before their heads hit the pillow," Libby said, entering the room and sitting down on the sofa next to Johnny.

"Are they going to be okay?"

"I think so. They were very frightened, of course. I think mostly they were worried about you. So was I. I've never seen a gunfight before. Weren't you scared?"

"The man that says he's not scared when he's facing somebody that's trying to kill him is a liar."

"But you seemed so calm, so sure of yourself."

"A man facing another man can't afford to have doubts. I've practiced drawing and firing a gun thousands of times ever since I was a young boy."

"Have you...have you killed many men?"

"I've never killed anyone that wasn't trying to kill me."

She tipped her face upward toward his. Their eyes met, locked, and held, staring deeply as if they were the windows to their very souls. She nestled her head into the hollow of his shoulder.

"Johnny," she whispered. "hold me."

His arms encircled her, drawing her to him. His face touched the softness of her neck. He inhaled the fresh fragrance of her. His fingers threaded softly through the locks of her flaming-red hair. His lips brushed her neck ever so lightly. Feather soft kisses traced a trail up to her ear and lingered there for a long moment. He lifted his little finger and traced the softness of her lower lip. A soft moan escaped from deep inside her throat.

She gasped and melted deeper into his strong arms. Their lips met. The sweetness filled him, devoured him, and melted his wildly beating heart. When the kiss ended, she again searched the depths of his eyes.

"I love you, Johnny Shooter."

Chapter XVII

Johnny and his team, as he had come to think of them, camped their first night out in a little alcove surrounded by a thick grove of cedar trees.

"Maybe this will give us at least a little protection from the wind," Johnny said, as he stepped from the saddle.

They quickly unsaddled their horses, watered them in a small stream, and unloaded the heavy pack saddles from the mules. Lobo and Bass built a small lean-to and coaxed a fire to life. Soon, coffee boiled on the fire and bacon was sizzled in the pan.

The wind lay quiet as darkness shrouded the land. The four huddled around the campfire with blankets clutched around their shoulders, eating their supper from tin plates.

"Reckon it will be colder or warmer where we're heading?" Smokey asked.

"Likely we'll find out when we get there," Bass said, draining his coffee cup. "We've a far piece to go before then. No need wastin' our worry."

"I wasn't worrying, just asking."

"Any idea how many we'll be up against, Mr. Johnny?" Bass asked.

"Nope. The information I got was that this colonel had himself a small army."

Smokey smirked and said, "Well, shucks, he ain't gonna have no army at all after we get through with him. It'll be like shooting fish in a barrel."

"We just want to be careful we ain't the fish," Bass said, lighting up his pipe.

"Anybody want to play a little poker?"

"Too blasted cold to play poker, Smokey," Bass said. "My hands is freezin'"

"You're just afraid I'll win all that reward money you got from our last assignment."

"That ain't likely to happen until hell freezes over."

"If hell is anything like the territory, that might just happen. What about you, Johnny, what are you gonna do with all your bounty money?"

"Ain't give it much thought. Deputy Marshals don't seem to last long around these parts. We best get some sleep, I want to be in the saddle before daylight."

For the next two weeks, Johnny pushed them hard. They rode from can-see-until-can't-see and averaged forty miles a day. When they happened upon a farm house, which was rare, they put up in the barn if there was one, or paid the farmer to allow them to sleep inside on the floor out of the weather.

Most of the dirt farmer houses were little more than a one-room sod hut. Isolated as they were, they were leery of strangers, especially those as well armed as Johnny and his men, at least until they presented themselves as lawmen.

The farther west they went, the warmer the weather got. The landscape changed, too. Instead of wooded and rolling hills, they now traveled through barren, sandy terrain. Large outcroppings of red sandstone stood like silent sentinels guarding some ancient treasure.

The only vegetation was clusters of mesquite bushes, tumbleweeds, and occasional patches of bunch grass. It was a God forsaken country where no man with a lick of sense would want to call home.

For the past week Johnny and his team followed the North Canadian River. Now they sat their horses on the shoulder of a sandy hillside and stared down at Camp Supply. Johnny learned that the fort was established in 1868 as a supply base for Major General Phillip Sheridan's winter campaign against the Great Plains Indians. It was the westernmost army post in the Indian Territory. In recent years the primary function of the soldiers was to escort cattle drives as they passed through the Indian Territory.

"We'll re-supply and rest up a couple of days," Johnny told his tired crew.

"Sounds good to me," Smokey said. "I feel like my tail is growed to this saddle."

The camp itself rested on a hill overlooking the junction of the Canadian River and Wolf Creek. It displayed a sturdy-looking wall of logs, obviously hauled from well downriver since there was no timber for miles in any direction. Johnny saw several large buildings of adobe brick inside the walled compound. Two large gates stood wide open in the center of the wall on either side.

An assortment of tattered teepees were scattered around the fort. This was common of most army forts in the territory.

Outcasts, freeloaders, and petty thieves survived on a meager existence, mostly on handouts and what they could steal.

Johnny heeled Blackjack forward into a long trot.

Their entrance through the open gate drew considerable attention. The two guards on the catwalk over the gate openly eyed them suspiciously.

"Captain of the guard," one of them called out loudly.

A young, spit and polish lieutenant appeared from a large building nearby and walked briskly toward them. He walked like he had a board strapped to his back as he approached Johnny and his little band. They reined to a halt.

"I'm first Lieutenant Homer Leonard. May I ask the nature of your business?"

"I'm United States Deputy Marshal Johnny Shooter. These are my men. I'd like to see your commanding officer."

"That would be Major Richard Sterling. Follow me."

"You men stable the horses and see to our gear. I'll be back directly."

Johnny followed the young Lieutenant across the parade ground and up the steps to an adobe building. Two flags flapped in the afternoon breeze above the roof. One was the American flag. The other carried the insignia of the Fourth Cavalry.

A young corporal shot to his feet and saluted smartly as the lieutenant pushed through the door. The officer returned the enlisted man's salute.

"Is the major in his office?"

"Yes, sir."

Tapping lightly on the large oak door, the Lieutenant waited.

"Yes, what is it?" A gruff voice from inside the office called out.

"Lieutenant Leonard, sir. There's someone asking to speak with you."

"Well, don't just stand out there, show him in."

The young officer pushed open the door and stepped aside. Johnny walked into the major's office. Lieutenant Leonard followed and closed the door.

"I'm United States Deputy Marshal Johnny Shooter. I work for Judge Isaac Parker out of Fort Smith."

"I'm Major Richard C. Sterling, Fourth Cavalry, United States Army and Commander of this outpost. Have a seat, Deputy Shooter. That will be all, Lieutenant."

The young lieutenant snapped a salute to which the major merely raised a finger in the general direction of his forehead while keeping his gaze fixed upon his visitor. The officer slowly took a cigar from a box on his desk, bit the end off it, licked the entire length of it, and stuck a match to it. Large billows of blue smoke drifted lazily toward the ceiling.

The commander appeared to be a big man. Obviously he ate well. His uniform jacket lay open, revealing red long johns stretched tight over a pot belly. His head was balding, but he wore a heavy, well-trimmed beard. His cheeks were large and puffy. His eyes looked glassy. Johnny guessed the man was a boozer.

"What brings you all the way from Fort Smith to our little corner of paradise, deputy?"

"Me and my men are on a special assignment by Judge Parker. We have information that a gang of outlaws are operating in the area called No Man's Land somewhere west of here. My information is they are led by a man that calls himself Colonel Marcus Solesby.

"They have been raiding in Kansas, Texas, and New Mexico Territory. Judge Parker wants them stopped."

"And just how do you intend to do that, deputy?"

"My orders are to locate their base of operations, arrest them if they surrender, kill them if they don't."

"And how many men did you bring with you to accomplish all this?"

"Three, besides myself."

The major leaned back in his chair gave a big belly laugh. When he recovered he leaned forward and pinned a critical gaze on Johnny.

"Deputy, I'm afraid you don't understand how things are out here. Allow me to enlighten you on a few things. By all accounts this Solesby fellow has well over fifty men that ride with him. They are well trained, well equipped, and well hidden. We've had a couple of run-ins with him over the last year or so, but generally, he stays out of our way and we stay out of his.

"My orders don't include going chasing off after a few outlaws. So, if you've come expecting help from the United States Army to do your job, I'm afraid you've wasted your time. My assignment is to protect the settlers in this area from raiding bands of savages and to escort the cattle drives coming up from Texas and New Mexico Territory through hostile indian territory.

"If this Judge Parker has no more foresight than to send four men to do a job it would take an army to do, then I've even less respect for his judgment than I already had. I have less than a hundred men under my command. I can't spare any of them."

Johnny let go of a long breath and stood to his feet. He slowly moved his hat from his hands to his head and adjusted it before he spoke.

"Major, I don't recall asking for your help. We stopped only to pay a courtesy call and make you aware of our assignment. With your permission, we'd like to replenish our supplies and rest our mounts a couple of days, then we'll be moving on."

"Well, uh, perhaps I misinterpreted your intentions."

"Perhaps you did."

Fuming, Johnny spun on his heels and stalked from the office.

He met Bass and Smokey halfway across the parade grounds. They carried their bedrolls. The two deputies took one look at Johnny, and then slid a quick glance at each other.

"You okay, boss?" Smokey asked.

"Where's Lobo?"

"We left him looking after our gear. After looking around at some of these soldier boys, we thought it best not to leave our stuff unguarded. Lobo said he'd rather sleep in the stable close to our packs."

"Good thinking."

"We ran into that lieutenant over at the stable. He said we could bed down in the enlisted men's quarters. We're headed over to stash our gear."

"After you get settled, let's go ahead and buy the supplies we need and get them packed up. I've got a bad feeling about this place."

"Is something wrong?"

"Not sure. Nothing I can put my finger on, I'd just feel better if we had our supplies in case we had to leave before we planned. I'll go on over to the camp store and make arrangements for what we need."

"We'll be right along."

Johnny made his way to the store and began selecting the supplies they needed. He was almost finished when Smokey and Bass entered. Together, they finished up and paid for their goods. By the time they had everything carried to the stable and loaded onto the packs, the bell rang announcing that it was chow time.

The four made their way to the chow hall and joined the long line waiting to be served. When it was Lobo's time to have food ladled onto his plate, the big sergeant skipped him and instead dished food onto Johnny's plate.

"You forgot my friend," Johnny said, giving the sergeant a hard look.

"We don't serve indians. They eat outside the camp with their own kind."

"This man is a United States Deputy Marshal. Serve him."

The young lieutenant Johnny met earlier walked up and heard the exchange.

"Sergeant, serve this man his food, and be quick about it. He's our guest."

The sergeant glared at the young lieutenant for a long moment. Finally the sergeant ladled a helping of red beans onto Lobo's plate and added a piece of corn bread.

"Would you and your men sit at my table for supper?" the officer asked. "I was just about to eat."

"Much obliged," Johnny said. "We'd be glad to."

When they were all seated at the lieutenant's table, Johnny flicked a quick glance around the room. All eyes gazed in their direction. They were obviously the topic of the many whispered conversations.

"Allow me to apologize for that incident. I'm afraid tensions are running high around here lately," Lieutenant Leonard said.

"What's going on, lieutenant?" Johnny asked. "Everyone seems on edge. Even the major seemed edgy this afternoon."

"He is. We've lost two patrols within the last three months. All of them slaughtered right down to the last man. The major blames it on the indians, but I'm not so sure."

"What do you mean?"

"Well, I led the squad that recovered the bodies of the last patrol. Twelve good men, all shot and scalped. At first I thought it was renegade indians, too, but then I began to notice some things that made me wonder."

"Oh, like what?"

"The first thing was the shod horses. Then there was the

boot prints, lots of them. I reported what I saw to the major, but he dismissed it and told me I was seeing things that weren't there. But I know what I saw. It wasn't indians that murdered that patrol."

"Who do you think it was?"

"All I know is both patrols we lost were found west of here. I believe they stumbled on something they weren't supposed to see and it cost them their lives."

"You're saying it was white men that killed the soldiers?"

"That's what I believe."

"Got any idea who?"

"Let me ask you a question," the lieutenant said, leaning close across the table and lowering his voice. "You fellows obviously are here on some sort of mission. Who are you after?"

Johnny stared at the officer for a long heartbeat before answering. *Can I afford to trust this young Lieutenant?* He decided that he could.

"We were sent by Judge Isaac Parker after a man that calls himself Colonel Solesby. He's supposed to be operating out west of here someplace."

"Uh-huh, most folks in these parts have heard of him, I don't know of anybody that's actually seen him though. Rumors are that he has a hideout someplace west of Little Beaver Trading post, but then again, nobody seems to know where it is."

"Think he might have something to do with your two patrols?"

"Maybe, I just don't know."

"The major said something this afternoon I found strange. He said, 'He stays out of our way and we stay out of his.' What do you suppose he meant by that?"

The lieutenant was quiet for a a few moments, obviously searching his memory.

"Don't know. I do know he restricted our patrols from ranging west. And we lost a trail herd about a month ago that we were supposed to be escorting. Some sort of mixup, and nobody got assigned to take them through the territory. All the trail hands were slaughtered just like our patrols, and the whole herd just disappeared into thin air."

"Didn't they leave a trail?"

"It was over a week before we learned about it. The major himself led the patrol that went to investigate. By then the trail was too cold to follow."

A young corporal hurried up to their table and saluted.

"Lieutenant Leonard, sir. The major wants to see you on the double."

The officer returned the corporal's salute.

"I better go. Good luck on your mission, deputy."

"Watch yourself, lieutenant."

Johnny and his crew lingered over their coffee until the mess hall cleanup crew chased them out. They moved outside and joined a group of soldiers sitting around a campfire not far from the stable.

At first the soldiers were cool to the deputies, but after a little bit they began to open up and talk freely. Mostly it was small talk of home, family, and sweethearts left behind. Soon they wanted to know what it was like being a Deputy US Marshal.

"Probably not much different than being in the army," Smokey told them. "Except you get shot at more."

"We've been getting more than our share in that department," one corporal volunteered.

"Yeah, that's what I hear," Smokey said. "I hear the indians have been hitting you pretty hard lately."

"Indians, my eye. They want us to think it's the indians, but it ain't."

"You better watch that kind of talk," another soldier warned.

"I reckon we better turn in," Johnny told his men. "I want to be in the saddle before first light."

Johnny, Bass, and Smokey headed for the enlisted barracks. Lobo headed for the stable to spend the night.

They paid little attention to the card game going on at the far end of the long barracks. They found their bunks, kicked off their boots, and crawled between their blankets.

"What's that awful smell?" A gruff voice from the direction of the card game asked. "Smells like something dead somebody drug in."

The card players all laughed.

"Oh, yeah," the same voice said even louder. "I remember that smell now. It's the stink of a nigger. They stink worse than an outhouse. Did somebody let a nigger into the barracks?"

Johnny glanced over at Bass's bunk. The big black deputy pushed to his feet.

"Easy, Bass," Johnny said quietly. "We don't want any trouble."

"Never walked away from trouble in my whole life, Mister Johnny. Don't intend to start now."

Johnny and Smokey shed their blankets and followed Bass as he approached the group of soldiers.

"Mister, you got somethin' to say to me, say it to my face."

The speaker was the big sergeant from the chow hall that refused to serve Lobo. He leaned back in his chair, tipping it up on its two back legs and eyed the black man in front of him with disdain.

"Okay, you are a stinking nigger and I hate niggers."

Bass's foot swept out and hooked the chair leg out from under the loudmouth. He crashed to the floor, uttering obscenities. Bass's bare foot lashed out again, landing solidly along the side of the big sergeant's head. The kick sounded like a mule's hoof landing against the man's head.

Several of the sergeant's companions leaped up from the table.

"Just have a seat!" Johnny barked. "You boys got no dog in this fight."

They took one look at the Colt Peacemaker in Johnny's hand and sat back down in their chairs.

Bass stepped backward a couple of steps and allowed the sergeant to climb to his feet. The big man rushed forward with his massive arms open wide, obviously intent on grabbing his opponent in a bear hug.

Bass sidestepped and landed a vicious left hand as the sergeant lumbered past. Bone snapped loudly as the blow broke the man's jaw. Blood spewed from the sergeant's mouth and a tooth flew halfway across the room.

Spitting blood and staggering to stay on his feet, the troublemaker turned to face the deputy. He let go a vicious roundhouse right that would have torn any man's head off. Bass blocked it with his left forearm and smashed a right directly into the man's nose. The sickening sound of crushing cartilage could be heard all over the barracks.

For a long moment the big sergeant teetered like a giant oak tree, and then crashed forward onto his face, totally unconscious.

Bass wheeled around and returned to his bunk without a word. Johnny and Smokey followed.

"Roll your bedrolls, fellows," Johnny said. "I think we just wore out our welcome."

* * *

In less than a quarter of an hour they passed through the gate of the camp and headed west. They rode until the sliver of moon told them it was past midnight, and then made a dry camp at the foot of a field of upthrust rocks. It had been a long, hard day. They tied the stock to a line strung between two scrawny mesquite trees, shook out their bedrolls, and crawled in.

Johnny lay in his blankets, staring up at the velvety blackness of the night sky. Tiny stars winked like faraway diamonds and reminded him of the night he and Libby sat in the porch swing and watched those same stars. Maybe someday they could do that again...maybe.

"Mr. Johnny, I'm feeling awful bad about what happened back there tonight," Bass said softly in the darkness.

"Forget it, Bass. You had every right to do what you did."

"Maybe so, but we shore had to leave with our tails tucked between our legs like a whipped puppy. I don't like that."

"It was time for us to leave anyway. There's something going on in that camp that ain't right. But we've got a job to do and don't need to concern ourselves with it, at least not right now."

It was a short night. Lobo stoked a fire to life and set a pot of coffee over the flames by the time Johnny rolled out of his blankets.

"Where we be headed now, Mr. Johnny?"

"There's supposed to be a small trading post along Beaver Creek somewhere west of here. As I understand it, it's an offshoot of the main Beaver Creek Trading Post down on the Red

River. Word is this colonel and his men show up there frequently. I figure that means their hideout is pretty close. We'll start there."

After a while, the coffee was ready. Johnny and Lobo sat close to the fire, sipped coffee, and watched the eastern sky gray up. Soon daylight crept silently across the desert.

Bass untangled his big frame from his blankets, shook out his boots, and stomped them on. "That coffee shore smells mighty good."

"Tastes even better," Johnny told him. "Bet some bacon and fried potatoes would go good with it too, that is, if we could ever get our cook out of bed."

"It ain't often you beats me out of my blankets."

"That's a fact."

After a good, leisurely breakfast, they saddled up and headed west. About mid-morning they came upon a small stream and watered their horses and mules. Lobo rode ahead to scout the trail. Just before sundown the indian topped a rocky hill and walked his horse to intercept them. He had a large buck deer slung across the saddle in front of him.

"Looks like we gonna have venison for supper tonight," Bass said, a big smile showing his pearly-white teeth.

"Fresh running water over ridge," Lobo told them. "That's where I kill deer."

"Then let's make camp there for the night," Johnny said.

Smokey took care of the stock while Johnny rustled up wood for a fire. Bass and Lobo skinned and cut up the deer.

As the red sun kissed the western horizon and slid quickly out of sight, the four deputy marshals leaned back against their saddles with full bellies and lingered long over a last cup of coffee. Life shore was good sometimes.

Chapter XVIII

Johnny and his men followed the slow, winding Beaver Creek westward. The next afternoon was half used up when they spotted the little Trading Post sitting on a high bank of the creek. It was sure nothing to write home about.

It was a flat-roofed structure made of logs. Dirt piled on the roof over the years had become hard-caked, at least until it rained, which was a rare occasion in this part of the country. A lean-to of smaller logs served as an excuse for a shelter for the horses and was surrounded by a makeshift fence of brush and limbs.

Dozens of beaver skins lay stretched out on a rack for drying. An assortment of various other animal skins were stacked along one side of the log cabin. Two hip-shot, saddled horses stood tied to a hitching rail out front as if they'd been there for a while.

Johnny and his crew sat their horses and studied the situation for several minutes.

"Could be those two horses belong to a couple of that colonel's bunch. How about if I ride in and have a looksee. You boys make yourselves scarce. I'll be back directly."

Johnny unpinned the badge from his vest and slipped it in his pocket. He heeled Blackjack and approached the little trading post at a slow walk.

He stepped down from his saddle and looped Blackjack's reins around the hitching rail beside the two horses, then pushed open the door.

Darkness from the room filled the doorway. So did the worst stench Johnny had ever smelled. Rotted meat, stale whiskey, and sickening body odor permeated the air and churned his stomach. He took a step backwards and filled his lungs with fresh air before stepping inside.

Three men and one fat indian squaw occupied the room. A long plank resting on two empty whiskey barrels stood along one side of the large room. A huge man—Johnny figured him to be the proprietor—leaned on the makeshift bar. A pot-bellied stove stood in the center of the room. A blackened coffee pot sat on top of the stove.

At a rough hewn table not far from the stove, sat two tough-looking characters. The squaw sat on the lap of one of the men. A jug of whiskey sat on the table between them.

Every eye in the place gazed up and down Johnny as he stood just inside the door, framed by the light from outside. He paused for a long moment, allowing his eyes to adjust to the darkness inside the room.

"Howdy there, stranger," the man behind the bar greeted.

Johnny swept the room with a slow, searching gaze but said nothing. He crossed the few steps to the bar and leaned his back against it, propping his elbows on the rough wood.

"I'm looking for Colonel Solesby. Anybody know where I might find him?"

The unshaven man with the squaw on his lap hooked the whiskey jug with a finger and turned it up to his lips. He took a long swallow, cleared his throat, swiped a dirty sleeve across his mouth, and turned an evil stare in Johnny's direction.

"Who's askin'?"

"Just a fellow that needs to find him," Johnny answered, meeting the man's stare without flinching.

"Asking too many questions in these parts ain't healthy." Johnny's voice was cold, flat, and emotionless when he answered. "I don't ask but once."

"Then what?"

"Then I get an answer."

"You got a smart mouth, stranger."

"And I've got a Colt Peacemaker that I'm gonna pull and shoot you right between the eyes if the next words out of your mouth ain't answering my question."

"Here now," the grizzled fellow behind the bar growled. "We won't be having that kind of threatening talk in my place."

"Ain't no threat to it. Just telling that fellow what's fixing to happen. Best you stay out of this, trader"

The fellow at the table shoved the squaw out of his lap. She landed with a thump on the dirt floor. He stood to his feet and pushed aside a heavy, long coat, revealing a Walker Colt tied to his right hip. He glared at Johnny.

"No man talks to me like that. I'm gonna—"

He never finished what he was about to say. Johnny's hand streaked down and came up with the Peacemaker in it, with the hammer pulled back to full cock, and aimed straight into the man's face.

"You gonna talk or you gonna die?" Johnny whispered.

Sudden sweat beaded on the man's forehead. He licked his dry lips. His gun hand shook uncontrollably. His eyes widened and walled white.

"The colonel would kill me if I told you."

"I'll kill you if you don't. What's it gonna be, die now by me or later by him?"

"Ride West to Twin Peaks. You'll see a..."

A blast from close quarters struck the man in the back, cutting his words. Johnny swung his pistol toward the shooter, the man sitting quietly at the same table. He'd slipped his pistol out and shot his partner before Johnny saw him make a move.

Before the man could cock his pistol and swing it toward Johnny, two shots from Johnny's Peacemaker punched gaping holes in the shooter's chest. He flipped backwards in his chair, dead before he hit the floor.

Flicking a glance over his shoulder, Johnny saw the trader grabbing for a sawed-off shotgun. Their eyes met for a brief instant. Johnny slowly shook his head. The man retrieved his hand and placed it palm flat on the bar.

Hurrying over to the fellow with the bullet in his back, Johnny rolled him over. His eyes were becoming glassy. Pink foamy blood oozed from the corner of his mouth. The bullet likely struck a lung. He wasn't long for this world.

"Finish what you were gonna say. What about Twin Peaks?"

The man's lips moved but no sound came out. He took a long, ragged breath, let out all of it. It was his last.

Johnny swung a look at the trapper.

"What about you? You must know where this colonel is."

"Mister, I don't know and I don't want to know. All I know is they come and they go. I got no idea where they come from or go to."

"How often do they come and go?"

"Sometimes a few days, sometimes a few weeks."

"Were these two part of the colonel's outfit?"

"I'd say so."

Shooter

"Oh, by the way, one more question. Ever see the army over this way?"

"The army? I ain't seen a blue coat in a coon's age."

"Much obliged," Johnny said over his shoulder as he headed out the door.

The days were sweltering hot and the nights were bone chilling cold. The air hung hot and heavy over the cactus strewn sandy creek bed where they had set up a temporary camp. A cluster of scrawny willow and mesquite bushes shielded their camping spot from prying eyes, but offered little shade.

One of them stood guard both day and night in case they had uninvited company.

More than a week past since Johnny's visit to the trading post. Not a soul had come or gone. The only human movement was the indian woman going to the creek for water twice a day.

Johnny and his men were careful to light a fire only at night and even then to make sure it was well hidden. They didn't want to take a chance of anyone seeing the smoke during the day.

On the tenth day following the shooting incident, Lobo was standing guard when he suddenly hot-footed it back into camp.

"Many riders come."

Johnny and his men grabbed their rifles and hurried to the sandy hillside from which they could view the trading post. They bellied down behind some low mesquite bushes and watched a dozen riders approach the post in a fast trot and a cloud of dust.

The riders reined down and pulled their mounts to a stop along the front of the trading post. One man pointed to the recently deceased's horses in the makeshift corral. A long and lanky fellow swung a leg to the ground and pushed open the door.

Johnny couldn't hear what was said from where they lay, but soon the tall fellow came out, gave some orders, climbed on his horse and wheeled it around. Two of the riders threw ropes over the heads of the horses in the corral. Then they all rode away.

"Follow them, Lobo, but be careful. We'll tag along aways behind."

Johnny, Bass, and Smokey waited a couple of hours, then mounted and followed Lobo. The tracks headed west.

Johnny figured they'd ridden twenty miles or so before spotting two towering peaks off in the distance that rose up from the sandy desert. Sure enough, the tracks headed directly toward them.

"Let's find a gulley or something and lay low until we hear from Lobo. Someone up high could spot us miles away."

An arroyo off to their left offered the concealment they needed, about ten feet deep and twice that wide. They reined their horses down into it, dismounted, and loosened their saddle cinches.

The night was near spent when Bass, who had been standing guard, shook Johnny awake. Lobo appeared like a ghost out of the dark.

"I find hideout. Small opening in side of mountain. It well hidden. Three guards, two high up on side of mountain, another guard inside entrance."

"Think we'll be safe here tomorrow?" Johnny asked.

"I found you, so can they."

"Then we better find us a better hole and crawl into it until we can figure out how to take them on."

"I find better place."

"Then let's go. We'll follow you."

Lobo led them to a nearby line of low hills honeycombed with a maze of arroyos and canyons. A thin trail took them down inside one of the canyons. It appeared to be a dead-end, but it doglegged to the right and narrowed. Large bounders, some the size of a small cabin, littered the bottom. A small spring bubbled from under the rocks and formed a little pool.

Johnny said, "How'd you find this place?"

"I follow birds and bees, they know better how to find water than man," Lobo told him, swinging down from his horse.

"Well, it's perfect for our camp. Let's set up housekeeping."

With everyone working together they set up camp in short order. Bass started cooking supper while Smokey watered and fed the horses from the supply of corn they'd brought along.

On the second day Lobo found a small game trail leading up the side of the steep mountain, which then led to a rocky ledge looking down into the colonel's valley stronghold.

Johnny and his men lay belly-flat and gazed down into an unbelievable sight. A lush green valley that was at least a quarter-mile wide and twice that long spread out below them. A spring-fed stream wandered through the valley and provided the lifeblood for the grass and green trees lining its banks before forming a rather large pond. The place was a literal paradise smack dab in the middle of the desert that surrounded it.

A hundred or more cows and horses munched contentedly on the fetlock-high grass. Several dozen tents were arranged in orderly rows along the stream. Thirty or more horses milled inside a large corral.

For three days Johnny and his men watched the activities of the colonel's army in the valley below. Each night they slipped back down the mountain and returned to their own camp in the canyon.

"Anybody got ideas how we can deal with the colonel and his army?" Johnny asked them.

They lounged around the small campfire after supper, sipping coffee.

"One thing for shore," Bass volunteered. "Ain't no way we can take 'em on in a straight up fight. They's way too many of 'em"

"I figure you already got something in mind," Smokey said. "What are you thinking we ought to do?"

Johnny grinned. "You boys ever chop cotton?"

"More'n I wants to think about," Bass said.

"My pa used to take me out to the edge of a big field of cotton. He handed me a hoe and told me he wanted that field cleaned of weeds and johnson grass. Well, sir, I looked at that field and it stretched out from here to yonder, row after row as far as the eye could see. I asked him how I could ever do what he wanted me to do. Do you know what he said?"

The men sitting around the campfire looked puzzled and shook their heads.

"My pa spit a stream of tobacco and said, 'Don't look at the field, son, just worry about one row at a time.'"

Johnny let that soak in for several long minutes. Then he spent the next hour explaining his plan.

Chapter XIX

Just after sunup, a horse galloped into the valley carrying a stark-naked rider. Someone spotted it and grabbed its reins and managed to pull it to a stop. The rider's hands were tied securely behind his back and his feet tied to the stirrups of his saddle. A gag made from his own sock was secured tightly in his mouth by a leather thong. A note hung around the rider's neck.

"Somebody better get the colonel!" The man holding the nervous horse shouted.

"Who is it?" Another man asked.

"That's Joe Tolbert. He was on guard duty last night," someone said anxiously.

Colonel Marcus Solesby emerged from his tent and hurried toward the gathering crowd of men surrounding a naked man on a horse.

He's an impressive fellow, Johnny thought, as he peered through his telescope from his perch atop the ledge of a nearby hill. The colonel appeared to be a man in his early to mid-forties.

He stood a head taller than the man who hurried along beside him struggling to keep pace with the colonel's long strides.

He wore dark trousers and was hurriedly buttoning the Confederate officer's coat as he approached the gathering of his men.

Johnny couldn't hear what they said, but from the gestures he could pretty well imagine what was going on.

They cut the naked guard loose from his saddle and lowered him to the ground. The colonel jerked the note from around his man's neck and read it.

Marcus Solesby,
This letter is to inform you that you, and all of your men are under arrest. You are all ordered to throw down your weapons, surrender, and ride single file out this valley. If you fail to obey immediately you will be considered resisting arrest and will be shot on sight.

Johnny Shooter
Deputy United States Marshal
Federal District Court
Western District of Arkansas and the Indian Territory
Fort Smith, Arkansas

Johnny watched as Solesby ripped the letter to shreds. The pieces were still fluttering in the morning breeze when Johnny feathered the trigger of the big .52 caliber buffalo gun in his hand. The explosion from it rocked into his shoulder like the kick of a mule and set his ears to ringing.

Down in the valley, Johnny saw the man next to the colonel lifted off his feet and slammed into the ground. *I missed the colonel,* Johnny scolded himself. *I should have let Smokey take the first shot.*

Shooter

From the hilltop across the valley another shot rang out and another of the colonel's men fell, his head exploding like a ripe watermelon. *That would be Smokey saying a howdy.*
He worked the lever and fired again. Another man fell.
Men scrambled for the limited cover in the valley. A few hastily swung onto the saddled horses nearby and galloped toward the entrance to the valley, apparently hoping to escape the withering gunfire from the mountaintops on both sides of the valley.

But instead, they rode headlong into hot lead from Bass and Lobo's rifles. Johnny saw one man blown from his saddle, somersaulting over the back of his galloping horse. Another doubled over, clung desperately to his saddle horn, then tumble to the ground, bouncing like a rag doll before coming to a stop in a heap.

Suddenly, a tremendous explosion from the direction of the entrance shook the ground. Rocks lifted toward the sky and a huge plume of dust rose, hung in the air, then drifted off to the east on a westerly wind.

Johnny hoped the dynamite did a good job. The entrance to the valley should now be closed, preventing any of the outlaws to escape.

For more than an hour the one-sided battle raged on. One by one the outlaws were cut down under the continuing fire from the hilltops. The barrel of Johnny's long gun grew so hot he couldn't touch it. He dropped it and picked up the spare he'd brought from Lobo and continued to fire. He knew that across the valley, Smokey must have done the same.

The men below took refuge behind anything they could find and the targets became fewer. The return fire ceased completely, Johnny figured, after the outlaws finally realized that those shooting at them were well out of rifle range and that they were only wasting ammunition.

How many Johnny and his men killed was impossible to know. One thing he did know, the odds were definitely getting better all the time.

By mid-morning it was over. The couple dozen or so still alive in the valley below waved a white handkerchief and came out of their hiding places with their hands over their heads. Bass and Lobo rode up carefully, keeping them covered with their rifles as they approached.

By the time Johnny and Smokey managed to climb down from their perches, make their way on foot through the tangle of boulders that blocked the entrance, and walk into the valley, Bass and Lobo had the twenty-three survivors lined up and securely tied with their hands behind their backs.

Johnny walked among them, examining each one with a searching gaze. When he stood in front of Marcus Solesby, he stopped. For a long moment he stared deep into the eyes of this evil outlaw, the cause of so many men, women, and children dying.

When Johnny spoke, his words came out like hot lead from the nose of a rifle.

"Marcus Solesby, for way too long you have robbed, stolen, and murdered innocent folks. You have lived by your own rules and thumbed your nose at the laws of God, of man, and of common decency. You've shown no mercy to your victims. Now you will be shown none.

"I'm going to ask you a question, but I warn you, I'm only going to ask it once. I want to know your involvement in the deaths of those army patrols. I want to know what happened to those cattle herds. I want to know the names of everyone in the army that was involved, and I want to know right now."

Johnny waited. His questions were met with stony silence.

"Fair enough," he said. "Bass, gather up all the food and water you can find and load it on to six of those horses. Smokey, you and Lobo untie these fellows one at a time and let them saddle their horse, then tie them up again."

While his crew went about their assigned chores, Johnny walked to the colonel's tent and looked around. He rummaged through all the papers he could find. He had no idea what he was looking for, but hoped to find something, anything to implicate an accomplice from the army. He was convinced the major was somehow involved. He found nothing.

By the time Johnny returned to the corral everything seemed ready. Six horses carried heavy packs of food and containers of water. A saddled horse stood by for each of the prisoners.

"See that each man leads his own horse, but we'll walk to the entrance. These fellows are going to clear it so we can all get through."

It took awhile. Some of the boulders brought down from the mountain by the dynamite were huge. Finally they cleared a path large enough for all the men and horses topass through.

"Just so you will know," Johnny told the gathered prisoners, "we're headed for Fort Smith, Arkansas. It's a long way. I asked a question back there awhile ago. Until I get my answers you will walk and lead your horse. If you fall, you will be dragged until you get back on your feet. If you refuse to go on, you will be shot. Anyone who answers my questions truthfully can mount up and ride the rest of the trip. Let's go."

It was mid-afternoon when they started the long journey. Johnny led the long column, Bass and Smokey rode on either side and Lobo rode drag.

By dusky-dark the prisoners were exhausted. They stumbled along in the sandy terrain, each step clearly a struggle. Some fell from time to time, then quickly climbed to their feet, obviously recalling Johnny's words.

Just before good dark Johnny pulled the caravan to a stop near a grove of mesquite trees. A small stream threaded along the edge of a large outcropping of sandstone before disappearing into a crevice.

"We'll stop here for the night."

The prisoners collapsed in their tracks. Lobo and Smokey took care of the horses, unsaddling, feeding, watering, and hobbling them for the night. Johnny scrounged up enough wood for a small fire and Bass began cooking supper.

"Cook only enough for us," Johnny told him. "Our guests get nothing but a cup of water. They'll eat when they start talking, not before."

There was a lot of grumbling from the prisoners, but still no one was willing to talk. One by one the outlaws were set down beside a tree and tied for the night. Then Johnny and his team settled down to enjoy their supper and a cup of steaming hot coffee.

By dawn they were up and moving again. The outlaws, use to riding instead of walking, complained of blisters and bleeding feet. They were reminded that they could ride any time they decided to talk.

Each man received one cup of water three times a day. On the second day Bass cooked up a stack of Johnny-cakes. Each prisoner got one of the fried biscuits and a cup of water, and then were tied up for the night. When trees weren't available they were tied to the back legs of a hobbled horse. Johnny and his team took turns standing watch in two hour shifts throughout the night.

On the fourth day they sighted Camp Supply. Johnny led his caravan within shouting distance of the army camp, but didn't stop. The whole camp turned out to witness the sight.

A squad of mounted soldiers, led by Major Sterling himself,

spilled out of the gate and headed directly toward them at a trot. The young lieutenant rode behind the major.

Johnny flicked a quick look over his shoulder and circled his finger in the air. His men immediately rounded the prisoners into a huddle. Then they withdrew rifles from their scabbards, and propped them against their legs, ready for action in case it came to that.

The major held up a hand and drew rein. His squad of soldiers stopped. The officer walked his mount forward to within a few yards of where Johnny sat his horse. Sterling's face flushed in anger, his hard-set eyes and blazed fire.

"What is the meaning of this, deputy? Who are these men?"

"I expect you know full well who these men are, major. This is the so called, Colonel Solesby and what's left of his army of outlaws."

The major looked clearly shaken. He cast a nervous look over the prisoners, his eyes pausing and focusing upon the outlaw leader for a long moment.

"Where...where are the others? I understood he had many more than this."

"Dead."

"Dead? All of them dead? How?"

"Like I told you, they were told to surrender, they decided not to."

"Where are you taking these men?"

"To Fort Smith. They'll stand trail in front of Judge Parker and then they will most likely hang."

"These men look awful. What have you done to them? Why are they walking?"

"Because I asked them a question and they ain't answered me yet. When they answer they get to ride, not before. They will answer my questions, though, it's just a matter of time."

"What sort of questions?"

"Oh, I reckon you got a pretty good idea what I'm wanting to know, don't you, major?"

"What's that supposed to mean?"

"You figure it out."

"I'm arresting your black companion for assault and battery. He's going to stand trial for what he done to my sergeant the other night."

"Not likely. Your sergeant's got a big mouth. He started the whole thing and my man finished it, that's all there was to it."

"Stand aside. I have jurisdiction here. I'm arresting that man."

Johnny slowly lifted his sawed off double barrel shotguns. His thumbed back both hammers.

"Major, I expect you're already in more trouble than you can say grace over. Don't make the same mistake your sergeant made and bite off more than you can chew."

Johnny could see the major was so flustered that his big belly was about to burst. His face was beet-red.

"You'd draw a shotgun on an officer of the United States Army?"

"I'd draw a shotgun on a loudmouthed blowhard that's sticking his nose in where it don't belong. Now get out of our way, we've got a long way to go."

"You'll be hearing from me, deputy. I'll have your badge for this!"

"I expect you'll be hearing from me, too, major."

The officer angrily jerked the reins of his mount and galloped back toward the camp. The lieutenant cut a grin and winked at Johnny before wheeling his horse and signaling the squad of soldiers to return to camp.

Johnny raised his hand and moved it forward. The caravan of prisoners got to their feet and, once again, set out on their long journey with their saddled horses walking along beside them.

Two days after they passed the fort, and five days of walking, the first man broke. Smokey brought the man to Johnny.

"Fellow here wants to have a word with you," Smokey said.

The man appeared somewhere on the sundown side of forty. He could hardly stand on his swollen feet. His lips were chapped and peeling badly. His breathing sounded hard and labored.

"What's your name?"

The man raked his dry tongue across chapped and bleeding lips. His eyes had a tired look, like he'd completely given up.

He mouthed the words twice before sound came out.

"Name's Dallas, Dallas Hiatt," his raspy voice managed to get out.

"You got something you want to say?"

"I, I was part of it. I helped kill those soldier boys."

"Why? Why did you kill them?"

"They happened on us when we were driving that herd of stolen cattle. The colonel ordered us to kill them and make it look like indians done it."

"Anything else you want to tell me?"

The man shook his head weakly.

"Give him food and water and put him on his horse and let him ride up front with me." Johnny told Smokey.

Within an hour another man decided to talk, then another, and another. Before the day was over more than half of the outlaws were in their saddles riding, while the rest still defiantly trudged along on foot.

Gradually the pieces fit together. Johnny now knew the whole story, at least most of it. As yet no one implicated anyone from the army. As far as the outlaws knew, everything they did was the colonel's idea.

It took a week. Only the Colonel and two of his men were still walking. All of the other outlaws were making the trip in their saddles and eating regular meals like Johnny and his men.

Johnny saw him when he fell and couldn't get up. Marcus Solesby, once the proud leader of the worst outlaw gang in the territory, was now reduced to an exhausted, beaten man. Smokey looked at Johnny. Johnny nodded his head.

Smokey untied his lariat from his saddle, made a loop, and threw it over the colonel's feet. He did a half-hitch with his rope around his saddle horn and heeled his horse into a slow walk. Solesby seemed oblivious to his being dragged. Johnny thought at first the man might be unconscious.

"All right!" the outlaw leader finally screamed. "What do you want? I'll tell you whatever you want to know."

Johnny walked Blackjack over to the man. He sat his horse and stared down at the broken, sniveling man.

"I want to know where you got your information about the cattle drives. Who was helping you?"

"It was the major. Major Sterling. He sent word when a drive was coming through. I give him a cut of whatever we got from the stolen herd."

"Where did you take the herds? How did you move them?"

"We drove them to a valley southwest of Dodge where the Cimarron River splits. A cattle buyer met us there and paid us cash money. Don't know what he did with them."

"What was his name, the cattle buyer?"

"Cooper, his name was Cooper, never heard his first name."

"What was the split? How much did the major get?"

"He got a third of whatever we got."

"How did you deliver the major's part, did you deliver it to him personally?"

"No, he always sent that big sergeant of his to collect."

"Anything else you want to tell me?"

"That's all I know."

"Put him and the others on their horses. It's still a long way home."

Chapter XX

Johnny and his men caused quite a stir when they began unloading from the ferry. It took the operator three trips to get the caravan of prisoners and all their horses across the river.

News spread like wildfire. It seemed as if the whole town crowded along the riverbank to witness the event. Even Marshal Fagan and Judge Parker were there. They stood on the little knoll beside the courthouse.

Johnny searched the crowd, looking for Libby. He finally spotted her, Riley, and Cathy standing not far from the marshal. Johnny lifted a hand and waved. Libby stood on her tiptoes and blew him a kiss.

As always, the newspaper reporters turned out in force shouting questions at Johnny and his deputies. They captured tomorrow's headlines with flash after flash of their cameras.

Several deputy marshals came to take charge of the prisoners and get them checked into the Hell on the Border hotel folks called the dungeon-like jail beneath the courthouse.

After the prisoners were off his hands, Johnny rode his way through the crowd to where Libby and the children stood waiting. He stepped down from a stirrup and swept Libby into his arms. After a long hug and a half dozen kisses, he released her and gathered both children into a big bear hug.

"Excuse me for a few minutes. Wait right here, I'll be right back."

Leaving Blackjack's reins in Riley's capable hands, Johnny walked over to Judge Parker and Marshal Fagan.

"Welcome home, Deputy Shooter," the judge said, reaching out his hand hand.

Johnny took the judge's proferred hand shook it. "It's good to be home, sir."

"I see you brought us a few visitors," Marshal Fagan said, smiling and sticking out his hand.

"Yep. Brought what's left of the colonel's army."

"I'll be anxious to hear your report," Judge Parker said. "Would nine o'clock be agreeable? I'd like Marshal Fagan to be present."

"Nine o'clock will be fine."

"I lost track of time," Johnny said around a mouthful of fried chicken. "What day is it, anyway?"

"Today is March 29th. You've been gone two months and seventeen days," Libby said.

"Seemed longer."

"What did you think of that part of the country?" Marshal Fagan asked.

"God must have been having a bad day when He made it."

"Yeah, I know what you mean. I rode through there once

several years back. Can't say I saw a single reason I'd want to linger there."

"What's it like, Mister Johnny?" Riley asked, pouring honey on his fourth biscuit.

"Looks a lot like a great big sandbox."

"Yuk! I shore wouldn't like that."

"You mean, you sure wouldn't like that," Cathy corrected.

"That's what I said. Pass the chicken, please."

"What happened regarding the shooting incident after I left," Johnny asked.

"Nothing. I attended the inquest," Marshal Fagan said. "Everyone agreed it was clearly self-defense. The case is closed."

"How long will your meeting last tonight?" Libby asked.

"Might take awhile."

"That's okay, I'll wait up."

"Sure was a mighty fine supper," Johnny told Miss Lila. "Three months of trail food wears thin after a while."

"What do you fellows do after supper when you are on the trail?" Miss Lila asked.

"Sometimes we play cards. Mostly we sit around the campfire sipping coffee and talking or thinking about home."

"Must be a lonely life," Libby said.

"Yep, sure is, especially when you're by yourself. Gives a man time to do a lot of thinking, though."

"Johnny, do you think we could go hunting sometime?" Riley asked.

"Sure don't see why not. Maybe I can get a few days off and we could go. I'll talk to the judge tonight."

"Really? Wow! That would be *great*."

"Right now I suspect you've got homework, young man," Libby told him.

"Yes, ma'am."

"Reckon we better be heading to our meeting with the Judge?" Marshal Fagan asked.

Johnny nodded. "It's a nice evening and we've got a little time, how about if we walked over?"

"Good idea."

"I'll be back as soon as I can," he told Libby.

The two lawmen left the house and walked slowly along the street toward town.

"You and your men did a remarkable job, Johnny. I still don't see how you managed to pull it off considering the odds stacked against you."

"I had a lot of good help. I can't think of three men I'd rather work with. To my way of thinking, they're the best there is."

"You and your team, as you call them, are making quite a name for yourselves. The way I hear it, the bad guys are saying the only thing worse than standing in front of Judge Parker is hearing that Johnny Shooter is on their trail."

"I had a good teacher."

"Johnny, I've told you this before, but I'll say it again. You are a natural born lawman. I've got two hundred deputies on my payroll, not a one of them could walk in your boots."

"Them are mighty flowery words. You must have another job you're wanting me to take on."

"Nope, just telling it like it is."

"I'm much obliged, marshal, but if I'm still alive come May, I aim to hang up my guns and marry Miss Libby."

"I kind of figured as much. Can't say I blame you, she's a beautiful lady. Shore hope word don't get around about you quitting though, that piece of news would make a lot of folks happier than a fly in a barrel of molasses."

"If it does, it won't come from me."

They climbed the stairs, paused to tap on the office door, and entered when invited. On each of Johnny's previous visits he had been forced to stand because the only chair in the office was the one behind the judge's big desk. Johnny always assumed it was some kind of authority thing to remind visitors who was in charge.

This time was different. There were two extra chairs sitting in front of the desk.

"Have a seat, gentlemen. Would you like a cigar, marshal? I know Mr. Shooter doesn't smoke."

They both took a seat and Marshal Fagan took the offered cigar.

"Congratulations on a job well done, Johnny, It was a long and seemingly successful trip."

"Yes, sir, you are right on both counts."

"Why don't you just start at the begining and tell us all about it. Tell us everything, both the good and the bad. Leave nothing out."

Johnny did so. When he got to the part about the major and his sergeant, he saw the judge pick up a pen and jot some information down on a piece of paper.

Johnny pulled no punches. He related the events exactly as they happened, right down to forcing the prisoners to walk until they answered his questions. When he was finished, he sat back and took a deep breath, then blew it out in relief.

"That's quite a story, Deputy Shooter. Well done. Splendid job, you are to be commended. This major, you say his name was Richard C. Sterling?"

"Yes, sir."

"And the sergeant, what was his name?"

"Sergeant Short is all I heard."

"Very well, I'll send a wire to General Sheridan first thing in the morning reporting your findings. I'm sure this Major

Sterling and his sergeant will be relieved of duty immediately and will face a court martial."

"Any word about the Choctaw Kid?" Johnny asked.

"We haven't heard a word of his whereabouts," Marshal Fagan said. "It's like he crawled in a hole and pulled it in behind him. I've had all my deputies asking around. No one seems to have heard a thing."

"Judge Parker, I was wondering if I might have a few days off. You remember Riley Buckner, the young man who lost his folks and lives with us at the boarding house? Well, I've come to think of him kind of like a son and I would like to take him hunting and spend some time with him."

"Of course. I think we can spare him for a few days, can't we, Marshal?"

"Yes, sir. I think he's earned some time off."

"Then take a week. Report back to me for your next assignment a week from tonight."

"Yes, sir, thank you, sir."

"Marshal Fagan is tallying up the rewards you and your men have coming. He'll settle up with you in a few days. Then if there is nothing else?"

"Goodnight, judge," Marshal Fagan said, standingup.

"Goodnight, Your Honor," Johnny said, also pushing from his seat.

"Goodnight, gentlemen."

Chapter XXI

Saturday

It was still dark. The pre-dawn grayness tinged the eastern sky as Johnny and Riley toed stirrups and swung into their saddles. Johnny wrapped the lead line to their pack mule around his saddle horn and reined Blackjack out of the stable. Riley followed close behind on the red and white pinto Johnny borrowed for him.

They headed for the ferry that would take them across the Arkansas River into the territory. Once they crossed the river Johnny planned to head east, cross Lee Creek, and then ride toward the Boston Mountains. He figured on setting up their camp beside a pretty mountain stream he spotted when hunting down the horse thief several months back.

Daylight blossomed when they walked their horses aboard the ferry. By now the ferry operator knew Johnny by name and greeted them as they came aboard.

"See you got you a new helper."

"Yeah, thought we'd ride up in the mountains a ways and get us a big buck. Riley, this is Elmo Gillis. He owns the ferry. This is Riley Buckner."

"Howdy, Riley."

"Howdy, Mr. Gillis."

"You kin folks to Mr. Shooter?"

"No, sir, he's my friend"

"Well, everybody needs a friend."

As early as it was, they were the only two passengers. Elmo pulled the ramp closed and began tugging on the heavy rope to pull the ferry across. Riley watched a minute then whispered something to Johnny.

"Riley wants to know if he could help you pull the rope?"

"Why shore, I'd be obliged for a strong looking young fellow like him to help. Grab ahold right there, son, and walk to the back of the barge like I do."

With Riley's help the big barge moved swiftly across the wide expanse of water and soon docked on the far side. Johnny and Riley thanked the ferry operator and led their animals up the ramp into indian territory.

They had to ride downstream aways before they could ford Lee Creek. Then all that lay in front of them were the foothills of the Boston Mountains.

Riley and Johnny rode stirrup to stirrup. Riley was so excited he hardly took a breath between sentences. He talked nonstop for the first few hours with Johnny mostly listening. *I reckon that boy could talk the hinges off a barn door.* Then he split a thin grin.

By mid-afternoon they drew rein at the spot Johnny had in mind for their camp. It was a beautiful mountain stream that rushed out of the Boston Mountains, around and over moss covered boulders. A small clearing surrounded by huge pine trees appearing to touch the sky grew beside the stream. Off to the right a long valley flanked by large mountains seemed the perfect place to find that big buck.

"We'll set up our camp right here," Johnny told his hunting partner.

"This is the prettiest spot I've ever seen," Riley exclaimed excitedly. "What do I need to do?"

"How about rustling up some wood? Find us some small stuff for kindling and some larger stuff too. There's an ax in the pack. It's liable to get cold before morning."

While Riley was off dragging up their wood supply, Johnny unloaded the pack mule and unsaddled their horses. He watered their stock then hobbled them on the thick grass nearby.

Before the sun sank behind the mountains they got a fire going and coffee boiling in their pot.

Johnny cooked their supper while Riley cleaned his rifle.

"Is this the way it is when you're on the trail, Mr. Johnny?"

"Well, sort of. Most of the time we don't find a spot quite this nice."

"How old do you have to be to become a deputy marshal like you?"

"Twenty-one, I suppose. Why do you ask?"

"Wish I was twenty-one so I could be a lawman like you."

"Well, you've got a few years before you need to think about something like that. Besides, there's lots of things better than being a lawman."

"Did you always want to be a lawman?"

"No, I guess I never gave it much thought."

"Mr. Johnny, would you teach me how do draw a pistol like you did the other night when you shot that fellow?"

"I think we better wait a while on that. Here, stir those potatoes before they stick to the frying pan."

After they finished their supper and washed their pots and pans in the creek, Johnny showed Riley how to turn his saddle upside down and use the soft padding on the bottom for a pillow. They sat around the campfire sipping coffee, talking, and gazing up at a perfect night sky.

"Bet Cathy and Miss Libby arc wishing they were out here with us."

"I expect."

"You're sweet on Miss Libby, ain't you?"

"Guess you could say that for a fact."

"Are you gonna marry her someday?"

"Maybe someday, if she will have me."

"She talks about you all the time when you're gone. Sometimes she stands at the window staring up the road and crying."

"She's a wonderful woman."

"Before ma and pa got killed, sometimes we all use to sit out on the porch and try to count the stars. I sure miss them something awful."

"I know you do, son. I miss my ma and pa, too."

"Did they die?"

"Some bad men killed them just like those men killed your ma and pa."

"What happened to the men who killed them?"

"I killed them."

"I'm going to kill the Choctaw Kid that killed my folks, too."

"How are you gonna do that?"

"Just as soon as I learn how to shoot a pistol I'm gonna go after him and find him and kill him."

"Is that why you wanted me to teach you how to shoot a pistol?"

"Yes, sir."

"Killing don't make a fella a man, son, and if you did that you would be arrested and tried for murder. Most likely you'd hang for it."

"That don't seem fair to me."

"No, it don't seem fair, but that's the way it is."

"But you killed the bad men that killed your ma and pa and you didn't hang."

"I almost did."

"But the Choctaw Kid's gotta pay for what he done to my folks and little brother."

"He will, son. He will. Let the law handle it, Riley. I promise you I'll find him. I won't stop until I find him and make him pay for what he done to your family."

Neither of them said anything more. A soft breeze whispered through the pines. The fire crackled. For a long time Johnny stared up at the stars, trying to work his mind around the problems he faced, and shake off the weight of the worry.

I love Libby—that's a natural fact. I love her more than life itself. But for me to make plans for the future is a waste of time. I have no future. What is, is. Ain't nothing gonna change that. All I have is now, today. The chances of me living out that six months I promised Judge Parker are slim and none. Besides that, now I've gone and promised Riley that I wouldn't stop until I find the Choctaw Kid.

What if by some miracle I did last out my time? If I haven't found the Kid by then, I still couldn't give up being a marshal. I've shore gone and done it again. But a promise is a promise, I can't let that boy down. I've got to find the Choctaw Kid. If I don't do it, the boy would—or die trying.

Finally he looked over and found Riley sound asleep. He quietly spread a blanket over the boy.

Shooter

* * *

Johnny shook Riley awake while the sky was still dark. "Coffee's on and that big ol' buck is waiting on us, time to rise and shine."

Like any boy his age, it took a few minutes for Riley to get his eyes to cooperate with his mind. He sat up bodily, but his eyes were still asleep. He rubbed them with his balled fist.

"Walk over and wash your face in the stream, that cold water will wake you up. Breakfast is almost ready."

By the time Riley made his way to the bushes, and then washed up in the icy waters of the mountain stream, he looked wide awake. They ate a good breakfast of bacon, left over fried potatoes, and warmed over biscuits that Miss Lila packed for them.

"Those deer will be out and moving just before good light. We want to be in position before then. We'll leave the horses and walk over yonder to that young pine thicket on the shoulder of the hill. I figure the deer will be munching the tender grass out in that clearing. That ought to give us a clear shot."

"I've never killed a buck before. Mostly I hunted squirrel and rabbit."

"I was about your age before I got my first buck, too. If you're finished with that last biscuit, we need to get moving."

Johnny ruffled the boy's hair playfully as they picked up their rifles and headed out.

By the time the eastern sky showed a tinge of gray they found a good spot and hunkered down in position.

"We need to sit real quiet and still," Johnny whispered. "Deer depend on both sight and smell to protect them against danger. We're downwind so they can't smell us, but they can spot the slightest movement."

Daylight crept silently over the mountain. The sky brightened. A slight breeze ruffled the pine saplings and filled the air with their sweet-smelling fragrance. Morning birds fluttered about, seemingly oblivious to the men's presence.

They waited.

Soon they saw the deer as it walked out of a pine grove less than a hundred feet to their left. It moved cautiously, only a few slow steps into the field, its head up and nostrils flaring. Its head swiveled left and right, sweeping the area for danger.

Apparently satisfied that no threat was nearby, the buck lowered his head and munched on the tender grass of the clearing. Every couple of bites his head came up, swept the area again, and then moved a few steps farther into the field. His velvety rack looked huge, Johnny counted twelve points. It was very a large buck.

He flicked a glance at Riley. The boy was wide-eyed and frozen motionless. Remembering his own first experience of buck fever, Johnny cautiously moved a hand to the boy's arm and gave him a reassuring squeeze. Riley's eyes cut a look and Johnny offered a single nod of his head toward the advancing deer.

Slowly, silently, Riley brought the Winchester to his shoulder. His hands shook, then steadied. His finger found the trigger with a soft touch, his eyes sighted along the barrel. Just like Johnny had coached him, the boy paused, took a deep breath, let it out in a slow slide, then squeezed the trigger.

The explosion shattered the morning stillness of the little valley. The recoil slammed into the boy's shoulder. The heavy 44.40 slug found its mark just behind the deer's right leg. The buck reared on his back legs, took a few running bounds, and then dropped in his tracks.

"I got it, Mr. Johnny!" the boy shouted, leaping to his feet. "I got it!"

Johnny's chest swelled with pride. He reached an arm and surrounded the boy's shoulder as they walked side by side toward the large buck.

They dined on venison steaks that night. Riley was rightfully proud of his first buck and could hardly wait to share his story with the folks back home.

Johnny's time off passed quickly.

Libby heard about a traveling New York Opera Company that was performing in Fort Smith on Saturday night and subtly *hinted* that it would be nice to attend. Johnny looked into it the next day and obtained four tickets for Miss Lila, Libby, Marshal Fagan and himself.

Both Johnny and James Fagan needed to purchase suitable clothes to wear, figuring their regular daily attire would not be suitable for such a grand occasion.

To Johnny, the evening was unforgettable. Libby insisted they mark the occasion by having photographs made. Johnny never had a picture made in his whole life, but agreed to Libby's request. They each ordered individual portraits as well as a group photograph. He had to admit it was a thrill for him to pose next to Libby and have their photograph made together.

Earlier Johnny made reservations at the finest restaurant in Fort Smith. The ladies were excited and carried the conversation during the meal of Baked Pheasant under Glass of which the waiter highly recommended.

Both Johnny and James Fagan agreed that the meal was okay, but would have preferred fried chicken.

Johnny didn't understand anything at all about the opera though he tried hard to pay attention. The best part of the whole thing was sitting next to the most beautiful lady in the entire place. He couldn't help noticing all the men stealing quick glances at Libby. That made him extra proud.

The good-bye was maybe the hardest thing Johnny had ever had to do. They went for a walk after supper. The moon was full and seemed only an arm's length overhead. Stars winked at them like diamonds scattered upon a black velvet cloth.

He remained quiet as they walked, trying to figure out how to say what must be said. Libby seemed to sense something was wrong. She stopped and looked him in the eyes, searching for an answer to her unasked question before the words were said. Their eyes met, their hearts in their lingering gazes.

"What's wrong, Johnny? You've hardly said half a dozen words all evening."

"It's the Choctaw Kid. I've got to find him. Vengeance is eating Riley alive. He asked me to teach him how to use a pistol so he could go after the one that murdered his folks and little brother.

"If I don't find the Kid and set things right, Riley is bound and determined to try it himself, and it would get him killed. I'll be leaving in a day or two."

"But how will you find this man?"

"I'll find him. I'll keep looking until I do."

Johnny watched Libby's face carefully. She wasn't exactly crying but her eyes were getting teary. Hot tears breached the rims of her lashes. Her voice frayed. A sob squirmed its way up her throat.

Seeing Libby shed tears made his heart ache.

"How long?" she asked.

"No way of knowing."

He gathered her into his arms and pulled her close and held her for a long time.

"I miss you every minute of every day when you are gone," she admitted softly. "You're the first thing I think of every morning and the last thing on my mind at night. I lie in bed every night and wish you were there beside me. I'm not ashamed to say that, Johnny, because I love you."

"I love you too, Libby, I truly do. Maybe when this is all over..."

He left it there. It was better left unsaid what his heart shouted out for him to say. He wanted more than anything to tell her just how much he loved her, how much he wanted her to be his wife, how much he wanted to spend the rest of his life with her.

But this wasn't the time.

"I've settled it in my mind, marshal." Johnny told his friend as he poured himself a cup of day-old coffee from the blackened pot in the marshal's office. He took a sip and felt the pleasant burn against his lips. He stared into the cup for a long time before he spoke again.

"I've got to find the Choctaw Kid, and I don't want to wait until he decides to crawl out of his hole to do it.

"I'd like it if you'd put out the word that I'm looking for him. Somebody knows where he is. Maybe that reward money will get to looking good and help to loosen up their tongue."

"Okay, Johnny, I'll shake the trees and see what falls out. I'll have all my deputies start asking around, but don't expect too much. The Choctaw Kid ain't just fast with a gun, he's smart. He ain't stayed alive this long by being stupid."

"No, but men like the Kid get to thinking they're better and smarter than anybody else, too. Men like that make mistakes. We all do. I aim to be around close when he makes his next one. I'd like to make the rounds of some of his old haunts and turn over a few rocks, never know what might be hiding under them."

"Just watch your back. Most things that hide under rocks don't want to be found, that's why they're under there."

"Reckon I could take Lobo with me?"

"I just figured you'd take your whole team."

"No need."

"You can talk to Lobo and see what he says. How long you figure you'll be gone?"

"Long as it takes."

"When you leaving?"

"I'll talk to Lobo and let you know."

Chapter XXII

Johnny and Lobo rode into Fort Gibson just after dusky-dark. The same old hosteler Johnny remembered from his last visit limped out to take the reins to their horses and pack mule.

"See ye back again, young fella. Ye still lookin fer the Choctaw Kid, I reckon."

"I reckon. Don't suppose he's hereabouts?"

Both Johnny and Lobo stepped down from their horses and stripped their saddles from their mounts.

"Haven't seen him in quite a spell. Hoping maybe somebody put a bullet in him. Couple of pole cats that run with him are in town, though."

"Is that a fact? What do these men look like?"

"One is a tall drink of water. Goes by the name of Gib Lowery. Thin as a rail and ugly as a fence post. You can't miss that one. He'd be about as hard to miss as a hump on a camel's back.

The other is a half-breed. Folks call him Chitto. Wears

his hair in braids under a black, floppy hat. Uses a cross draw gun rig. They usually hang out at the Lucky Lady saloon."

"We'll be staying over at the hotel for a day or two. Take care of our stock and see they get extra grain and a stall."

"Say, what ever happened to that young boy whose folks was killed?"

"He's fine. His name is Riley Buckner. We found his sister. They both live in Fort Smith now and are doing well."

"Glad to hear it, he seemed like a good boy. It's shore too bad about his folks."

"Yeah, it was the Choctaw Kid who murdered them."

"He ain't worth the powder it would take to blow him to Kingdom Come."

"That's a fact."

A squat little man with a bald head and thick glasses apparentlky replaced the brassy woman that was on the desk when Johnny visited before.

"We've got us a powerful longing for a soft bed with clean sheets," Johnny told the desk clerk.

"Yes, sir. Just make your mark there in the book. That will be rooms five and six upstairs. I'll have Maggie change the sheets."

Johnny paid the man and they climbed the stairs. They found their rooms and stashed their gear. After wshing up, they headed for the Chow Hall Café. There they ate a leisurely meal of biscuits and beef stew and relaxed over a second cup of coffee.

"Let's mosey over to that saloon and lay a loon on those two gents the old hosteler told us about. We gotta start somewhere."

"What you think about going in separately. I watch your back."

"Good thinking, might be smart for you to hide your badge, too."

Lobo removed his badge and slipped it into his pocket.

"Give me a few minutes before you come in," Johnny told him.

Johnny left the café and walked up the dusty street to the Lucky Lady saloon. A loud, tinny sounding piano and boisterous laughter filtered through the swinging doors as Johnny pushed inside. It was obvious this was the soldiers' favorite watering hole.

The place was crowded. A long mahogany bar with a huge mirror took up most of the left wall. Crowded poker tables were scattered throughout the large room. Soldiers filled most of them; a few hard-looking civilians sat bunched at a table near the back.

At the bar, men stood shoulder to shoulder. A big man with a sour look, sloshed drinks into glasses as fast as he could pour and collect the money. Johnny found a space and shouldered into it.

"What'll you have, mister?" The barkeeper asked, wiping his hands on a dirty towel.

"Got coffee?"

As the man poured a cup of thick, black brew from a black coffee pot he took Johnny's measure.

"You new in town?" the barman asked as he set the coffee in front of Johnny. "Don't recollect seeing you before."

Johnny dropped a coin onto the bar and fisted the thick cup.

"Looking for a fellow."

"Does this fellow have a name?"

"Calls himself the Choctaw Kid. You know him?"

The barkeeper's eyes slanted a look down the bar. Johnny's gaze followed the barman's. The two men the old hosteler told him about stood aways down the bar.

"Yeah, reckon I do."

"Seen him around lately?"

"Nope, hope I never see him again. He's bad news. Couple fellows down the bar hang around with him some. You might ask them, though I wouldn't advise it."

"Give them a beer on me."

"It's your funeral, mister."

The barkeeper drew two beers and carried them down the bar. He said something to the two men and pointed a meaty finger at Johnny. Out of the corner of his eye, Johnny saw Lobo slide into a recently vacated spot at the end of the bar.

The ugly one pushed away from the bar and sauntered up to Johnny like a bantam rooster. His half-breed partner hung back, angling away from the bar.

"I'm obliged for the beer. I hear you are asking about a friend of mine," the man said.

The old hosteler had been right. The man was ugly. His weathered and pock-marked face and deep-sunk eyes gave him a look of evil. His gray hair was long and looked matted. He wore an army single action Frontier Colt tied low in a cutaway holster on his right leg. His right thumb was hooked into his gun belt only inches from the pistol. His left hand carried the mug of beer Johnny bought him.

"If you call the Choctaw Kid a friend, I am."

"You got a name?"

"Johnny Shooter, Deputy United States Marshal."

Gib Lowery's jaw dropped, his eyes widened a notch. A look of surprise swept across the man's ugly face. It was clear he'd heard the name before.

"Why are you looking for him?"

"He's wanted for murder. There's a thousand dollar bounty on him, dead or alive."

Another look of surprise. This was obviously news the man hadn't heard before.

"You looking to collect that reward?"

"I'm gonna either arrest him or kill him, whichever he chooses. If he's a friend of yours, tell him that for me."

"You better bring your lunch cause that'll be an all-day job."

"I doubt it, I hear tell he's slow as molasses."

"You'll find out how slow he is if you ever face him. He's might near as fast as me."

"You fancy yourself as some kind of gun slick?"

"Some have tried me. I lost count after the first dozen or so. They're dead. I'm still alive and kicking."

"Just deliver the message I gave you."

For a few heartbeats Johnny thought sure the man was gonna get up enough nerve to draw. His hand hovered just above the butt of his pistol, and then abruptly he turned and walked from the saloon. The half-breed followed.

The barkeep walked up, leaned close pretending to wipe the bar, and said in a low voice.

"Watch your back."

Johnny and Lobo hung around Fort Gibson two days. Word of why they were in town spread quickly. Everywhere they went folks clearly knew who they were and why they were in town. After a good breakfast of biscuits and gravy, they walked to the livery with their rifles and bedrolls over their shoulders.

"Ye fellows shore stirred the pot while ye was in town. Ain't a soul in a hundred miles hadn't heard about ye callin the Kid out."

"Think it'll work?"

"Ye can bet your britches on it. The kid's got it in his head he's the fastest gun around. He won't take kindly to ye makin him look bad."

"In case anyone asks, tell them we're heading for Tahlequah."

The Choctaw Kid turned over and pulled the blanket tighter around his neck. It was a chilly morning in the spacious cave even with a fire going. The aroma of boiling coffee filled his nostrils. He sensed a presence and blinked awake. Sam Starr stood glaring down at him.

"You've used up your time, Kid," the big indian said. "Either pay up or ride on."

"I paid for two months."

"Two months are come and gone. You want to stay, you got to pay."

Anger festered down in the Kid's gut. *I got a notion to blow a hole in that fat indian's belly.* Then he remembered the guards on Starr's payroll. He knew he'd never make it out of here alive if he shot the indian.

"I was thinking about leaving anyway. I've got a gut full of this place. That slop you call food ain't fit to feed the hogs."

"I don't want you around anyway, you're too hot. Word is that new deputy marshal, Johnny Shooter, is on your trail. He's bad medicine. Be gone before breakfast or you'll leave feet first." Sam Starr told him, turning his back and walking away.

The Kid slanted a look at two men with rifles standing nearby. *Old Sam don't take no chances. He covers his backsides before he makes a move. I best ride out while I still can. Johnny Shooter, huh? I've heard talk of him. Well, he better ride clear of me or I'll add another badge to my collection.*

After saddling up, he swung a leg over his saddle and slanted a look northeast. Gigging his horse, he headed toward Tahlequah.

Reckon it's time I look in on Little Star. I got me a itch that needs scratching.

Johnny and Lobo rode into Tahlequah at mid-day. They took two rooms in a rundown excuse for a hotel, the only one in town. Johnny spent half of the afternoon relaxing in a tub of hot water and the rest in the barbershop.

At dusk they went to the café and ate a thick, juicy steak and all the trimmings, then relaxed over another cup of coffee.

"We'll ride out to Sadie's Place in a bit and look around. Maybe the Kid's got lonesome to see that little indian gal of his. Let's do it the same way we did in Fort Gibson, I'll go in first then you follow later.

"This is a tough place, so be ready for anything. If I go upstairs, you go around back. The last time he jumped through a window and got away."

"He won't get past me."

They finished their coffee, paid the lady, and left. Th ey bordedtheir pack mule at the livery and rode the two miles out to the den of iniquity.

"What day is this?"

Lobo only shrugged.

"Must be Saturday night. Look at that line of horses at the hitching rail."

They found an empty spot off to the side and tied their mounts.

"Load up your sawed-off shotguns and keep your eyes open and your finger on the triggers," Johnny said.

He strode up to the open double doors and paused, sweeping the crowded room with a slow, searching gaze.

He spotted Little Star immediately. She was dancing with a young, tough-looking gun slick. His long blond hair hung loose to his shoulders from under the wide brimmed Stetson. He wore a pearl-handled Colt thonged down on his right hip.

That fellow sure looks familiar. I've seen that face before. Of course, I remember now, that's Utah Kelly. I've got a wanted poster in my saddlebags with his face on it.

The piano beat out a slow, easy tune. Several bar girls danced with potential customers. A dozen others hustled drinks from some poor suckers.

Well, that answers one of my questions. The Choctaw Kid shore isn't here or his little gal wouldn't be rubbing herself all over Kelly.

Johnny took another look around the room before stepping inside, and threaded his way through the jam of men crowed around the bar. He found a hole and squeezed into it.

When the bar keep came, Johnny ordered coffee. The man eyed him for a long moment when he brought the cup. "Don't I know you?"

"Maybe so, maybe not. I stopped by once before. I'm Deputy United States Marshal Johnny shooter out of Fort Smith."

"Oh, yeah, how could I forget. It took me a week or more to clean the blood off the floor from your last visit."

"Seen the Choctaw Kid around lately?"

"Nope."

"Mind if I have a word with Little Star?"

"Suit yourself."

Johnny picked up the cup of coffee with his left hand and walked across the room. The piano stopped playing, but the gun slick and Little Star were still locked in an embrace on the dance floor. As Johnny drew near, Little Star whispered something to Kelly. She took his hand and they started for the stairway to her room.

"Little Star, I'd like a word with you," Johnny said.

They both turned and looked at Johnny. Little Star showed no sign of recognition on her face or else too much whiskey clouded her memory.

"Who are you?" the gunfighter demanded.

"I'm a fellow that wants to talk to the lady for a moment."

"Well, I'm the man that's taking the lady upstairs. Get lost."

"Your name Utah Kelly?"

"What if it is?"

Johnny wanted to postpone the confrontation with Kelley until after he finished talking with Little Star, but that didn't look like it was going to happen.

"Then I'll put it this way. I'm United States Deputy Marshal, Johnny Shooter. I've got a warrant for your arrest, dead or alive. I'm gonna talk to the young lady. I can do it before I arrest you or after."

"I don't care who you are, nobody's arresting me."

The young gun slick squared around to face Johnny. His hand hovered within a hair's breadth of the Colt on his right leg.

Since the piano no longer played, many of the folks in the room heard the exchange and started hurriedly pushing, falling against and over one another in their mad rush to get out of the line of fire.

"Like I said, the paper on you says dead or alive. I'll either arrest you or kill you. Your choice."

In that fleeting split second every gunman can sense rather than see, Utah Kelly drew lightning swift, sure as light. In less than a heartbeat, Utah snatched the Colt from his holster and thumbed back the hammer in a draw too fast for the eye to see. Instinctively, Johnny's mind told him that the outlaw had beaten him to the draw.

Two guns barked. Smoke billowed.

As if in slow motion Johnny saw the orange blast from the

nose of Kelly's colt even as he felt his own Peacemaker explode. He braced himself for the bullet he knew was about to slam into him.

It did.

It felt like a mule had kicked him. A sharp pain stabbed at his left side. The air grew fetid with the rotten egg odor of gunpowder.

He saw Kelly's body stiffen and stumble backward, his eyes widen in a surprised look. A red splotch blossomed in the center of his chest. The outlaw twisted, stumbled over a chair in a backwards dance of death and fell to the floor.

Johnny dropped the coffee and grabbed at his side with his left hand. His hand came away wet and slick. He looked down. The bullet had struck him just above the hip bone.

A warm flush surged over him. Suddenly he felt weak. The room spun. He needed to sit down. His legs went weak. Then the world went black.

Chapter XXIII

He was floating on a beautiful white cloud. The cloud felt softer than Ma and Pa's feather bed. He was so sleepy. His side hurt. Why did his side hurt so badly? He struggled to open his eyes. The light hurt. His eyes wouldn't focus. Everything looked fuzzy.

"I think he's coming around," a strange voice said.

Johnny blinked his eyes to gain focus. A face floated up in front of him. It was an old, gray haired fellow with tiny spectacles that set on the end of his nose.

"How you feeling, Mr. Shooter?"

"Who are you?"

"I'm Doctor McKinney. You've been shot. You've lost a lot of blood and been unconscious for quite a while, but you're going to be fit as a fiddle in a few weeks. You were bleeding like a stuck hog when your partner, here, brought you in."

That's when Johnny saw Lobo standing nearby.

"How you doing, Johnny?"

"Not too good, don't feel like."

"Like doctor said, you be fine. Here, thought you might want slug doctor took outta your side."

Johnny took the heavy .44 slug and rolled it between thumb and finger. He stared at it for a long moment.

"Did it hit any bone or something vital?"

"No, sir," the doctor answered. "You were lucky. It tore up your side pretty good but didn't hit anything that won't heal if you give it a few weeks."

"Can I ride?"

"I wouldn't advise it. What you need is a couple of weeks in the bed to give that wound time to heal."

"What happened to Utah Kelly?"

"They bury him tomorrow," Lobo told him. "You got him good in chest. He dead before he hit floor."

"Where are we, anyway?"

"We in Tahlequah. I brought you doctor's soon as I could after shooting. I send telegram to marshal this morning. Not hear back yet."

"Looks like you're gonna have to play nursemaid to me for a couple of weeks."

"Doctor say there is boarding house down street. Say food good. Lobo think better than hotel."

"Most anything would be better than that flea trap."

"I talk to captain of the Cherokee Lighthorse Police. I tell what happen. He say he file report. That be end of it."

"Reckon you might as well see if you can make arrangements at the boarding house, then. We'll lay up there until I can ride."

Lobo nodded once, spun and headed for the door.

***

Lobo made arrangements for two rooms in the Cherokee Boarding House and talked three of the Lighthorse Police into helping him carry Johnny down the street. The doctor loaned them a stretcher to make the move.

Within an hour Johnny found himself resting in a soft feather bed in a spacious room. Mrs. White Eagle was the owner of the boarding house. She was a heavyset, full-blood Cherokee who mostly nodded her head and hardly ever spoke.

Johnny made himself comfortable just as Lobo walked in with a telegram in his hand from Marshal Fagan. Johnny took the telegram and read it quickly.

Sorry to hear about your accident<stop>Libby leaving within the hour to join you<stop>Bass and Smokey will escort her<stop>Judge Parker said to take your time and recover.

James Fagan
United States Marshal

Johnny could hardly believe it. Libby, coming here?

Libby knew something was wrong the moment Marshal Fagan opened the door and walked in.

"What is it?" She asked her heart in her throat. "What's wrong? Has something happened to Johnny?"

"He's all right. He's been wounded, but the doctor says he will recover in a few weeks. I thought you'd want to know"

"Where is he?" she asked, swallowing a huge lump in her throat.

"He and his partner are in Tahlequah, over in the indian territory."

"I'm going."

"That's not a good idea, Miss Libby. It's at least two days of hard riding."

"I don't care. I'm going."

"I'd advise against it, but if you are bound and determined to go, I'll send Johnny's other two partners to escort you. Wish it was where I could take you myself, but I've got some things I can't turn loose of right now."

"When can they be ready to leave?"

"I can have them ready within the hour. I'll rent a buckboard from the livery, he's got a doctor's rig that he rents out from time to time. One of them can drive and the other ride escort. I'll have them pick you up here. Are you sure you want to do this, Miss Libby?"

"I'm sure."

Less than an hour later, Smokey and Bass pulled up in front of the boarding house. Smokey drove the team of matched black horses that pulled a single-seat, covered buckboard and Bass rode up on his gray gelding. Libby was ready and waiting.

Smokey took her valise and put it in back along with their trail supplies. The marshal came up with an extra bedroll and blankets for Libby.

In minutes they were already crossing the ferry into indian territory. The sun shone near noon high.

The Choctaw Kid was still fuming as he left Robbers Cave and gigged his black and white pinto into a lope. He wanted to put as much distance between him and Sam Starr as possible. *One of these days I'll catch that fat indian alone and I'll blow his head off.*

One thing for sure, he had to get his hands on some money.

He was flat broke. What money was left after paying Sam Starr, he lost in poker games during his two month stay.

Guess I'll have to rustle up a few of the boys and figure out some way to make us all some fast money. But right now I don't have enough to buy a beer. Wonder if Little Star is missing me? Shore would like to see that sweet little thing. Maybe I ought to ride on over to Tahlequah and pay her a little visit. Why not? I ain't got nothing else to do.

Darkness claimed the rugged countryside by the time the Choctaw Kid reined his pinto to a stop at the edge of the tree line. For long minutes he sat his saddle and watched the area surrounding Sadie's Place.

His dark eyes examined every horse tied at the hitching rails, every shadow, and every tree. He hadn't survived the outlaw life this long by being careless.

Finally convinced that no one lurked in the shadows, he heeled his horse forward. Swinging to the ground, he half-hitched his pinto to the rail then approached the wide open door and paused. From long years of habit, and without even thinking, he lifted his pistol from its holster, spun the cylinder to assure himself it was fully loaded, and then returned it to the greased holster tied to his leg.

His gaze swung a slow, searching sweep of the large room. The occupants at the long bar were mostly Cherokee. Four local businessman were totally engrossed in a poker game at one of the tables. Two bar girls looked on, with their arms surrounding the shoulders of potential customers.

Three tough-looking hombres sat at a table near the back. The Kid came close to smiling when he recognized two of them as Gib Lowery and Chitto. He didn't know the third fellow. He walked into the room and crossed to where his two companions sat and pulled out a chair.

"Bout time you showed up," Gib said, swallowing the last of his beer.

"Who's your friend, here?"

"This is Crazy Ed, he's all right. I've known him a while. We met when we were both serving time up in Illinois."

"Told you not to call me that!" the man growled.

"Call you what?" Lowery shot back.

"What you just did."

"Well, that's your name, ain't it? That's what everybody calls you."

"That ain't my name. Don't like to be called that. I killed a man once for calling me that. My name is Ed"

"You mess with me and I'll put a bullet in that crazy head of yours."

Ignoring his companion's comments, Gib turned his attention back to the Choctaw Kid.

"Where you been, Kid?"

"Busy."

"Busy staying ahead of that law dog, I reckon."

"What law dog?"

"The one everybody is talking about. Shooter is his name, Johnny Shooter. He's a deputy darshal what works for the Hanging Judge in Fort Smith. Surely you've heard about him? He's one tough piece of work. He braced us down in Fort Gibson, asking about you. Tried to goad me and Juno into drawing on him. That fellow is crazy mean. He said he heard you were slow as molasses."

"He said that? What's his problem?"

"Right now his problem is a slug in his side. He's laid up over in town at a boarding house. He braced Utah Kelly as big as you please right here in Sadie's, night before last. Told him he was either gonna arrest him or kill him and Utah could choose which it would be."

"He went up against Kelly? No wonder he's nursing a bullet. Utah is the fastest I ever seen."

"Well, I reckon he weren't fast enough. He's deader than last year's daisies, and all Shooter got was a bullet in his side."

"What did this marshal and Kelly get into it about?"

"We weren't here, mind you, but the way I hear it, Utah was heading upstairs with Little Star and Shooter wanted to talk to her. Kelly objected and so it came to a head."

"What did this marshal want to talk to Little Star about?"

"Most likely about you. You got all them marshals riled for some reason, they're all looking for you."

"I ain't hard to find."

"You better make yourself scarce if you want to stay healthy."

"Don't be telling me what I better do. Where is my gal?"

"Some stranger took her upstairs a while ago."

"That no-good tramp, I'll teach her to mess around on me. Go get the horses and wait for me. Have my pinto waiting, too. We might have to leave sudden like."

Taking the stairs two at a time, the Kid quickly arrived at Little Star's bedroom door. He tried the knob but the door was locked. Lifting a booted foot, he kicked the door in. The door splintered and flew from its hinges.

The stranger rolled off the bed and made a grab for his pistol hanging on a nearby chair; he didn't make it. The Choctaw Kid's pistol appeared like magic in his hand. It belched flame and hot lead.

Two holes appeared in the man's chest. The force of the bullets slammed him backwards into the bedside table. Walking across the room, the kid stood over the fatally wounded man who stared up at him wide-eyed.

"You picked the wrong girl, mister," he said before calmly raising his pistol and shooting the dying man between the eyes.

On the bed, the naked Little Star stared unbelieving, both hands over her mouth trying to stifle the scream in her throat.

"You just can't get it through your head that you are my girl, can you?" he yelled, lashing out with his pistol. The blow struck Little Star along her cheek. The sickening sound of crushing bone sounded loud in the room above her scream. In a fit of rage, he struck her again and again with the barrel of the pistol, each blow ripping, crushing, and tearing her face. Blood splattered over the bed, coloring the dingy sheets crimson red. She lay unconscious, and still he lashed out until Little Star's face was nothing more than a pulpy mass of unrecognizable raw flesh.

Someone rushed up to the opening that was once a door. Wheeling, the Kid emptied his pistol without even looking to see who it was. A body fell in the hallway with a loud crash. The victim was the bartender.

Pausing long enough to reload his pistol, he hurried down the stairs and through the saloon, swinging his pistol back and forth, his darting black eyes daring anyone to attempt to stop him.

On the street, his three outlaw partners waited nervously, holding a tight rein on their mounts and looking anxiously in every direction. The half-breed held the pinto.

Toeing a stirrup, the Choctaw Kid swung into the saddle, and then wheeled his horse and triggered two shots at the door of Sadie's place to discourage any followers.

"Where we heading, Kid?" Gib Lowery shouted.

"I'll let you know when we get there," the Kid shot back. "Now let's ride."

* * *

Bass, Smokey, and Miss Libby kept the buckboard team at a steady trot all afternoon. By sundown they drew near Webber Falls.

Bass rode alongside the buckboard and called out to Smokey. "Appears to be a little stream up ahead beside that grove of cedars. Maybe we ought to make camp."

"It's not dark yet," Libby said, "Couldn't we go on a little farther?"

"Could," Bass replied. "But the horses need water and graze, there might not be either one up ahead."

"Sorry, I didn't mean to question your decisions, I'm just anxious to get there."

"I understand, ma'am. We've been making good time. At this rate we ought to be in Tahlequah by noon the day after tomorrow, I figure."

Smoky pulled the team into a small clearing among a thick grove of cedar trees. A small stream ran nearby. Smokey unhooked the team from the buckboard while Bass scrounged up wood and kindling for a fire.

"Let's get a fire going to chase off the chill," Bass said.

He coaxed a fire to life and put on a pot of water to boil for coffee. Libby unpacked roast beef sandwiches and one of the apple pies she baked the day before.

By the time supper was over, darkness claimed the land. The night was clear and chilly. Stars flooded the sky. They sat around the campfire sipping coffee and watching the flames leap upward into the blackness of night.

"Do you think Johnny will be all right?"

"He'll be fine, Missy," Bass assured her. "Johnny is one hard number. One little ol' bullet ain't gonna stop Johnny Shooter, no way, no how."

"He's the gentlest man I've ever known."

"Johnny's a natural born lawman. I've been in this line of work a long time. Johnny Shooter is the best I've ever seen at what he does."

"He doesn't talk about exactly what it is he does. I know, of course, that he's a Deputy United States Marshal and that he seems to have some sort of special relationship with Judge Parker, but beyond that, I know very little about his work."

"Like I said, Miss Libby, Johnny is a top-notch lawman. Reckon I best leave the explaining to him."

For a long time they said nothing more. Bass lit his pipe. Smokey pulled his blanket up around his chin and tipped his hat low over his eyes. In minutes he was snoring.

Libby stared up at the night sky. A million tiny stars winked like fireflies in the velvety blackness of the sky. Her mind replayed the last time she and Johnny stared up at that same sky.

She remembered his gentle touch, the way he looked at her, the thrill that swept over her every time he was near. *Oh Johnny, I love you so very much.* She wiped tears from her eyes.

Johnny lay in the comfortable feather bed and stared at the ceiling. He was well aware that he'd made a mistake and that it almost cost him his life. *"There's always somebody faster,"* he recalled Marshal Fagan telling him. Well, I met the first one. There's bound to be others. I made the mistake of giving him the edge. I won't make that mistake again.

He yawned, tried to stretch until the sharp pain stabbed at his side, and glanced around the room.

The bedroom where he lay was a large, tastefully furnished room on the first floor of the two-story boarding house. Lobo had explained the layout. There were six rooms *to let* downstairs and four upstairs. Other than Johnny and Lobo, there was only one other guest, a fellow wh oworked in the local hardware store. There was an outside door down the hall that led to the street, but Lobo's room was between Johnny's room and the door.

As it did more and more frequently lately, his mind flashed to Libby. Wonder if Lobo remembered to talk to Mrs. White Eagle about rooms for Libby, Bass, and Smokey? I've got to remember to ask him.

A soft knock on the door scattered his thoughts.

"Come in."

The door opened and the boarding house owner waddled into the room carrying a tray heavy with food. She smiled that snaggle-toothed smile of hers and set the tray across Johnny's legs.

"There's enough food there to feed a whole family for a week," Johnny commented.

Mrs. White Eagle only widened her smile and turned to leave.

"Has Lobo said anything to you about needing three more rooms for some friends who are coming?"

The woman nodded her head and held up three stubby fingers and headed for the door. *Well, I reckon that was a yes,* Johnny thought, shaking his head. *I wonder if she can talk? Come to think of it I've never actually heard her say a word.*

Turning his attention to the tray setting on his legs, he again shook his head: Three pieces of fried chicken, mashed potatoes with gravy, corn on the cob, hot yeast rolls, a large slice of mincemeat pie, and a whole pot of steaming coffee. *If I eat like this for a week, I won't be able to climb aboard my horse.*

Another knock sounded on the door, this one louder.

"Come in."

Lobo opened the door and stepped to the chair sitting near the bed.

"Want some lunch? I got enough for both of us here."

"White man eat too much. Make belly pooch out like White Eagle squaw."

"Can't argue that point. I talked to Mrs. White Eagle about rooms for Miss Libby, Bass, and Smokey. From the nod I got from her, I got the idea you have already made the arrangements but wanted to make sure."

"She indian. Not talk much."

"Now there's a natural fact."

"Your woman be here tomorrow."

"What makes you think she's my woman?"

"You like wide-eyed calf when you get telegram."

"Yeah, I suppose you're right. Sure will be good to see her."

"I be in next room. You need, you call." With that Lobo rose and left Johnny alone.

Johnny lifted the sheet and stared down at his flat stomach for a moment, then smiling, picked up another chicken leg to eat.

A wide-eyed calf, huh?

Chapter XXIV

The Choctaw Kid and his three companions reined up on a hog-back ridge a couple of hours ride north of town and sat their saddles, staring for long time at the area surrounding the entrance to a cave he'd used before.

Satisfied that no one was around, they gigged their horses down the hillside and across the small stream that ran in front of the cave.

"We'll hold up here a day or so, then we're gonna pay that deputy marshal a visit and finish what Kelly started. I'm tired of that fellow dogging my trail. After a while a man gets so he can almost hear his shadow."

The three outlaws only nodded their heads. Choctaw Kid knew they wouldn't dare disagree. They swung from their saddles, tied their horses, and went to inspect the cave.

After they built a fire and put on water to boil for coffee, the Kid called them together.

"Gib, first thing in the morning I want you to ride back

into town and find out everything you can about that place where this deputy is staying, how bad he was hit, and who is with him.

"I want this guy dead. We're gonna hit him fast and hard and I don't want any surprises, understand?"

"Yeah, Kid, I understand."

"While you're in town, pick us up a few supplies."

"You got any money?" Gib Lowery asked. "I'm busted."

"No, I don't have any money, get some."

"Where am I supposed to get money?"

"Who cares where you get it, just get it and bring us some supplies, and get back here with the information. If I have to do everything in this outfit, I don't need you."

The next day, near dusky-dark, Gib Lowery walked his bay mare down the dusty street of Tahlequah. His shifty eyes swung to and fro, searching for any sign of danger. Shopkeepers were moving merchandise from the wooden boardwalks in front of their stores, inside, making ready to close for the day. Workers trudged wearily toward home, having finished their labor for another day. The hitching rails in front of the town's numerous saloons, that later in the evening would be crowded, were now mostly empty.

Gib decided he needed a beer. He rained his mare toward the Aces High saloon. Stepping down, he threw a half-hitch around the rail with the reins and stepped up onto the boardwalk in front of the swinging doors. He paused with a hand in his pocket to finger the single half-eagle he kept rat-holed for emergency situations.

Pushing inside the afternoon darkness of the room with a long-legged gait, he took it in with a sweeping gaze. Besides the barkeeper, only three early customers sat at the scattered tables. Two were typical Cherokee barflies, the other wore the familiar rough uniform of the Cherokee Lighthorse Police.

The man was a short, squatty sort of fellow. He wore a battered, black-felt hat pulled down tight over long braids. The Union uniform jacket looked too small for his thick chest. He wore a Smith & Wesson in a worn holster strapped high on his right hip on the outside of his uniform jacket. Judging by the looks of the policeman, he'd been throwing back drinks for the best part of the afternoon.

Sensing an opportunity, Gib pushed his last coin toward the barman.

"Give me two of whatever the policeman is having."

Scooping up his change and the two drinks, he sauntered over to the Cherokee policeman's table.

"I make it a habit of showing my appreciation for their work in keeping the peace by buying law enforcement officers a drink. Reckon I could join you?"

The indian was at least two sheets in the wind. He looked up at Gib for several long moments through glassy eyes that tried hard to focus on the stranger who offered to buy him a drink.

"Do I know you?" he finally slurred.

"I'm Gib Lowery. And you are officer...?"

"Samuel Gray Wolf at your service," the man said with an exaggerated flourish. He reached for the offered drink, stared at Lowery for a minute, then lifted the glass to his lips and threw it back with one gulp.

"I hear good reports on your Lighthorse Police Company. You been with them long?"

"Bout a year, I reckon."

"I heard some talk about a shooting out at Sadie's Place a few nights ago, you hear about it?"

"Most everybody heard about that one, I reckon."

"Somebody said some deputy marshal out of Fort Smith shot Utah Kelly. Is that what you heard?"

"Shot him deader than a doornail."

"Kelly was supposed to be pretty quick with a pistol, wasn't he?"

"Yeah, but that marshal was quicker, I reckon. He's still alive. Kelly was buried out in boot hill yesterday."

"Is that a fact? Was the marshal injured at all?"

"Yeah, he took a bullet in the side, nothing too serious. So happened I helped lug him over to the Cherokee Boarding House after the doctor patched him up."

"You don't say. What's that lawman's name again?"

"A fellow everybody in the territory is talking about, Johnny Shooter."

"Shooter? Are you sure about that? I think I know that fellow. Maybe I'll just drop by and say howdy. What room is he in?"

"We carried him in the side door, second room on the left. The man who travels with him is in the first room."

"Has he got anybody else traveling with him?"

"Don't think so. Why all the questions, mister? What did you say your name was?"

"It's not important. I'm just a friend of Marshal Shooter. Think I'll mosey on over and shake his hand."

Downing his drink and smiling to himself at his own brilliance, Gib pushed from the chair and walked from the saloon. Mounting up, he asked a passer-by how to find the White Eagle boarding house.

Following the man's instructions, he soon found it and rode slowly by the large boarding house on one of Tahlequah's three main streets. It set on a large lot surrounded by giant oak trees. No other houses appeared close enough to be a problem.

Right proud of himself, now all he had to do was come up with enough money to buy some supplies like the Choctaw Kid ordered. He didn't cotton to being told what to do, especially from somebody the law was looking for as hard as they were the Kid. Sooner or later some of those marshals were gonna find him. Gib didn't want to be within shooting distance when they did. Come to think about it, that thousand dollar reward on the Kid shore would buy lots of beer and women. *After we take care of that wounded marshal, Johnny Shooter, that reward might go even higher. Now that's a thought that needs some more thinking.*

He reined his horse into an alley next to the mercantile store. Dismounting, he looked around carefully, and then crept to the back door. Using his long Bowie knife, he jimmied the back door open and quietly slipped inside.

Finding a tow sack, he quickly gathered it half-full of supplies. In a few minutes he mounted his horse and galloped back towards the hideout.

Anticipation tickled along Libby's skin and sent goose bumps racing down her spine as Smokey reined the buckboard down the main street of Tahlequah. The trip proved long and difficult, not so much physically, although Libby never before camped out a single night in her life. But she felt frustrated because it took so long. Johnny needed her. She wanted to be there for him.

Bass reined his gray gelding up at a mercantile store and asked directions, then moved alongside the buckboard and pointed to a side street.

When the big, two-story house with a small, simple sign out front identifying *Cherokee Boarding House* came into view,

Libby's heart leaped inside her chest. She wanted to jump from the buggy, run as fast as her feet would carry her into the house and throw herself into Johnny's arms. Instead she let out a long breath on a ragged sigh.

Bass dismounted and looped his reins through a large ring on a hitching post. Smokey pulled the team to stop, wrapped the long reins around the brake handle, and hurried around to help Libby to the ground.

Lobo was expecting them. He strode from the side door and walked to meet them. He lifted a finger to his floppy hat acknowledging Miss Libby, and then all three deputies exchanged handshakes.

"How's Mr. Johnny," Bass asked.

"Eating Mrs. White Eagle outta house and home."

Smokey and Bass chuckled. "Then he must be feeling fit."

Grinning, Smokey said, "We better get Miss Libby in to see him. I've been worrying she was about ready to jump outta the buggy and run the rest of the way."

"I believe I could have run faster than you drove," she cracked back, smiling good naturedly.

They headed to the side door and trooped inside. Lobo led the way down the hallway, opened the door to Johnny's room, and stepped aside. Libby literally flew across the room. Johnny reached up with his right arm and drew her close. Smokey, Bass, and Lobo quietly slipped out the door to give them a few minutes alone.

The three deputies rejoined Libby and Johnny at mid-afternoon and visited until Mrs. White Eagle brought Johnny's supper. She motioned to the others their supper was on the table. She didn't have to tell the deputies twice.

After supper, Libby and Johnny talked far into the night. Finally saying goodnight, Libby slipped quietly down the hallway to her own room.

They came in the deepest part of the early morning hours. Only silence accompanied their coming, two through the front door and two through the side door that opened onto the street.

Something, a sound, a sinister presence, whatever it was, nudged Johnny from a sound sleep. He listened, and heard nothing but silence. Then a board squeaked in the hallway. Someone was outside his door. Could it be Libby, or maybe Lobo? He waited.

Thin light from a quarter moon filtered through the curtains of the single window. The uneasy feeling that often precedes danger, set off alarm bells in his mind. Turning back the covers, he slipped quietly from bed and lifted his pistol from the holster hanging on the bedpost, thumbing back the hammer.

He sensed, rather than heard, the almost indistinguishable movement of the doorknob turning.

On an impulse, he rearranged his two pillows and pulled the cover over them to resemble a sleeping body in the bed, and then slipped silently to his hands and knees on the far side of the bed, away from the door.

The door slowly opened. Dim silhouettes of two figures crept soundlessly into his room. Whoever they were, it was clear they were there to do him harm. Still, to erase any remote chance there might be another explanation, he waited.

Two nearly simultaneous, explosions erupted. Two orangey-red blossoms illuminated the semi-darkness of the room. Two heavy slugs thudded into the pillows under the covers of Johnny's bed. His own pistol bucked in his hand, once, twice, three times. A man screamed, cursed, and collapsed to the floor. The second man wheeled and dashed out the door.

Down the hall, Johnny heard a door slam open, then another. Pistols barked. Booted feet pounded in the hall. Voices shouted. More shots sounded from both ends of the hallway. The unmistakable thump of another body hitting the wooden floor reached his ears.

Johnny pushed painfully to his feet and struggled across the room to the door. Chancing a quick look, he felt the breath of a bullet singe past his ear and splinter the facing of the door. He flattened his back to the wall beside the door and listened.

The next sound he heard tugged his heart into his throat. Libby screamed.

"I'll kill her!" A gruff voice shouted. "I'm getting out of here and taking this little gal with me. Anybody tries to follow, I'll blow her brains out!"

Throwing caution to the wind, Johnny ducked around the corner of the door and into the hallway, his pistol out in front of him. He turned left toward Libby's room ignoring the sharp pain in his side and hurried down the hallway.

The door to her room stood open, he shot a look inside, but the room was empty. Libby screamed again, this time from outside the front door. He sensed a presence behind him in the dark. He swung his pistol that direction.

"Boss, is that you?" Bass's familiar voice eased the tension on Johnny's trigger finger.

"It's me, they got Libby. This way, she's out front."

An exchange of shots from toward the back told Johnny that Lobo and Smokey were after somebody.

Bass raced ahead of Johnny through the front door and out into the yard. By the time Johnny reached the door he heard galloping hoof beats and Libby's screams fading into the distance of the night.

"I couldn't shoot," Bass told Johnny sadly. "I was afraid I might hit Miss Libby."

"You done right. Get our horses. I'll check on the others. I'm going after her."

Bass turned and ran toward the little barn out back where they stabled their horses. Johnny went back inside.

He lit a lamp and began inspecting the house. The first body he found was the ugly man he once saw over in Fort Gibson, Gib Lowery. The man was dead. Down the hall, another body sprawled half in and half out of the side door, this one a complete stranger to Johnny.

Lobo and Smokey were still unaccounted for. Part of his search was satisfied when Lobo stepped over the dead man in the doorway, his pistol still smoking.

"Where's Smokey?" Johnny asked.

"Not see him."

A knot of fearful anticipation snarled deep inside his stomach, Johnny turned and made his way toward Smokey's room. Lobo followed.

He was there. Lying where he'd fallen, his pistol still clutched in his right fist. Blood from two ugly bullet holes soaked the top of his long johns and painted the braided rug underneath him a crimson red.

Johnny knew instinctively that Smokey was already dead, but he checked his pulse anyway. For a moment Johnny knelt beside his fallen amigo with his head bowed. Wet tears escaped his eyes and trailed across his cheeks. A knot swelled up in his throat, he swallowed, but it wouldn't budge.

Bare feet padded cautiously down the hallway. Another circle of lamplight approached the door and Mrs. White Eagle appeared. For a moment she just stared at Smokey's dead body, then turned and padded back up the hall.

Bass appeared, took one look, and swiped off his hat.

"Oh, me," he whispered in his hoarse voice. "Oh, me."

Jerking a sheet off the bed, Johnny spread it over his partner's body.

"Bass, would you mind watching over things here? I'm sure the Lighthorse Police will be here shortly. Explain what happened, then follow Lobo and me as soon as you can. We're going after Libby."

"Yes, sir, Mr. Johnny, I shore will. You get that fella, you hear?"

"We will. Let's go, Lobo."

Chapter XXV

The Choctaw Kid rode through the night. The red-haired woman lying belly-down across the saddle in front of him struggled mightily. His right hand clamped tightly over her mouth had finally shut off her screaming, but her feet and fists still flailed away at him.

Once he rode a distance away from the last house, he pulled his pinto to a stop and flung the woman to the ground. Leaping from the saddle he grabbed a handful of hair and pulled her face around, then backhanded her with a closed fist, knocking her unconscious.

With a rawhide thong he tied her hands behind her back. Jerking off his dirty red neckerchief, he stuffed part of it into her mouth and wrapped another leather strip around her head to hold the gag in place.

He had no idea who she was, only that she would make a good hostage in case anyone followed, and he had no doubt they would.

He neither knew nor cared what had happened to his three companions. One thing for sure, if Gib Lowery wasn't dead, he would be the next time the Kid saw his ugly face. Lowery led them smack-dab into a trap.

Hoisting the woman back across the saddle as she had been before, he climbed on behind her and heeled the pinto toward his hideout cave.

The sound of hoof beats behind him reached his hearing. He swung his pinto off the trail into a small grove of trees and waited, pistol in hand.

In the faint light of breaking day he recognized Chitto, the Choctaw half-breed that ran with Lowery. The Kid gigged his horse out of the trees.

"Where's the others?"

"Dead."

"Just as well, saves me the trouble of killing them. That partner of yours said the only men with that marshal was the indian. I counted four back there. He led us right into a trap."

"Him not partner, no white man partner. Why you bring white woman?"

"She's our ticket out of a tight spot if one comes up. Come on, let's get back to the cave. Soon as it gets light enough I want you to hide our tracks. I don't want anybody tracking us to the cave, got it?"

Chitto merely nodded his head once, and held his mount back as the Kid rode on ahead.

Lobo led the way. The tracking proved difficult and slow in the light of a quarter-moon. He walked bent close to the ground, the reins to his horse in his hand. From time to time he knelt, traced a finger around a hoof print, then rose to proceed. Marshal Fagan always said Lobo was the best tracker he had ever seen, Johnny saw why. Few men could track hoof prints in the dark.

Johnny rode slumped over in his saddle. The sharp pain in his side tore at him, causing his head to spin. He reached a hand to his side and pulled it away bloody. His wound had opened up just like the doctor said it would, but even if it killed him, he had to go on. Libby needed him. He swallowed the pain and rode on.

Grayness tinged the eastern sky. It would soon be light, which would speed up the tracking.

As they neared a long line of low hills, Lobo pulled his mount to a stop. The trail led them to a long shelf of solid rock and then simply disappeared.

Lobo slid off of his horse, knelt, and examined the rock surface. He dropped the reins to his mount and walked in ever-increasing circles. Johnny gritted his teeth against the pain and waited.

Suddenly Lobo stopped, knelt, and pointed to a small pebble no larger than a thumbnail that looked dislodged, and then hurried back to his horse and swung into the saddle.

"Indian with Choctaw Kid and Miss Libby. He try to hide trail. You not worry, Johnny, Lobo find."

Libby awoke slowly. She hurt all over. Her jaw ached where her captor had struck her, her stomach throbbed from riding belly-down across a saddle for no telling how long. Her hands hurt from the tight binding cutting into her wrists, and her lips were dry and cracked from the gag tied in her mouth.

She opened her eyes, not knowing what to expect. She found herself lying on her side on a dirt floor of what seemed to be a cave of some sort. A fire crackled nearby. The aroma of coffee reached her nose.

Careful to move only her eyes, she saw an indian kneeling on his haunches near the fire, slicing something into a frying pan with the biggest bone-handled knife she had ever seen. Swinging her gaze further, it locked with what appeared to be another indian, but he was dressed in white man's clothing. He stared directly at her, a rifle lying across his legs.

"I see our guest finally woke up," he said, with hardly a trace of an accent.

Libby only stared at him, intense anger burned in her eyes. The other indian glanced briefly over a shoulder at her, then returned to what he was doing.

Where are we? Is Johnny alive? Was he killed in all that shooting? Who are these men? Why did they kidnap me?

She didn't like the way the outlaw was staring at her but was helpless and completely at his mercy. She seriously doubted this man even knew the meaning of the word *mercy*.

She watched as both men poured steaming coffee into tin cups and sipped the sweet-smelling liquid while salt pork fried in the pan.

"Wonder who we got here?" The one in the white man's clothing said, "She sure is a pretty filly. Bet she could keep a man's blanket warm on a cold night."

His indian companion only grunted and sipped his coffee. A slight sound outside the cave twisted his head around. He set his cup on the ground and picked up a rifle lying nearby. Without a word, he rose and slipped quietly out of the cave.

The remaining outlaw also rose, levered a shell into his own rifle and leaned it against the wall beside Libby. He grabbed a handful of hair and yanked her to her feet. Holding her with his left hand, he withdrew his pistol and let it hang loosely in his right hand.

True to his word, Lobo found the outlaw hideout just after sunup. Tying their horses aways off, they deer-footed through the bushes to a point where they had a good view of the entrance to the cave.

Johnny was bleeding badly. Lobo wadded a piece of his shirt and tied it tightly over the wound to slow the blood, but the bandage quickly soaked through. He could feel his strength ebbing away. If the showdown didn't come pretty soon, Johnny knew he would be of little use in the fight that was sure to come.

"You wait," his companion whispered, and disappeared into the bushes.

Johnny jacked a shell into his Winchester and hunkered down behind a log. He was close enough to the cave to smell the coffee and salt pork frying. He could only guess what had happened, or was happening to Libby. He willed his mind not to think about it.

Then he heard a twig snap to the left of the entrance. He couldn't imagine Lobo letting that happen, unless he did it deliberately. Knowing Lobo, that was a real possibility.

A movement at the front of the cave caught Johnny's attention. The indian outlaw emerged cautiously, rifle at the ready. He paused for a moment, listening intently, then moved silently toward some heavy bushes to the left.

The outlaw went perhaps thirty feet when suddenly a flash of light sped through the air. The indian dropped his rifle and grabbed at a knife protruding from his throat. He pulled frantically at the long blade, finally wrenching it from his body. Blood gushed in a steady stream from the hole the knife left.

The man staggered around and around, choking, gurgling, and drowning in his own blood. Finally, he sank to his knees, then fell face forward and lay still.

With the indian outlaw out of it, Johnny could wait no longer. Climbing painfully to his feet he staggered toward the right side of the cave even as he saw Lobo taking up a position on the left side.

Darting a quick look, Johnny was terrified at what he saw. Libby stood bound and gagged. A helpless, frantic look held her face captive. Behind her stood the Choctaw Kid, his pistol pressed against Libby's temple.

Fear clamped its sharp talons deep into Johnny's heart. A sick feeling of helplessness churned his stomach. He figured the Kid knew he had noting to lose. He'd kill Libby as quickly and easily as he might squash a bug.

"You must be the famous Johnny Shooter!" the outlaw shouted. "If you come one step closer, I'll blow this pretty lady's brains out."

"Don't be stupid. The only way you're gonna walk out of here alive is to turn that lady loose."

"She's my ticket out of here. Now back off!"

"Turn her loose, Kid, I won't say it again."

Lobo readied his Winchester, training on the outlaw. Johnny brought his own rifle up, laying the sights directly on the Choctaw Kid. *What should I do? I can't let him walk out of here with her. I better do something fast, my legs are getting weak. I won't last much longer.*

The outlaw stood behind Libby, his left arm wrapped tightly around her neck, his right hand held the pistol to her head, but his leg ...his left leg was extended to the side, using it to brace his body. Making up his mind, Johnny lowered the nose of his rifle and fired.

The outlaw's left kneecap exploded, completely shattered by the rifle bullet. His left arm instinctively dropped from Libby's neck to his knee. Libby spun away from his grasp and flung herself to the side.

Johnny heard Lobo's Winchester thunder and saw the outlaw's right knee disintegrate. The Kid collapsed to the cave floor, screaming in pain, dropping his pistol as he did. Johnny staggered forward and kicked the pistol away from the outlaw.

Lobo moved to Libby's side and quickly cut the leather strips to the gag as well as to her hands.

"Take her outside and wait for me," Johnny said, his words barely above a whisper and as cold as an outhouse in the dead of winter.

Lobo helped Libby to her feet and led her toward the entrance.

"It'll be all right," Johnny told her as they passed. "I'll be right along."

The Choctaw Kid wallowed on the floor of the cave, screaming obscenities and clutching at his shattered kneecaps. Johnny stood over him and reveled at the agony the man was experiencing.

"It ain't so much fun when it's happening to you, is it Kid? Just so you will know, I'm gonna kill you, but it's gonna be slow and hard. Before I'm finished, you'll beg me to shoot you."

Shifting his rifle to his left hand, he withdrew his pistol and shot the outlaw in his right elbow. Bone fragment flew in every direction. Only a thin strand of flesh held the Kid's arm to his body. The screams and curses grew louder and more desperate.

The next shot completely severed the killer's left arm at the elbow.

"Kill me!" The Choctaw Kid screamed between wracking sobs. "In the name of God, kill me!"

Johnny scooped up both the outlaw's rifle and the pistol lying nearby, and turned toward the entrance.

"I promised you would die slow and hard, take your time. *Adios.*"

"Where you going? You can't leave me here like this!"

"Wanna bet?"

Epilogue

Judge Isaac C. Parker
Oct. 15, 1838—Nov. 17, 1896

Judge Parker served as judge of the United States Court for the Western District of Arkansas for twenty-one years, fourteen of which he remained unique in that he was the only judge in the history of our country to allow no appeal for the condemned. He is buried in Fort Smith, AR.

James F. Fagan

James Fagan was sworn in as United States Marshal in July, 1874. He died in 1936 and is buried in Little Rock, AR.

Bass Reeves

Bass Reeves served as Deputy United States Marshal for thirty-two years, longer than any African-American in history.

During his career he killed fourteen men in the line of duty. He died Jan. 13, 1910

Henry (Lobo) Whitehorse

Lobo was shot and killed in the line of duty in January 1875.

Johnny Shooter

Johnny and Libby were married in Judge Parker's chambers on June 1, 1876. The judge handed him a full pardon and their marriage license at the same time. They adopted Cathy and Riley Buckner and bought a small horse ranch in the Boston Mountains near the present day Mountainburg, Arkansas community. Over the years, Johnny continued to serve as a part-time U.S. Deputy Marshal when Judge Parker had a particularly difficult outlaw to deal with.